D0364869

THE GOOD THIEF'S GUIDE TO AMSTERDAM

ALSO BY CHRIS EWAN

The Good Thief's Guide to Paris

THE GOOD THIEF'S GUIDE TO AMSTERDAM

Chris Ewan

Minotaur Books ⧖ New York

This is a work of fiction. All of the characters, organizations, and events portrayed in this novel are either products of the author's imagination or are used fictitiously.

THE GOOD THIEF'S GUIDE TO AMSTERDAM. Copyright © 2007 by Chris Ewan. All rights reserved. Printed in the United States of America. For information, address St. Martin's Press, 175 Fifth Avenue, New York, N.Y. 10010.

www.minotaurbooks.com

The Library of Congress has catalogued the hardcover as follows:

Ewan, Chris, 1976–
    The good thief's guide to Amsterdam / Chris Ewan.—1st U.S. ed.
        p. cm.
    ISBN-13: 978-0-312-37633-8
    ISBN-10: 0-312-37633-2
    1. Novelists, English—Fiction. 2. Thieves—Fiction. 3. Figurines—Fiction. 4. Americans—Crimes against—Fiction. 5. Detective and mystery stories—Authorship—Fiction. 6. Amsterdam (Netherlands)—Fiction. I. Title.

PR6105.W36 G66 2007
823'.92—dc22

                                                          2007033226

    ISBN-13: 978-0-312-57082-8 (pbk.)
    ISBN-10: 0-312-57082-1 (pbk.)

    First published in Great Britain by Long Barn Books

    First Minotaur Books Paperback Edition: May 2009

            10 9 8 7 6 5 4 3 2 1

For Jo

ONE

"I want you to steal something for me."

It wasn't the first time I'd heard those words, though usually the person saying them liked to warm up to it first. Not the American. He got straight to the point, casual as you like. If I was a lesser writer, I'd tell you it set alarm bells ringing inside my head or that a chill ran down my spine. In truth, it just made me listen a little harder.

"You've made a mistake," I told him. "I'm a writer, not a burglar."

"Some writer. I've been following your work. You're good."

I smiled. "A hack with a pricey education, nothing more."

"Oh sure, as a writer. But as a thief, now that's a different story. You've got talent, kid, and that ain't easy to find around here."

Around here was Amsterdam. To be exact, around here was a dim-lit brown bar on a northern stretch of the Keizersgracht canal, a twenty minute stroll or a ten minute bicycle ride from my apartment. It was a cramped space, warmed more by the closeness of the walls than the fading embers in the fire across from our table. I'd been here before, though only in passing, and the name had meant nothing to me when the American suggested it as a meeting point. Now here I was again, a glass of Dutch beer in front of me and a tricky proposition beyond that.

The American had contacted me through my website. Most suspense writers have a website nowadays and you can go there to find all kinds of information about me and my writing. There's a page for each of the burglar books I've written to date and a *News* section with details of any readings I'm involved in, as well as some personal stuff my fans might care to know, such as where I happen to be living while I'm writing my latest novel. There's also a link that allows readers to e-mail me and that was how the American had been in touch.

A job for you, he'd written. *Name your price. Hear me out at Café de Brug. 10pm Thursday (tomorrow).*

I had no idea who the American was, of course, and far less reason to trust him, but then again, the lure of a new job was something I'd long since given up trying to fight. Because the truth, in case you haven't already guessed, is that I don't just write books about a career thief – I also happen to be one.

"This talent you're referring to," I said. "Supposing it did exist."

"Supposing, I like that."

"Well, just supposing, then, that I really do have this talent – I'm curious how you'd like me to use it."

The American checked over my shoulder, towards the doorway, then over his own shoulder, towards the rear of the bar. When he was satisfied that his neck worked just fine and that nobody was eavesdropping on our conversation, he reached inside the front pouch of his windbreaker and removed a small object that he placed on the wooden table before me. The object, it turned out, was a monkey figurine, about the size of my thumb. The monkey was sat on his haunches, knees up around his chest, with his front paws covering his eyes and his mouth wide open, as if in shock at whatever it was he'd just seen inside the windbreaker.

"See no evil," I said, half to myself, and the American nodded and crossed his arms in front of his chest.

I picked up the monkey for a closer look. From the weight and the dry, gritty feel of it, I could tell the figurine had been rendered in plaster of Paris, which went some way to explaining why the finish was not very precise. The look of astonishment I'd read on the monkey's mouth could just as easily have been intended to show fear or even dumb joy by its maker. All things considered, it was hard to imagine it was worth more than a handful of pounds, or even dollars or euros for that matter.

"There are two more of these monkeys," the American said, not altogether surprising me. "One covering his ears, the other covering his mouth."

"You don't say."

"I want you to steal them."

I tilted my head to one side. "Supposing I could ... obtain them for you. I'm not sure it would be worth my while."

The American leaned towards me and cocked an eyebrow. "How much to make it worth your while?"

I thought about a figure, then doubled it.

"Ten thousand euros."

"You want it tonight?"

I laughed. "But this is worthless," I said, tossing the figurine back to the American, who scrambled to catch it before it struck the table.

"Not to me, kid," he told me, carefully dusting the monkey down and then placing it back inside the pouch of his windbreaker. "What do you say?"

"I'll think about it. Another beer?"

I stood and picked up our glasses without waiting for his answer and crossed to the bar, where a not unattractive blonde was filling some finger dishes with cashew nuts. She was tall and lean and tanned in that year-round Scandinavian way that never fails to make me feel impossibly English. You could tell she was used to fools like me hitting on her and when her eyes met my own, it was with a look that was like a ready apology.

"Twee pils astublieft," I managed, meanwhile holding up two fingers just in case the fact I was stood before a beer tap at a bar with two empty beer glasses left her in any doubt as to what I was aiming to buy.

"Of course," she said, in clipped English.

She pushed her hair behind her ear, then took one of the glasses and began to fill it, and meanwhile I tried to think about something other than the freckles on her neck and ended up considering how the American had found out about me instead. It was intriguing, alright, because I was always careful to keep my thieving a secret, and that was one of the reasons I travelled around so much. The only person I talked about that side of my character with at all was back in London and here in Amsterdam I'd carried out just three jobs in the past four months, none of them the type of thefts to draw much attention. True, one of the jobs had been a commission, but the man who'd hired me was a Belgian who passed his instructions through a Parisian fence I happened to trust and it seemed unlikely the Belgian would have told the American about me, given we'd never actually met. So how had the American known to contact me? And why on earth did he want me to steal two worthless figurines?

"Your beers," the blonde said, scraping the froth from the top of the half-pint glasses with a plastic spatula and placing them in front of me.

"That man," I said, indicating the American with a nod of my head. "Has he been in here before?"

"Yes. He is an American."

"Does he come here a lot?"

She pouted. "Many times, I think."

"You know his name?"

"No," she said, shaking her head. "But he is polite, always tipping"

Of course he was. I laid a few extra notes on the table and collected our beers.

The American was in his late fifties, I guessed, though it was hard to gather much else about him. He had a thick head of grey hair, cut in a jagged, youthful style, and he looked relatively fit for his age. The windbreaker suited him, making him appear sporty, like the type of guy who enjoyed sailing in his spare time, and I had it in mind to pay attention to his hands and look for signs of rope chaffing when he pulled me out of my thoughts by saying, "You want to know my name, all you gotta do is ask. It's Michael."

"Michael ..."

"You don't have to say it so slow."

"I was waiting for your surname."

"Now that could be a long wait. The monkeys," he went on, "are in two locations. It's important to me that you take them both. It's also important that you take them on the same night."

"Two separate locations?"

"Uh huh."

"In Amsterdam?"

"That's right. Two places, fifteen minutes apart by foot."

"And these places are private dwellings?"

"Private dwellings," he echoed. "Jeez. One's an apartment and the other's a houseboat, alright? You don't have to worry about alarms and you don't have to worry about being disturbed because the night you do this, both places'll be empty."

"How come?"

"Because the men that live in these two *dwellings* will be having dinner. Here. With me."

I gave this some thought. I wasn't crazy about what I was hearing.

"Sounds complicated," I said. "Why don't you take the monkeys yourself? I can't imagine they'll be missed."

"For one," he said, hitching an eyebrow, "the guy in the houseboat has a safe and he's kind of guarded about the combination. The other guy, he has an apartment in the Jordaan – it's on the top floor of a five storey building and he happens to have three door locks I know of."

"But no alarms."

"None."

"You're sure?"

"Listen, you can't have an alarm on a houseboat – you get a storm or a barge goes by too fast, the movement of the canal water'll trigger it."

"And the apartment?"

"Like I said, it's on the fifth floor. Way I see it, the guy figures he don't need no alarm."

"These locks ..."

"Won't be a problem for you. Me, I don't have the keys or your talent, which is how come we're having this conversation."

"Something else occurs to me," I said. "Supposing these two men value their figurines in the same way you do, well, what if they go home after your meal and notice the figurines are gone – they'll suspect you."

He shook his head. "They trust me."

"Maybe. But if they do suspect you and they come looking for you, well, you can see how my name is liable to crop up."

"Not from these lips."

"You say. But I don't like it."

"Well try this for size – I don't plan on being any place they can find me. We meet at seven and we'll be done eating by ten – that gives you three hours to do your job, which I figure is plenty of time. The bar here closes at eleven and I have it in mind for you to meet me with the figurines at a half after ten. If all goes to schedule, I'll be out of Amsterdam before midnight. And I ain't coming back."

"You're leaving the Netherlands?"

"Well now, there's no need for you to know that, is there?"

I paused, tried something else.

"The timing's kind of tight. Say I can't get into this safe."

"You'll get in."

"Or I can't find the figurine in the apartment."

"Guy keeps it under his pillow."

I frowned. "He sleeps on it?"

"Sleeps with it for all I care. But you'll find it under his pillow."

I backed away from him and looked about the room. The blonde was wiping down the bar with a damp cloth, her hair dancing around her face. The only other customers were three Dutch men drinking beer at a table near the front door. They were laughing and clapping one another on the back, grinning toothily as if life simply didn't get any better. Behind them, sheet rain blasted against the picture window, blurring the outline of the lighted canal bridge I could see on the other side of the glass. I sighed, and gave it to him straight.

"Listen," I said, "I'm going to have to say no. I don't know how you found me and that's part of the problem. The other thing is you want this done tomorrow night and that's a concern for me. I like to look around a job before I get inside of it and you're not giving me the time I need."

The American laced his hands together on the table and tapped his thumbs against one another.

"Say we double your fee?"

"It's funny," I told him, "that just makes me more nervous. See, I have to think it's vital to you now, for whatever reason, that this thing is done tomorrow night. And the fact you'd pay me twenty thousand makes me think there's twice the risk I'd considered in the first place."

"Risk is a part of it. So's the reward."

"It's still a no."

The American grimaced, shook his head wearily. Then he reached inside the sleeve of his windbreaker and removed a square of paper. He hesitated for a moment, looking me in the eyes once more, before sliding the paper across to me.

"Kid, I'm gonna take a chance. These here are the addresses. I want you to keep them. Say tomorrow night comes around and it gets to seven o'clock and you change your mind."

"That's not going to happen."

"And you're confident about that. But why don't we leave ourselves open to the possibility that you just might reconsider your attitude? This way, you have the details you need and everything's in your control. You make the decision."

I held his gaze, and, fool that I was, reached out and took the piece of paper.

"That's right, kid," he told me. "All I'm asking you to do is think about it."

Two

And think about it I did, for most of that night and throughout the following day. I thought about it when I should have been proof reading the manuscript that was sat on my writing desk and I thought about it when I took my lunchtime stroll and then when I went out for a packet of cigarettes around three. And damn if I wasn't still thinking about it when I found myself stood opposite the window of Café de Brug at a quarter after seven later that night.

The American was in there alright, sat at the same table, and he had two men with him. The men were younger than the American and there was a European vibe about the way they dressed, though whether they were Dutch or not I couldn't tell without hearing them speak. They wore matching leather jackets and light denim trousers but physically they were complete opposites. The man with his back to me was heavy-set, with a thick neck and a shaved head whereas his friend was rail-thin, almost ill-looking, with a pinched quality about his face that made it look as if he'd sucked too hard on a cigarette and had forgotten to exhale. Were they the men who lived in the houseboat and the apartment in the Jordaan, and if they were, which was which? I had the thin man pegged as the boat owner, because I couldn't see him making it up and down five flights of stairs each day without a team of medics in support and a troop of cheerleaders up ahead, but the wide man didn't strike me as the type to have enough cash to live in the Jordaan. But then, why judge a book, you might say, because I sure as hell hoped I didn't look anything like a burglar.

Hand inside my pocket, I fingered the piece of paper with the two addresses written on it. For a moment, I had it in mind to run through the situation once again, to weigh up the pros and the cons that were confronting me, but really there was no point. I mean, who was I kidding, stood outside the café, pretending I had a decision to make? There was more chance of me turning down a midnight tumble with the blonde bartender than walking away from the job now. So I backed off from the window and crossed over the canal bridge and took a few turns this way and a few that, and before very long I found myself stepping down from the street and onto the painted metal deck of a grand old Dutch barge.

I guess that's something that might surprise some people – that most professional thieves tend to avoid breaking into a place in the middle of the night. Sure, there are less people around then, but if anybody does happen to spot you crouching before a locked door at three in the morning, well, they're going to be pretty suspicious. On the other hand, if you tackle that same lock at, say, half past seven in the evening, you risk being seen by more people but there's also a fair chance they won't be concerned about it. After all, burglars only operate after midnight, right?

As it turned out, this particular burglar didn't have to worry either way. For one thing, it was already dark and there was a raw bite to the wind that was keeping people inside their homes and off the streets but, more to the point, it took me longer to pull my micro screwdriver and set of picks from my pocket than it did to snap back the lazy old cylinder lock on the door to the barge.

I rapped on the door and waited long enough for somebody to answer before opening it fully. There were no stirrings or rumblings or, in fact, noises of any kind, which didn't come as a great surprise because the interior of the barge was in darkness and I knew (or at least thought I knew) that the owner was out for the evening chewing on minute steak. I knocked once more and when I was sure there was nobody at home, I stepped inside, locked the door behind me (for all the good that would do) and flicked on a light switch. I suppose some people might be surprised about that too, but it's just common sense – putting a main light on suggests you have a right to be some place whereas flashing a torch beam around a property is just another needless giveaway.

The interior was large and open-plan, a seventies mishmash of wall-to-wall wooden panelling painted yellow, with a shag-pile brown carpet and orange window curtains. I drew the few curtains that were still open and took a moment to look around. There wasn't a great deal of furniture, just a large bed at the bow end of the boat covered in twisted sheets and discarded clothes, a plastic kitchen table stacked with dirty plates and take-away food containers, and a threadbare couch with sinking cushions that faced a television that dated, at a guess, from the last time the room had been decorated. There was also a good deal of built-in storage around the edge of the room, some of it covered in plaid seating cushions, and a small cubicle that protruded from one wall where I assumed the bathroom was to be found.

I raised my hands and cracked my knuckles, like a concert pianist or, more accurately, a thief with mild arthritis. Then I flexed my fingers, waggling them in the air as if I was capable of tuning in to some cosmic presence and divining the hiding place of the safe. My fingers made a faint swishing noise as I did this because I was wearing disposable surgical gloves from a box I had at home which, in turn, I'd taken from the city hospital during a recent visit (for my arthritis, naturally). I was wearing the gloves out of habit – my fingerprints weren't on record anywhere outside of the UK and it was unlikely anyone would look for them here – but habit and routine were my friends, the surest way I knew of protecting myself against costly mistakes.

But I digress. The safe.

Finger waggling aside, the best way to find it was to conduct a reasoned, methodical search, beginning at the front of the boat and working my way along either side, port then starboard, checking each cupboard and cubby hole and cavity until I reached the bedroom area at the rear, assuming it took me that long. And this was the approach I would surely take, in just a moment, after I'd tried a few things first.

So now, if I were a safe, where would I be hiding? Antigua? Hmmm. The bathroom? No, not there. The kitchen? What kitchen? Above the bed? No sign of it. Behind the not-quite-straight picture of a field of tulips hanging on the wall above the couch? Ah, I thank you. Our boat owner, it would appear, was not afraid of the odd cliché or two.

Neither, sadly for me, was he a fan of the classic combination lock safe. Now this was a shame because I've spent more evenings than I'd care to remember with my ear pressed against the metal doors of one or two of the more common makes, listening for the tell-tale click of contact points on a drive cam dial, plotting the numbers these clicks correspond to onto graph paper and coming up with the sequence of digits necessary to open the once impregnable door. All that practice was wasted here, though, because the safe in front of me had an electronic lock. Ten digits in all, from zero through to nine, housed in a no-nonsense keypad. I could try listening for clicks, but it wouldn't do me any good, since an electronic lock doesn't make any noise. Or I could try every possible combination for what might very well turn out to be the remainder of my time here on earth, though I was a little short on patience for that. No, an electronic lock was a difficult customer, alright, and I knew of only three ways around it.

The first, and the least appealing, was to torch the thing. You see, safes generally fall into two categories – they're either burglar-proof or fire-proof. Amazing as it may seem, it's rare to come across a domestic safe that does both jobs for the simple reason that it would make the safe very expensive. So while burglar-proof safes are designed and manufactured to resist attempts to break into them, they lack fire protection. Which is all well and good, but didn't help me very much, since I didn't have time to lay a controlled fire that could reach the kind of intense heats necessary to buckle the metal casing and, more to the point, taking that approach would likely transform the safe into an oven and cook the very item I was aiming to steal.

The second, and much more preferable method, was to use the code. Forgive me for stating the obvious here, but the truth is that no matter how many times and ways we're told not to, most of us keep a written record of the codes to our credit cards and mobile telephones and, yes, our safes, and more often than not we keep these handy notes right beside the very items the codes are meant to protect. So I had a good look for the code. I looked on the fascia of the safe itself, on the wall surrounding the safe, on the front and then the back of the painting that had been hanging in front of the safe, in the nearby cupboards and drawers, in the not so near cupboards and drawers, in the bathroom, among the dirty linen, under the bed. And I didn't find a thing. Not a digit. But it was worth a try.

All of which left me with my final option, which although similar to the second is a little more devious, even though it's based on the most simple of facts – in order to open an electronic lock, you have to press the keypad. And if you press the keypad, come now, what does that mean? Fingerprints, yes! Lots of them. And assuming you don't change your code all that often (or even better, ever) your fingerprints can tell the resourceful burglar which buttons to press, although sadly, not which order to press them in. Incidentally, the only way I can think of avoiding this trap is to wear gloves whenever you access your safe, but then, who wears gloves inside their home, other than your friendly neighbourhood burglar?

If I'd had a little more time, I could have used a particularly neat trick and smeared a little ultraviolet ink on a nearby surface the owner of the boat was liable to touch before opening the safe, such as the picture frame, and then returned at my leisure with a black light (which would have complemented the décor nicely) and got the code that way. But sadly, time was not on my side and I was left to rely on the next best thing – a fingerprint kit.

So, from among the small collection of burglar tools in my pocket, I removed a make-up compact that I'd re-filled some months beforehand with fingerprint powder. I popped the compact open, removed the small brush that was clipped inside and began to carefully dust each numbered key. When I was done, I blew the excess away, then turned off the overhead lights for a moment and angled the beam of my pocket torch over the keypad until I could see what I was looking for. And there they were – four keys smeared in layers and layers of prints – the mystery numbers being 9, 4, 1 and 0. Once this bit of magic was done with, I put the overhead lights back on, wiped the fingerprint powder from the keypad as best I could and began to enter various combinations of the code I'd obtained, working on the assumption that it consisted of just four digits. At some point around ten minutes later, when I was deep into a fantasy that involved me punching the keypad way into next Sunday, I finally heard the welcome clunk and whirr of the locking mechanism retracting and, wouldn't you know it, the door to the safe popped open.

Being a resourceful type, I pulled the door fully back and peered inside. It was only a small space and it contained just four items. First off was a crumpled photograph of two men stood in front of a muddy river, holding fishing rods and tackle boxes, smiling to camera. I recognised one of the men as the thin man from the café and the second figure was almost certainly his father. Beneath the photograph was a stack of euro notes. I picked them up and counted them. The bills were in denominations of one hundred euros and there were sixty of them altogether. I put the bills back where I'd found them, next to a tan coloured bar of what looked to be cannabis. Beside the cannabis was the monkey figurine. The monkey was clutching his ears, as if he was afraid I'd been planning to blow the safe apart. I picked him up and hefted him in my palm and he felt exactly like the figurine the American had shown me. I slipped him into my pocket and had a think about what to do next.

What I decided to do next was pocket the money. Sure, I was being paid over the odds for the job I was carrying out, but that didn't mean I had to pass on a little extra cash when it was right there waiting for me to take it. And while the cannabis held no attraction to me – Amsterdam was hardly a seller's market and if I was ever in the mood for a smoke, I would likely get a much better high from the cheap weed being sold in any number of coffee houses within walking distance of my apartment – I took the drugs too. That way, if the thin man happened to check his safe when he got home he might not automatically assume that the person who'd broken in had been after the figurine. Or at least that was my theory.

With the safe emptied of everything except the photograph, I closed and re-locked the door, hung the painting back on the wall as I had found it and turned off the overhead lights. Then I opened the curtains I'd drawn and made my way outside again, locking the door to the barge behind me and removing my gloves.

I checked my watch. It was already a quarter to nine and I would have to get a move on if I was to meet my deadline. With a casual flick of my wrist, I tossed the cannabis over the side of the barge and into the dark canal waters below and then I stepped up onto the pavement and went in search of a bike.

THREE

Bicycles are stolen all the time in Amsterdam. It's one of the reasons why all the bikes are so old – nobody wants to invest in something that's likely to be taken at any moment. The funny thing is how many locals are willing to replace their stolen bikes with other stolen ones. They buy them from the thieves who operate in Dam Square, keeping the whole racket alive.

I couldn't tell you how many bikes are stolen each day but I know it's a lot. So it stands to reason that there are more than a few bike thieves around. Virtually all of them, it seems to me, use bolt cutters to break through the bike chains and padlocks as quickly as possible. In that sense I'm unusual because I like to use my picks. If a padlock is straightforward enough, I'm almost as fast as a pair of bolt cutters anyway, and my picks are a lot less awkward to carry around. And as an added bonus, I don't destroy the owner's lock, which is often worth more than the bike in the first place.

On this occasion, I chose a bike with Dynamo lights and a comfortable-looking saddle and then I removed the lock and chain in less than a minute. After that, I locked the chain back around a railing and peddled clean away. It turned out the gearing was a little higher than I would have liked but I couldn't do much about that because the bike only had one gear. The brakes were operated by pedalling backwards, something that's illegal in the UK, and though the Dynamo hummed willingly against my back tyre, the front lamp barely flickered. But I enjoyed the ride nonetheless. It lasted a little over five minutes and when I reached the street I was after, I was almost sorry to get off and leave the bike resting against a tree.

The building the apartment was housed in was typical of the

Jordaan. Dark-stoned, tall and thin, it had a gabled roof and an old winching hook extending from its very highest point. It was part of a terrace of perhaps forty similar buildings that each overlooked the Singel canal, and a fine location it was too.

I climbed the steps to the front door and cast my eyes over the buzzers that were affixed to the door frame. The uppermost buzzer, which I assumed belonged to the fifth floor apartment I was after, had no name written on it. I leaned on the buzzer and waited. Given the age of the building, and since there was no speaker positioned nearby, I didn't think I'd operated a modern-day intercom system and so I allowed the occupant enough time to either open a window and yell down at me or to descend the full five floors and open the door. I waited for the minute hand on my watch to complete two revolutions and, when nothing had happened, I gave the buzzer one more ring and waited some more. Eventually, switched-on chap that I am, I deduced that nobody was in.

Of course, the lack of an intercom system cost me not only time, but also an easy way into the building. With a modern apartment block, I could always buzz one of the other apartments and have an unsuspecting person admit me. I couldn't do that here, though, because anyone I buzzed who happened to be in would have to come and open the door, meaning I'd need to somehow talk my way inside while giving them a chance to remember my face. It was unlikely to work and even if it did it was risky.

The front door itself was a mighty thing, fully two feet taller and wider than standard, as though it hoped to deter me through intimidation alone. Fortunate for me, then, that the lock that had been fitted to it was about as resistant to my charms as any one of the near-naked women who danced in the red-lit windows only a few streets away. And just like the more commercial of those particular ladies, the door accepted my credit card, which I slid up the frame until the snap lock slid back. There was a second lock, with a recessed bolt, and it would have been an altogether trickier prospect had the good people who lived in the building decided to engage it.

I eased the door open and stepped inside. Ahead of me was a near vertical staircase that I began to climb in a style not dissimilar from climbing a ladder. The steps were wooden and full of unpredictable creaks and groans and part of me worried that a nosy neighbour might be drawn out from one of the other apartments to ask me who I was. The other part of me cussed the fool who'd built the staircase on such a fun-house angle in the first place. It made me think that anyone who lived above ground level had to be relatively young and healthy and that if I needed to get away from them in a hurry, it wouldn't be straightforward. A nasty image of me slipping and falling and breaking my leg in several places appeared in my head and I winced as I heard the imaginary sound of my femur snapping repeatedly, like an ice cube plunged into a glass of tap water.

I made it to the top floor eventually. I may have stopped twice to catch my breath and to allow the acid to leak away from my thighs, but I didn't encounter anyone else and I was grateful for that. The door I was looking for was at the far end of the hallway and as I squared my shoulders and faced up to it, I experienced a tingle of nervous energy at the thought of entering yet another space that was forbidden to me. This time, part of the buzz was the challenge the locks presented. There were three of them, just as the American had said, but they were of a different order to the locks I'd bypassed earlier. The reason for this was that they were *Wespensloten*, meaning literally, Wasp Locks. *Wespensloten* were the most expensive locks on the Dutch market, and for good reason too. I'd bought several when I first arrived in the Netherlands and it had taken me a while to become familiar with their particular quirks. My big breakthrough only came when I dismantled one of the locks and then rebuilt it in order to understand what was proving so awkward. The answer was that there was an extra set of pins at the base of the cylinder as well as the top, but knowing that still didn't make the lock a cinch and it would usually take me a few attempts to pick my way through.

But before I confronted the locks, I knocked firmly on the door and waited again. When nobody came to see what I wanted, I felt safe enough to slip my surgical gloves on and remove my torch from my pocket. I shone the torch beam around the edge of the door, checking for any tell-tale wires. The American had been right about everything he'd told me so far, but it was my neck on the line if I got caught, so I wanted to be as sure as I could be that there was no alarm. I couldn't see any wires, and while that was hardly conclusive, it was close enough for me to get started.

I decided to tackle the top lock first, and the bottom lock second, because they were both snap locks and likely to be easier than the dead-bolt in the middle. So I got out my micro screwdriver and my picks and, torch in mouth, began to probe away at the internal pins that were preventing the bolt on the top lock from sliding back. Soon, the torch became uncomfortable against my teeth and my jaw began to ache, and, since the light wasn't really helping me a great deal anyway, I pulled the torch out of my mouth and slipped it back into my pocket. I worked my jaw around until it cracked and once it felt comfortable again I resumed teasing and probing away inside the lock cylinder, being rewarded every once in a while with the muffled tick of a pin lifting up to rest upon the delicate internal ledge I was visualising in my mind. Before very long, I had the top set of pins raised and at that point I turned the pick upside down and probed at the bottom set of pins. It was fiddly stuff, but I was stubborn enough to want to do the job right without breaking down the door, and I stuck at it until the last pin fell into place and the force I was applying through the screwdriver caused the cylinder mechanism to rotate. Now the difficult part was over, I wedged the cylinder open and repeated the same procedure on the bottom lock until a little while later that was undone too.

That only left the middle lock, something I delayed tackling for a little while longer by pausing to catch my breath and to wipe the sweat from my forehead with my coat sleeve. When at last I turned my full attention to the lock, I realised with a groan that it was a *Wespenslot Speciaal*, a product that for once lived up to the name the marketing people had conjured for it. The *Speciaal*, you see, worked on the same basic principles as the two locks I'd already disarmed but it also had a few other tricks besides, none of which are worth going into, save to say that they require a little more thought and a good deal more ingenuity, and while that might be something capable of amusing me in the comfort of my own home, it was a good deal more irritating when it happened to be preventing me from entering someone else's. So I cussed my luck and I gritted my teeth and I sighed, and then I got myself together again and began to focus on the damn thing, tackling the pins to begin with and then turning my hand to all kinds of jiggery-pokery and improvisation and sheer brute force until, in a shade over five minutes, I had the cylinder ready to turn. And it was then that I discovered something nasty I should probably have seen coming – the locking mechanism wasn't connected to a simple door-bolt, it was attached to a much larger steel rod that was braced right across the back of the door.

Now this was a problem, and the reason it was a problem was because I didn't seem to be able to transfer enough force through my micro screwdriver to move the rod and I hadn't had the foresight to bring a bigger screwdriver along with me. I stepped back and thought for a moment and what I decided was that I didn't have enough time to get hold of the right tool for the job. The wrong tool would just have to do. So, closing my mind to all the things that could very likely go wrong, I twisted as hard and as fast as I could on the tiny screwdriver and, to my considerable relief, the steel rod gave way before the screwdriver snapped.

With the final obstacle negotiated, I removed my prods and picks from each of the locks and then I eased the door open and peered around it, looking for the infra-red blink of any movement sensors. When I didn't see any, I stepped in way over the doormat in order to avoid any pressure sensors and then I checked under the mat to finally satisfy myself that the apartment really had no alarm. Once I was convinced, I closed and re-locked the door behind me, switched on the main lights and set off in search of the bedroom.

The apartment had two bedrooms as it happened, both situated at the rear of the building, away from the canal views afforded by the picture windows in the front sitting room. One of the bedrooms was tiny and it contained only an unmade camp bed with no pillow. I moved passed it and on to the second, much larger bedroom, which was dominated by a large double mattress in the middle of the floor. I knelt down beside the mattress and felt under the single pillow that was resting on it. Then I felt inside the pillowcase. Then I pulled the pillow out of the pillowcase and turned the pillowcase inside out. But there was nothing there.

I put the pillow back as I had found it and searched under the duvet cover and around and then underneath the mattress. After that I checked the pillowcase once more and then I sat back and scanned the room. It was empty aside from a large wooden trunk. The trunk had a small padlock on it and I picked it open without a great deal of thought and had a look inside. There were plenty of clothes there, as well as a blister pack of what looked like headache pills and a scattering of condoms in various colours. I dug a little deeper and my fingers touched something cold and hard. I knew what it was before I pulled it out of the trunk but I pulled it out anyway.

The object was a handgun. Sure, my knowledge of guns is rudimentary at best, but any fool could tell it was deadly. Holding the gun made me think for the umpteenth time that I really should learn something more about firearms. That way, whenever I happen upon one (which is more often than I care to think about) I could remove the bullets or do something destructive to the trigger that would prevent it from firing. But for some reason, I'm reluctant. Maybe it's because learning about guns is something the bad guys do. Or the police.

Since I couldn't disarm the gun, I began to think about hiding it instead, a tactic I'd resorted to once or twice in the past. The problem, of course, was that the only place to hide the gun inside the bedroom was the trunk and I had a funny feeling its owner might look for it there. One possibility was to take the thing with me but I didn't like it. Imagine if I got stopped and searched outside the apartment by a passing police officer and he happened to find my burglar tools *and* the gun on me. Not an appealing prospect.

And one I really shouldn't have been wasting my time on. After all, the real issue was where the monkey figurine had got to. If it was still in the apartment, finding it wasn't going to be as easy as finding a wall safe. Yes, the apartment was sparsely furnished, but the monkey figurine was only a few inches tall and it could be hidden just about anywhere. And that was supposing it was still here in the first place. The American had insisted that it would be under the pillow and it simply wasn't.

I checked my watch again. It was just shy of 9.30, which meant I only had an hour left until I was supposed to meet the American and just half an hour until the wide man and the thin man would be finishing their meal. The margins were getting uncomfortably tight and that was assuming the American didn't make them any tighter by bidding his companions an early good night. Was that so unlikely? After all, the American didn't know that I'd changed my mind, even if he'd hoped I might.

Ten minutes. That was all I was going to allow myself and it wasn't much time at all. I certainly couldn't dither any longer. But where to begin? I shook my head and raised my eyes to the ceiling, perhaps hoping for some kind of a clue. Which is funny, because I actually found something much better – a ceiling hatch.

The hatch was immediately above my head and I hadn't noticed it before because it had been painted the same colour as the rest of the ceiling. And wouldn't you know it, the thing was positioned right above the trunk. Curious, that.

In a flash, I slipped the gun inside the waistband of my trousers and then closed the lid of the trunk and climbed up onto it. Standing on tiptoes, I pushed the hatch up into the roof space and carefully slid it to one side. Then I felt around the opening with my finger tips. The wood was rough and grainy and covered in dust. I felt right around the wooden frame and still I didn't find what I was looking for. But I had a funny feeling about it all the same and so I popped my torch into my mouth and, with a well-timed leap and a heave, contrived to pull my head up into the opening. Of course, I hadn't had the foresight to turn the damn torch on and so I had to heave myself higher until I had my elbows resting on the inside edge of the hatch and I could reach for my torch with my free hand. I clicked it on and shone the beam around the cold, damp-smelling interior. There was nothing of any consequence in front of me and so I used my elbows to work myself around, legs dangling into the room below, turning almost a complete circle before I saw the monkey figurine. It was just beyond the wooden frame of the opening, resting on its side on the spongy loft insulation, wide-eyed in surprise, with its front paws clamped to its mouth. I reached for the thing and gripped it in my hand and wondered how in hell it could be worth all this effort.

I wondered even more when I heard a sharp bang, loud in the hallway, followed by a second bang and the rip of splintering wood.

FOUR

There were more splintering and ripping and cracking sounds, less violent now, as if the intruder was clearing the split wood away from the hole he'd punched in the door. Then I heard the locks being turned and I figured the intruder had reached his hand through the hole to get at them.

Not, you understand, that I was just hanging around waiting to see if I was right. In point of fact, as soon as I'd heard the first thud I'd heaved myself up into the roof space and I was now busy sliding the hatch back into its housing as quietly as I could. Light from the bedroom was visible around the edge of the hatch but I was pretty sure I had it positioned right. I'd find out soon enough if I was wrong.

I flashed the torch around the loft space, just to make sure my weight was positioned on the wooden joists rather than the padded insulation and the flimsy ceiling board below. Then I switched off the torch and waited.

The door to the apartment opened and somebody stepped inside. They paused for a moment, perhaps surprised that the lights were on and wondering if they should have knocked first.

"Hallo?"

It was a man and he sounded Dutch. It occurred to me for a second that I could respond and that maybe just the sound of my voice would send him running. Then it occurred to me that I should banish ideas as stupid as that one from every last cell in my brain.

We waited, the intruder and me, and when he finally decided that the apartment was as empty as he'd imagined, he began walking in my direction, the noise of his footsteps resonating with the wooden struts I was balancing upon.

He seemed to dismiss the small second bedroom just as quickly as I had and then he made his way into the main bedroom and paused, just a handful of feet below me. Had I left something down there? I didn't think so. In fact, I was sure I hadn't. And I'd put the bedding and the mattress back as I'd found them, and the lid of the trunk was closed too. There was always the possibility that I'd disturbed some dust when I'd been searching around the roof space and that it had fallen into an incriminating pile on the floor below, but that was unlikely, and the intruder would need some keen eyesight to spot a sprinkling of dust from across the room.

I mention the dust because it was a scenario, albeit a little far fetched, that I'd worked into one of my early burglar books. My series character, Faulks, had crawled inside the ventilation system in a Berlin art gallery with the intention of waiting until the gallery closed and then lowering himself on a wire to steal a particular painting, only to accidentally knock some debris through a grate, just in front of a watchful old museum guard. The guard had peered upwards, his suspicion aroused, and Faulks, being a quick thinking type, had made some scuttling noises with his fingernails inside the ventilation shaft. His impromptu rat impression was convincing enough to make the guard shudder, though I couldn't see how that would help me in my current situation.

What in blazes was he doing down there?

Carefully, I lowered my head and pressed my ear against the hatch. But it didn't help in the slightest – it just seemed to amplify the swirling noise of the blood in my ears. I tried peeking through the tiny crack at the edge of the hatch but all I could see was a blur of light. I leaned back and listened some more, straining my ears above the percussion of my heartbeat. There was some kind of movement, though I couldn't be sure what it was. My best guess was that he was searching the bedding, because what kind of noise would that produce anyway? Nothing loud, that was for sure.

Whump.

Now that sounded like the mattress being dropped onto the floor, as if the intruder had lifted it up to search underneath it. More footsteps. A slow creaking noise and a low-level thud. My guess was that he was searching the trunk. He didn't spend long on it. Then I heard him slide the trunk across the floor, perhaps to check if there was something below it, a move I hadn't thought of, and a few minutes later I heard long, deliberate ripping noises. This I thought I understood – he was slicing through the bed covers, which suggested he had a knife with him.

The knife was not a nice thought. I mean, who carries a knife unless they're the type of character to use it? I had visions of a scarfaced, one-eyed drifter, passing his blade from one hand to the other, just itching to cut up the hapless burglar who happened to have backed himself into the wintry roof space above him.

But then, the odds of him finding me were slim, and even if he did, there was always a chance I could somehow talk my way out. I'd managed it in the past. One time, I'd even been caught red-handed by a home owner happily pocketing her best silverware and had managed to walk clean away after giving her a rough appraisal of her collection's worth.

But what was I thinking? I still had the gun stuffed in the waistband of my trousers for God's sake. Which come to think of it now, was kind of worrying, because I hadn't even paused to try and work out if the safety was on before I pushed it towards my groin and began crawling around an enclosed space.

As nimbly as I could, I rolled onto my side and eased the gun from my trousers, then aimed its weighty barrel down at the hatch. The intruder could feel free to poke his head up now, I thought, and if he wanted me to I could blow it clean off his shoulders.

I ended up holding the gun like that for long enough for my wrist to begin to ache, and meanwhile, the ripping and slicing noises continued. Then, just as abruptly as it had begun, the ripping stopped, and the intruder moved on to the second bedroom. I set the gun down, shook some feeling back into my wrist and used my torch to check the time on my watch. It had gone ten o'clock, which meant the wide man could be home at any moment. And he knew about the hatch, even if the intruder hadn't spotted it yet.

I turned the torch beam onto the monkey figurine, wondering what was so special about it. The monkey stared up at me beneath the glare, like a petrified interrogation suspect. He was still covering his mouth with his hands, as if he was afraid he might spill his secret, or worse, squeal and give away our hiding place. I was all set to lean hard on the little fucker to make him talk when I heard the man's footsteps again, moving with more purpose this time, though thankfully they were heading away from me. After that, I heard the front door swing open and the noise of his footfall began to fade away to nothing.

He'd left, I was fairly sure, but I waited another few minutes just to be certain. Then, when I was convinced beyond all doubt that he was gone, I eased up from my crouched position and stretched the cramp out of my legs and my back. Once I'd regained a little movement, I slid the hatch carefully open and swung my legs around and down into the ceiling space below. Then, leaning as far as I could to the side, I lifted up a square of the loft insulation and buried the gun beneath it, pocketed the monkey figurine, lowered myself from the hatch and dropped to the bedroom floor.

I could, at that point, have moved the trunk back to its original position and stood on it to reach up and slide the hatch cover back into place. But really there was no point. My successor had made such a mess of the bedding and the mattress that the room looked as if a sorority house pillow fight had got out of hand. Shredded fabric and feathers covered the floor all the way to the doorway and I didn't have a hope of putting things back as they'd been. And even if I could have magicked up a fresh and identical set of bedding, the gesture would have been pointless because of the mallet-sized hole that had been left in the front door of the apartment.

So I dusted myself off and got out of there as quickly as I could, leaving the door ajar and drumming my way down the five flights of stairs until I reached the front door to the building, which, it turned out, had received similar treatment to its cousin upstairs, although this time the lock itself had taken the brunt of the mallet's force.

I slipped through the door and out onto the street, sucked in a mouthful of chill air, and, for just a moment, found that I had something to smile about. My bike was still there.

FIVE

Café de Brug was empty when I returned. The lights were off and the door was locked when I tried the handle. I was only a few minutes late but there was no sign of the American. I wondered for a moment if he might whisper to me from a darkened side alley but that kind of thing only happened in the pages of my mystery novels. I looked around anyway and found that the street was deserted. If I'd wanted to, it was the perfect opportunity to break into the café, though I couldn't see what purpose it would serve. In the end, I tried the door handle again and then banged my palm hard against the glass.

Within moments, the blonde bartender appeared from a back room. She switched the lights on and hurried to the door to unlock it for me, not even pausing to see what I wanted. Her movements were rushed and she looked anxious. I wouldn't say the colour had drained from her skin, because her tan was too established for that, but the animation was certainly gone from her face. She locked the door behind me and then stood and chewed on her lip and clutched her hands and pushed her hair behind her ear and gave off a hundred other less obvious signals that she was worried half out of her mind.

"They took him," she told me, breathlessly.

"The two men?"

She nodded. "An hour ago. To his apartment."

"You're in on this?"

She hesitated. I pulled one of the monkeys from my pocket and showed it to her. As soon as she saw it, something seemed to catch in her throat and then she nodded, her blue eyes transfixed by the figurine.

"What's your name?"

"Marieke."

"And your connection with the American?"

She met my eyes and blinked and I knew right away what a dumb question that had been. Then she looked again at the monkey figurine and I slipped it back into my pocket.

"You don't think he'll be back?" I asked.

She shook her head, as if clearing her mind of the spell the monkey had cast over her. "He said he would be here all night," she told me. "That he would not leave."

"But something changed his mind."

"It was them."

"Right." I looked about the café for some kind of inspiration. I seemed a little short of inspiration as it happened. "This apartment you mentioned, you've been there?" I asked.

She nodded.

"You'd better show me."

The blonde disappeared into the back room behind the bar again, leaving me to push any doubts I had about what I was doing to the deepest, darkest corners of my mind. When she returned, she had on a padded winter coat and she was carrying a set of keys that she used to lock the café door with before leading me away across the canal bridge and along a series of cobbled streets, her heels echoing in the darkness. It was just starting to drizzle and I turned my collar up and plunged my hands into my pockets as I paced along beside her. I didn't like the way things were shaping up – first the second monkey not being where it should have been, then the gun and the intruder, and now this. The whole situation reeked of trouble and I had a fair idea how it might end, but I also had a girl who seemed as if she could use a little help and, just maybe, twenty thousand euros to collect.

The American's apartment building, Marieke told me, was on St. Jacobsstraat, not too far from Centraal Station. The street itself was a second-rate off-shoot of the Red Light District, lined with squalid bars and coffee houses and peopled by tourists who'd wandered cluelessly off the Damrak only to be approached by shady types selling drugs. One of the pushers followed us for a while and asked me if I wanted to buy some Viagra for the lady. We ignored him until he left us alone, meanwhile passing street-level windows lit with coloured fluorescent tubes where the prostitutes behind the glass seemed bored by the whole charade. One of them was sat on a wooden chair in a Lycra bikini, legs splayed and high heels pressed against the glass, texting someone on her mobile phone.

We were half way along the street before Marieke turned and faced up to an ill-fitting door beside one of the coffee houses. The door was covered in flyers and graffiti and looked like it had been forced open one too many times. She fitted a key into the spring lock and led me inside a communal hallway that was lit by a bare, wall-mounted light bulb, and that stank of stale reefer smoke. We went up a floor in silence, me trying not to make too much noise or attract her attention as I slipped my throwaway gloves onto my hands, Marieke occupying herself by fumbling with her keys.

It turned out she needn't have bothered. The door to the American's apartment was ajar.

I moved past her and walked through the door and found myself inside a cramped, windowless bed-sit. The place was barely furnished but it was neatly kept. In one corner there was a single bed with a dark green bedspread and white sheets. On top of the bed was an open suitcase. I sorted through the case quickly. It was filled with neatly folded clothes and there were some travel documents and a small laptop computer inside, but nothing else of consequence. Beside the bed was a chest of drawers, and all of the drawers were open and bare. On the opposite side of the room was a small wooden table and two foldaway chairs, a single burner stove connected to a gas canister and a free standing sink with a couple of scratched water glasses draining on it. Ahead of us and just off to the side was a second door.

Marieke moved towards the door ahead of me but I put my hand on her arm and went first. I wasn't greatly surprised by what I found; only that he was still alive. He was slumped in the porcelain bath and covered in a lot of blood. The blood was thick and oxidised and dark as good ink. His skull had caved in above his left temple and I could see white flakes of what looked like bone fragments amid the blood that had matted in his hair. His right hand was hanging over the edge of the bath, fingers bent right back at a gruesome angle, but though his eyes were closed and he was clearly unconscious, his chest rose and fell in a fitful way.

Behind me, Marieke shrieked and dropped her keys to the floor, which was better than fainting I supposed. I turned to usher her out of there and back into the other room and it was at that point I heard the sirens for the first time, followed by the screech of car brakes. Seconds later, somebody kicked through the front door of the building and shouted "Police!" up the stairway.

Call me old-fashioned, but I don't tend to hang around when that happens. Marieke was glassy-eyed and shaking but I did what I could in the circumstances.

"You came alone," I told her. "I wasn't here. You came up here and you found him like this and that's all that you know. Marieke? Understand?"

She slumped to the floor, head lolling, and I couldn't be certain whether she'd got it or not. I didn't have time to make sure. The window in the bathroom was a sash and I opened it and climbed out onto the flat roof below. Then I turned around and jumped up to pull the window shut behind me and after that I ran away as fast as I possibly could.

Six

I stayed in bed until late the next morning, then spent the early afternoon printing off a final copy of my latest novel. Once the pages were all lined up and ready to go, I stretched an elastic band around the bundle, added a short handwritten note to the cover page and slipped the package into a large brown envelope. Then I walked the envelope to the central post office where I handed over enough euros to guarantee a next day delivery to London and after that I made my way to Centraal Station and purchased a return ticket to Leiden, the nearby university town.

I needed some time away from Amsterdam, if only for a brief spell, and Leiden seemed as good as any place else. Getting there involved nothing more strenuous than a thirty minute train ride and once I'd bought a takeaway coffee and a fresh packet of cigarettes to smoke during the journey, I was glad to drop my bones into a window seat on the bottom level of a double-decker train carriage and gaze sightlessly out through the dirt-streaked glass at the backs of moving houses and office buildings, and then the hinterland estates and after them the stretches of bleached highway tarmac leading towards Schiphol airport. The train stopped on time at the underground airport station and most of my fellow passengers left the carriage to wheel plastic suitcases towards the escalators at the far end of the platform. Once the train pulled away again, I continued my journey with nothing to distract me other than the hypnotic drone of wheels on track and the occasional draw of nicotine.

I don't remember much of what I did in Leiden. My feet carried me around the cobbled streets and along the canal pathways, I'm sure, but my mind was in another realm entirely, zoned out of my physical surroundings altogether. I often get that way when something big happens to me. Just to order my thoughts I need a change of scenery, but the nature of the scenery usually doesn't matter a great deal. I could have been in Africa or the Antarctic and the effect would have been much the same. All I needed was a little alone time, a feeling of space within which to clear my mind, and no more than three hours later something had clicked enough for me to climb back aboard an Amsterdam-bound train and return to the city.

Two wholly uneventful days later, my agent, Victoria, called me from London to discuss the book I'd mailed to her.

"It's wonderful Charlie," she began, which struck me as a good sign.

"You're not just saying that?"

"Of course not. It's one of your best so far."

"Because I was kind of worried about the ending."

"You're always worried about the ending."

"This time in particular."

"What are you worried about? The briefcase? You think anyone's going to read back and notice it couldn't have made its own way to Nicholson's apartment?"

"Oh crap," I said, striking my forehead.

She waited a beat. "Listen, it's not a huge problem."

"The hell it isn't."

"We'll work it out."

"*We* shouldn't have to. I should have caught it myself. What else? If I missed that I must have missed other things too."

"Nothing big. Really. It just needs a little tidying here and there."

"You're sure? Because this one got way more complicated than I planned."

"Complicated is a good thing."

"Only if I can put all the pieces together," I said, reaching for a pen and a nearby pad of paper.

"You will. I know it. And the briefcase is the final piece."

"Well, it should be," I agreed, drawing the outline of a briefcase on my pad and then crossing it through and stabbing it with my pen for good measure. "But why do I get the feeling that if I solve that one it'll just throw up another hitch?"

"It might. But where would we be without hitches?"

"Oh, I don't know. The bestseller lists? Award ceremonies? Colour supplements?"

"It'll happen Charlie."

"Yeah, right. Just as soon as I work out how to move a briefcase from a police evidence room to an apartment without giving away the killer's identity."

"Maybe the briefcase has wheels?"

I smiled and threw my pen to one side. "Yeah, or maybe I forgot to mention in chapter eight how Nicholson made his money by inventing a teleport machine."

"I liked my idea better."

"You always do."

"Anyway," Victoria said, treating me to one of her more theatrical sighs, "how's Amsterdam?"

I sighed myself. It was a good sigh, as it happened, so I did it again.

"It's Dutch," I told her, when I was done admiring our vocal ranges.

"Wow," she said. "You know, I'm pretty sure that's why I agreed to represent you – your dazzling powers of description, and all."

"You want tulips and clogs and windmills?"

"They have windmills in the city?"

"I've seen a few."

"And Dutch people wearing clogs?"

"Tourists buying clogs. The moment I see a Dutchman wearing clogs and riding a bicycle, I'm moving on."

"But for the time being you're staying put?"

"Well, that kind of depends," I said.

And it was then that I told her about my most recent caper; about the American and the monkey figurines and the houseboat and the apartment and the intruder and the stunning blonde and the almost-corpse the American had become. And while I explained everything to her, Victoria listened with barely an interruption, which is one of the things I like most about her. In fact, her capacity to listen to the finer details of whatever scrape my thieving has got me into since we last spoke is only bettered by her ability to pinpoint plot-holes at a hundred paces and the tendency she has to ask the right questions at the right time, which is something she did the moment I reached the end of my story.

"So this American's not dead?"

"Not yet, anyway," I told her. "I called the hospital this morning. They said he was in a coma."

"They just told you that?"

"Well no, I had to explain that I was Mr. Michael Park's personal physician first."

"And they believed you?"

"It was a nurse. I don't think she knew the procedures. And I guess maybe my accent helped a little."

"Hmm. Wait though, how did you get the American's name?"

"It was on the travel papers I found in his suitcase," I told her. "And it was in the newspaper report too."

"You can read Dutch now?"

"The story was covered in the International Herald Tribune."

"Oh. You think he was someone important?"

"I don't know. Maybe. Or maybe it was a slow news day and the mysterious beating of a Yank in a Dutch brothel house caught the editor's attention."

"They called it a brothel house?"

"They did, although as far as I could tell it was just a lousy bedsit in a pretty colourful neighbourhood."

"With the main colour being red."

"Actually," I said, glancing up from my desk to the moving leaves on the tree in front of my window. "I've noticed that a lot of the brothels use plain fluorescent lights. Although electric blue seems kind of popular too."

"You've carried out a survey?"

"I'm just giving you some of that description you like so much."

"Cute," she said, and I could picture her grinning. "But just going back to these monkey figurines for a minute – do you still have them?"

"The two I stole, yes," I said. "I had a look for the third one in the American's suitcase but it wasn't there."

"You think the men who beat him took it?"

"That would make sense."

"And then they went home and found they'd lost their own figurines."

"I suppose so."

She paused, trying to act casual about the question she really wanted to ask. "Charlie, how much do you think these figurines might be worth?"

"I have no idea," I told her. "If I'd seen them in a place I was robbing, I'd have passed them over as worthless."

"Which they're clearly not."

"So it would appear. I mean, nobody would beat a guy like that just for fun, I don't think."

"Plus you said you thought he'd been tortured."

"I did? Oh, the broken fingers, you mean. Yes, I'm not sure why they did that."

"Well," Victoria said, "people generally only use torture if they want information, right? Unless they're sadists, that is, but that can't be the case here because they stopped at the one hand. Which means either the American told them what they wanted to hear or they figured he wouldn't tell them anything at all."

"Or they got disturbed in some way. Or squeamish. Or any one of a thousand other explanations. None of which we'll ever know."

"Yes," she said, sounding deflated. "But supposing he did tell them what they wanted to know, he could have given them your name, couldn't he?"

"It's possible."

"More than possible?"

"Honestly? I don't think so. I mean, they had no reason to ask anything about me. The way I see it, they were after the third figurine. They didn't know the American had hired me to steal their figurines on the same night. So once he told them where the third figurine was, they had no need to ask any more questions."

"I suppose not."

"And that's not to mention that they haven't come looking for me."

"True. There is something else though Charlie. The man with the knife who broke into the apartment after you – where does he fit into it all?"

"Your guess is as good as mine. But one thing did occur to me – I turned the American down at first, yes? He was hoping I'd carry out the job anyway, and he was right about that, but he didn't know I would for certain. Say he got nervous the next day and hired some-one else at short notice – someone who didn't have what he called "my talent"."

"Which he didn't. Because he used a mallet to get in and he made a hell of a mess."

"Well, a mallet or something similar, but you take my point. Plus he was looking for the same thing I was because he started his search under the pillow."

"And he knew to leave just after ten o'clock."

"Exactly."

Victoria paused and made a humming noise as she considered my theory. I scratched my earlobe, waiting for the outcome.

"But if you're right," she said, "the American took one hell of a chance. Imagine if you two had run into each other."

"We pretty much did! But I guess from his point of view, and going on what happened to him later, he had to be sure someone would get him the figurines."

"Right. Hey, you know what you could have done? Gone back to the café after you found the American to see if someone else was waiting for him."

"Yes, I didn't think of that until the following day. But I'm not sure I could have done it anyway. What if the police had taken Marieke back to the café? I think there's a good chance she might own the place or at least live above it. And supposing she saw me waiting there and pointed me out. It's kind of far fetched but it could have happened."

Victoria didn't respond. Her mind was off on another track, pur-suing other ideas. I waited for her to conclude her thoughts and when she next spoke, it was with a certain hesitancy, as if something terrible had just occurred to her but she didn't want to worry me unduly.

"Charlie, what if the men beat the American like that because he'd already told them what they needed to know? What if he'd told them your name after all and they were just tying up loose ends?"

"You're beginning to depress me."

"Well, don't you think you should consider moving on? I mean, you've finished your book and these men sound dangerous."

"They don't just sound it. But the book's not finished yet and I'm not ready to leave Amsterdam. I like it here."

"Right. Plus there's the girl, I suppose."

"Excuse me?"

"The blonde, Charlie. Don't think I didn't notice the time you spent describing her."

"Marieke? Oh, she's attractive enough. But I hope I'm not quite that transparent."

"Come on, another damsel in distress? You love that stuff."

"Do I now. Listen Vic, if you want the truth I suppose it did occur to me that the American could have given the men her name. But that's really not my concern. I get the feeling she knew what she was letting herself in for."

"There is something else though, isn't there?"

"Well, there's my twenty thousand euros for starters. I did the job I was hired for, after all. But suppose the American doesn't make it and I can't collect, the way I see it I already have two of the figurines. Maybe if I can just find the third one ..."

"Charlie ..."

"I'll be careful."

"But why take the risk? You have the six thousand euros you found and maybe I can try for a little more for this book."

"*If* I can solve the briefcase problem."

"Well, yes. But how about I place some calls?"

"I don't think so. Not yet anyway. Wait until I've had a chance to think it over. And listen, Victoria? I'm going to have to go. There's someone knocking on my door. Take care, okay?"

"Like I'm the one who needs to take care," she said, as I went to lower the receiver. "I mean, what do I have to worry about? A paper cut?"

SEVEN

The man I found on the opposite side of the door to my apartment looked every inch the police officer. He was of above average height (although perhaps not for a Dutchman) with an upright stance that gave him the appearance of a soldier standing to attention. His hair was neat and clipped close to his head and a sober rain coat hung from his angular shoulders, concealing a charcoal suit. The only thing vaguely out of the ordinary were his spectacles, which were frameless and achingly modern, the kind of glasses a Swedish designer might wear.

"Mr. Howard?" he asked.

"Charlie Howard, that's right."

"I am Inspector Burggrave from the Amsterdam-Amstelland police force. I would like to talk with you please."

What he said fell somewhere between a request and an order and the distinction was blurred enough for me to usher him into my living room without another word. Antagonising police officers, I've found, is just about the quickest way to make your life a misery. Still...

"Do you mind if I ask how you got inside my building Inspector? Usually visitors have to buzz me from downstairs."

"Somebody was leaving," he said, without elaborating any further.

"I see. And they just let you inside?"

He nodded.

"You didn't mention you were a police officer?"

I received a puzzled look, as if I was labouring the point.

"Forgive me," I said. "But this is a communal building and I tend to think those of us who live here have certain responsibilities to one another. Especially where strangers are concerned. Could I trouble you to show me your identity?"

He sighed and reached inside his coat with a practised gesture, removing a leather folio that he flipped open before my eyes. I scanned his name and rank.

"That's fine then. Can I get you a drink?"

"No," he said, returning his ID to his pocket.

"A seat?"

The Inspector remained standing, behaving as if he hadn't heard me at all, and meanwhile he looked around my living room, taking in the piles of books on the floor and the coffee table, my writing desk and laptop, the copy of my latest manuscript and beside it my telephone and an ash tray containing a few cigarette butts. His eyes passed over the framed first edition of Dashiell Hammett's *The Maltese Falcon* hanging on my wall and on to the picture windows overlooking the Binnenkant canal below and the houseboats moored along the water's edge. You learn to get used to the way a policeman treats your home – how they inventory everything as if it's their God-given right to nosey around anyplace they please. Burggrave was no different, although perhaps a little more thorough than most.

"Do you have your papers?"

"I'm sorry?"

"Your immigration papers."

"Oh. I don't have any," I told him. "European Union and all that."

He blinked behind his highly polished lenses. "Your passport then."

"One moment," I said, and left him while I went into my bedroom to fetch my passport. When I returned, I found him studying the cover art on the Hammett novel up close.

"Are you a book lover Inspector?"

He just looked at me. "It is a famous book?"

"Quite famous."

"Most people hang pictures on their walls."

"Well, I'm not really that into art. At least not in the conventional sense."

"You have heard of some of our Dutch masters?"

"One or two," I admitted. "Though I've never really cared for Van Gogh."

I handed Burggrave my passport and he opened it at the back page and studied me intently over the top of it, as if he suspected he would find a discrepancy between my passport picture and my face. Then he removed his pocket book and a pen from his coat and began jotting down my details.

"What is your business in Amsterdam, Mr Howard?"

"I'm working on a book myself," I said, gesturing to my manuscript. "I'm a writer of mystery novels. Perhaps you've read one of them?"

"I have not," he said, concentrating on his note making. "Maybe you are not so popular outside of your own country."

"I sell very well in Japan."

"Japan is not the Netherlands."

You could see why they'd made him an Inspector.

"Is this just a routine check?" I asked, gesturing to my passport.

"You were contacted by a man several days ago, Mr. Howard. Wednesday evening."

He glanced up and held my eyes.

"I'm afraid I don't remember that," I said, as evenly as I could.

"He sent you an e-mail."

"Really? I don't recall it at all, but then I have been working quite hard recently. You don't happen to know his name, do you?"

Burggrave studied me some more, looking for some kind of giveaway. I smiled as pleasantly as I could and cocked my head to one side.

"His name is Park."

"No," I said, shaking my head and acting as if I was trying hard to remember. "I'm afraid that name means nothing to me."

"We have his laptop. It tells us you read his message."

"Oh," I said. "Oh wait. Yes. I did have one message now you mention it and I suppose it could have come from this man. I deleted it right away, you see, because it was so odd. He asked me to meet him in a bar, as I recall. Usually my readers might send me a question about one of my stories or ask if I can sign a book. It's rare for them to want to meet me."

"Did you meet him?"

I widened my eyes in surprise, then shook my head no.

"Of course not. Do you smoke Inspector?"

I darted away from his gaze towards my desk and picked up a packet of cigarettes. I made a show of searching for a lighter, looking beneath my papers and inside the uppermost desk drawer, then left him for just a moment to go to the kitchen, indicating with the unlit cigarette in my hand and a roll of my eyes what it was I was after.

In the kitchen, I let out a breath I hadn't known I'd been holding and tried to think where to take things next. The reality was I had few options. I'd set a course now and I'd have to follow it through and see where it took me. Lying to a Dutch police officer about meeting a man who'd been beaten close to death probably wasn't my smartest move ever but it could still turn out okay if I played it right. After all, I got the impression Burggrave hadn't looked into my background yet and if I gave him no cause for suspicion he might never place the phone call to the British Embassy that would tell him all he could care to know about my record.

I reached for the top of the stove, grabbed the box of kitchen matches I kept there and returned to the living room. I was just about to light up when Burggrave motioned towards the lighter that was positioned quite visibly on my desk.

"Right before my eyes," I said, throwing my hand up. "I'm always doing that."

Burggrave gave no indication as to whether he believed me or not. I don't suppose it really mattered. I reached for the lighter and lit my cigarette, the flare reflecting in his spectacle lenses.

"So you did not meet Mr. Park?" he asked again.

"That's what I said."

"But you did not tell him this?"

I exhaled smoke into the room.

"Reply to his e-mail, you mean? No, I didn't. I suppose that was rude of me. But you see, you can never be sure what these people want or how, well, normal they are. I had thought that by not answering he'd assume I hadn't read his message."

"But your computer sent him a message telling him you had."

"A read receipt, I believe it's called. I had no idea about that."

"So it is possible he went to this bar."

"Café de Brug – the Café on the Bridge, I believe. I know it, you see. And I suppose he could have gone. Why is it of interest to you, if you don't mind my asking?"

Burggrave studied me again, as if he was registering precisely what my face was doing so that he could gauge what effect the words he was about to use would have on me.

"Mr. Park is in hospital. He was attacked."

"Oh God. At the café?"

"In his apartment."

"And you wondered if I might know something about it?"

Burggrave nodded carefully.

"Well I'm sorry I can't help," I said. "What does Mr. Park say about it all?"

"He is asleep."

I frowned, trying to act as if I was confused by the discrepancy between the grave look on his face and the words he'd spoken.

"You mean he's unconscious?"

"He could die."

"God. I'm sorry to hear that. I only wish I could have helped further."

I extended my hand to shake but Burggrave just looked at it with mild distaste before moving towards the door of my apartment.

"You will be staying in Amsterdam, Mr. Howard?" he called over his shoulder.

"Until I finish my book."

"I may speak to you again?"

"Fine. But Inspector, my passport?"

Burggrave paused. I opened my palm and held it out to him and after a moment's hesitation he reached inside his jacket and passed the red folder back to me.

"Forgive me," he managed, through gritted teeth.

"Not a problem," I replied.

EIGHT

I sat at my desk for some time after he'd gone, smoking and looking out of my window at the patterns the wind was making on the surface of the canal. I thought about trying to work on my manuscript and the briefcase problem Victoria had spotted but I knew it would be pointless. My mind was on another course now, preoccupied with the mess I'd got myself in. I wondered how wise it had been to lie to Burggrave and then I thought about whether Victoria was right and I should just leave Amsterdam altogether. It wasn't as if I had anything holding me down: my possessions fitted in two holdalls, my rent was payable on a weekly basis and I would be walking away from my latest bout of thievery with close to six thousand euros in my pocket. It was a nice fantasy, so far as it went, but that was all it could be. The fact was I'd told Burggrave I was staying for the foreseeable future and it would look suspicious if I left. And besides, I had a feeling I might be missing out on a pretty intriguing opportunity if I did go.

Leaning back in my chair, I pulled the central drawer out of my desk and set it down on the floor by my feet. Then I felt around in the space where the drawer had been until my fingers found what I was looking for. I stood the two monkey figurines on my desk in front of me, the one covering his ears and the other shielding his mouth, and I held my face in my hands and thought about the third monkey, the one covering his eyes, and then I thought about how I was seeing about as little of my current situation as he was. How much was the complete set of figurines worth? Who even collected these things? And could they be moved on without too much difficulty?

I sighed and knocked the monkeys over onto their heels with a flick of my fingers, then scooped them up in my hand, put on my overcoat and scarf and stepped outside into a wintry, rain-laced breeze.

When I reached Café de Brug, it was almost full inside. Customers in knitted jumpers and woollen hats were warming their hands around mugs of Koffie Verkeerd and one or two were eating slices of spicy apple tart with whipped cream. The clientele seemed almost entirely Dutch and I felt self-conscious as I approached the young man behind the bar and interrupted the background chatter with my English.

"Is Marieke here?" I asked him.

The man squinted at me. "Who are you?"

"We're friends."

The man squinted at me some more and I resisted the temptation to warn him against stepping outside the glass door of the café in case the wind froze his features that way.

"Is she here?" I tried again.

Reluctantly, the man picked up a telephone and, when it was answered, mumbled some Dutch into it. I caught the word "Engelsman" but it was about all I managed. Some way into his short conversation, the man paused, looked me over, and seemed to provide a cautious description. I told him my name was Charlie but he chose to ignore me and hung up instead.

"She is upstairs," he said, directing me towards a door marked "Privé" at the far end of the room. "She waits for you."

I left the man to practise his squinting and walked past the few remaining tables and on through the door. A flight of wooden stairs took me to a second floor landing where I found Marieke looking down at me. She had on a pair of leggings and a baggy sweatshirt, her hair was unwashed and tied loosely at the back of her head, and she wore no make-up. But even with the scowl she gave me, which was far more severe than her friend's downstairs, she still had the ability to make me forget what it was I'd been thinking about.

"We need to talk," I said, not quite meeting her eyes.

Marieke studied me for a moment, then turned and walked

through the doorway behind her. I followed, soon finding myself in a light-filled room overlooking the front of the building, and beyond it, the bridge that spanned the Keizersgracht canal and that had given the café its name. A set of wicker lounge furniture filled the middle of the room, and there was a double bed and a clothes rack in the far corner, plus some nearby metal shelving units containing stock items for the bar: coffee beans, beer nuts, napkins, that kind of thing. Marieke sat herself down on the wicker sofa and folded her legs under her and I chose to perch on one of the armchairs and rested my elbows on my knees and rubbed my hands together for warmth.

"I need to know what's going on," I told her. "You have to tell me who you've spoken to and what you've said. Everything, in fact."

"Michael is alive," she told me, after a pause. "I do not think you care, but he is alive."

I softened my tone. "Of course I care."

"In the hospital, a machine breathes for him. He sleeps always. His fingers..." She shuddered.

"I said I care, Marieke."

She looked at me hard, clenching and unclenching her hand. I wasn't sure what she saw in me then and was even less sure that she liked it.

"Why did you run?" she asked, finally.

"You know why."

"Because you are a coward," she said, jerking her chin at me.

"Maybe. But if I'd stayed, it wouldn't have helped Michael. I don't know that I could have explained what I was doing there. I had my burglar tools on me. I didn't know you, not really."

"It was wrong."

"Yeah, well Michael paid me to do things that were wrong. I have a feeling he did some bad things himself in the past."

"He may never open his eyes again."

"I know that. I spoke to someone at the hospital."

"You have been there?" she asked, scrutinizing me, her lips pressed together.

"I used the telephone. I didn't think it was safe to go. I'm not sure you should go either. I'm not sure about much of anything right now."

"Perhaps you should keep running. Coward."

I sighed. "Look, the police came to see me this morning."

Her eyes narrowed. I could see I'd at least got her interest.

"They asked me about Michael. They knew we met. They said they found out through his computer but I'm not sure I believe them."

"How else would they know?"

"That's what I wanted to ask you."

"Ha," she said, throwing her hands up. "You think it was me? You think I am a coward too?"

"I think you were upset. In shock. You may not have known what you were saying."

"I told them nothing."

"I'm not saying it was deliberate. It's possible you don't even remember. Shock does that. You might have told them about me meeting Michael. Maybe you didn't tell them much more than that. Maybe they filled in the rest."

"You think I am stupid? I told them nothing."

"Alright," I said, making a calming gesture with my hands. "But they still knew. They didn't know if it was important but they knew to come and talk to me."

"What did you say?"

"That we never met."

"And they believed you?"

"I'm not sure. Did you tell the police about the two men Michael was with?"

She glanced towards the floor. "Of course."

"You know them?"

"No. I described them."

"Did the police know who they were?"

She shrugged. "I do not think so. They wanted to know if Michael had met them before."

"And?"

"I said I did not know. It's true," she told me, eyes wide. "I never met any of Michael's friends."

"Some friends."

"But that is what he called them to me."

"How about the monkeys?" I tried. "Did you tell the police about them?"

She shook her head, slowly.

"What is it with them anyway? How much are they worth?"

"They are worth nothing."

"You're sure? Because when I showed you one of them the other night... Your eyes."

"Yes?"

"They opened up. Like I was holding a bright light in my hands."

She began to smile then, as if she might laugh at me, but she managed to control herself and rested her chin on her hands.

"I had not seen him before," she said, simply. "The one covering his eyes, yes. But not the others."

"But what do they mean, Marieke? To you? To Michael?"

"Do you have them with you?" she asked, peering at me.

I shook my head.

"Where are they?"

"Someplace secure."

"Take me to them."

"Not just yet. I don't know what I'm involved in here. They give me protection."

"You will have your money," she said coldly.

"Maybe. But right now all I want are some answers. Why not tell me about the second thief? Did you know about him?"

Marieke's face tangled into a question mark, her lips pursed together to form the dot at the base of the curve her eyebrows and nose were describing.

"So you didn't. I think I believe you. There was a second man, Marieke. He broke into the apartment in the Jordaan while I was there. He was looking for the same thing I was."

"I do not know about this second man," she said.

"I think Michael hired him. I think he wanted a back-up when I said no to him."

"But why would he do this?"

"Because he needed the monkeys on that night in particular. He was very specific about it. It bothered me at the time, though not as much as it should have done."

Marieke unfolded her legs and found her feet, moving to the window at the front of the room. She wrapped her arms about herself and stared at her faint reflection in the window glass. I watched her watching herself, caught up in the circularity of the image. Those freckles on her neck again. Tiny blemishes. Calling out.

"He only wanted you," she said. "Nobody else. You were recommended to him. Someone in Paris. A friend."

"That can't be right," I told her. "I know a man in Paris but he would have told me about this."

"Not if Michael did not want him to."

"Yes. Even then."

"You think so?"

"Yes," I said. "The man I'm thinking of passes work my way. It's how he makes his money. But I have to trust him for it to work. He knows that."

She hitched her shoulders. "Perhaps Michael had to trust him too."

"Not in the same way."

"Of course in the same way," she said, turning to me, her face as open as I'd seen it so far.

"No," I pressed on. "You don't understand. This man is a fence."

"Yes?"

I looked at her expectantly, waiting for my words to register somewhere inside her thick head. They didn't though. They began to register inside mine instead.

"Marieke," I said, "what is it Michael did for a living?"

"You do not know?"

I shook my head.

"But he is like you, Charlie."

"Exactly like me?"

"Yes. A burglar, ja?"

NINE

I sat in my desk chair, fingers laced together behind my neck, and tried to work out how to solve the problem I'd run into.

Nicholson was my killer. For once, I'd known it right from the beginning of my book, and I'd known how to prove he was guilty too. It was all about the briefcase, one with a grizzly secret inside – the right hand of his victim, Arthur the butler. I had my hero, Faulks, figure it all out – how Nicholson wanted Arthur dead so he could get inside the home of Arthur's employer and take back the photograph he was being blackmailed with, how he'd created an alibi by having his wife believe that he'd spent the evening in his study, how Nicholson had, in fact, caught a cab across town, talked his way inside Arthur's apartment, choked him, cut off his hand, and then taken his hand back across town in a briefcase he'd found in Arthur's apartment, at which point he'd used Arthur's keys to get in through the front door and then his cold, dead fingers to open the electronic safe by means of the fingerprint scanner. What I hadn't noticed, until Victoria pointed it out to me, was that I had Faulks pull the briefcase out from inside Nicholson's study to prove his guilt, at which point Nicholson broke down and confessed, but I hadn't explained just how the briefcase had moved from Arthur's apartment, and then latterly the safe storage complex at the police evidence room, to the inside of Nicholson's home.

It was a hitch alright. In the past, I'd solved problems just like it by having Faulks break into places and move the evidence about as he wished. I couldn't do that here, though, because the briefcase was in the heart of a police station, and no matter how fanciful I might allow my burglar books to become, I drew the line at having Faulks burgle the police. One way of sorting it out was to introduce a new character, say a street-wise cop that Faulks could talk into helping him. Maybe the cop would get the collar in return for loaning Faulks the briefcase? It wasn't a bad idea but I didn't like it because it would involve too big a rewrite. If the cop was to have a role like that, he had to appear early on and I'd need to develop a few scenes where Faulks could talk to him and gain his trust and it all sounded like far too much work. Besides, if things worked that way, where was the surprise for the reader when Faulks opened the cupboard in Nicholson's apartment and pulled out the briefcase?

Just as I was wrestling with that very thought, my telephone rang and I answered it. It was Pierre, returning my call. Now I'm pretty sure Pierre isn't his real name but the truth is you need to use a name when you talk business with someone, and since he was French and he lived in Paris, Pierre had always struck me as an appropriate choice. For his part, Pierre didn't care what I called him, so long as he got a share of each job he passed my way and his cut of any stolen goods I needed him to shift.

"Charlie, you have business for me in Amsterdam?" he began.

"Perhaps," I said, leaning back in my chair and propping my feet up onto the surface of my desk, ankles crossed. "Though it really depends on you, Pierre. On how much I can trust you, to be exact."

"Charlie. Please," he said. "We are friends. We do not talk like this."

"Not usually, no" I said, glancing to my right and straightening the picture frame that contained my Hammett novel. "But then I hear things have changed. I hear you give my name to anybody who wants it."

There was a pause on the other end of the line. I cleared away a dust spot from the glass of the frame.

"Americans, Pierre," I prompted. "Admirers of my work. Does that mean anything to you?"

"Charlie – "

"Take your time. This had better be good."

"He is a friend, too," Pierre said, carefully. "An old friend. He wanted the best I knew in the Netherlands. You are my best, Charlie."

"That's reassuring. Did he tell you what he was after?"

"Only your name. I said I would contact you, like we agree, but he did not like this."

"Why not?"

"He did not say."

"You knew he was a thief?"

"Of course. It is why I knew him," he said, with a note of surprise.

"And it didn't make you suspicious that he wanted to hire some-one else?"

"A little, oui. But many men lose their courage."

"You figured that was what it was?"

"Twelve years, it is a long time, no?"

I sat up in my chair and gripped the receiver closer to my ear. "What's this about twelve years Pierre?"

"You do not know?"

"Know what? Was he inside?"

"He did not tell to you?"

"No, he didn't," I said, reaching for my pen and testing the ink on the top sheet of my manuscript. "What was he in for?"

"Why, he killed a man."

"Murder?"

"Non. This man, he try to be a hero – to stop Michael taking his diamonds."

"So he was a jewel thief?" I asked, meanwhile sketching the out-line of a prone body with a question mark planted right in the cen-tre of it.

"Diamonds, Charlie. This is what he would steal. Only diamonds."

"And someone tried to stop him?"

"A guard, oui."

"And he killed him?"

"It seemed so."

I thought about that for a moment. About the man I'd sat oppo-site in the poorly lit café. About how he'd seemed just about as nor-mal as you could imagine. Not a convict, I wouldn't have said. Not a killer.

"Where was this?" I asked, sketching out a diamond roughly the size of the body I'd drawn.

"In Amsterdam."

"And he went to a Dutch prison?"

"Oui."

"They didn't deport him?"

"What is this deport?"

"Throw him out of the country. Send him back to the States. I thought that was what happened."

"This I do not know."

I went over the hook of the question mark again with my pen, building on the layers of ink until the lines became blurred. Then I ground the biro around and around the dot.

"Pierre, did he tell you anything about the job? Did he want you to sell something on?"

"Non. Mais – it was not diamonds?"

"No. It was monkeys."

"Monkeys?"

"Figurines," I said, casting the pen aside and rubbing at my eyes. "Cheap-looking. A set of three. One covers his eyes, one covers his ears, one covers his mouth. You've heard of them?"

"But of course."

"You figure they could be worth much?"

"I do not know. It would depend on many things."

"Worth killing for?"

"He killed?"

"Not this time," I said, then sighed. "The thing is, he's in hospital, Pierre. And he's none too healthy from what I can make out. I'm really not sure what you've got me involved in here."

"This I did not know," he said, in a wistful tone. "It saddens me to hear it. He was someone I could trust. Like you."

"I've never killed a man."

"Non. But what can I do?"

"You can find out about these monkeys. See if there's a market for them."

"But of course. It is nothing. I will begin right away."

"And Pierre, no more giving my name to people. Especially not convicted killers."

I hung up and drummed my fingers on my manuscript, syncopating my thoughts. Three monkeys, three burglars, three men in the café. Everything in sets of three, like a combination lock I didn't know the sequence for. And how many deaths so far? Almost two that I knew of. I just hoped there wouldn't be a third.

TEN

A short while later, I called Victoria and got straight into it.

"Listen, I've been thinking," I said. "What if there were two briefcases?"

"Go on."

"Well, supposing Faulks could get his hands on a second briefcase and plant that in Nicholson's study."

"An identical briefcase."

"Exactly. Remember, Faulks is trying to open the safe when he hears Nicholson come in, and so he hides in the closet. But let's say this time he leaves the door open a bit so he can see exactly what kind of make the briefcase is."

"And he can also see who the killer is. Which ends your book on page 10."

"Stupid of me. So try this. Faulks gets the make of the briefcase from someone at the police station, maybe one of the female officers, in return for a steak dinner. It's a common make, so he goes out and buys a copy."

"Except if the *real* briefcase is with the police, and if everyone knows it, including Nicholson, they'll also know it's a plant."

"Damn."

"And the briefcase is only part of it, Charlie. You need the hand. You need to pop open that case and thrust that bloody hand right in Nicholson's face. In the reader's face, too. That's your climax."

"So I get another hand."

"Another hand? How are you going to do that? Cut off Arthur's left one?"

"No of course not. What about Arthur's niece, the actress?

Suppose she isn't an actress so much as a special effects designer?"

"You want a prosthetic hand?"

"It's not so much I want one," I said. "I just thought maybe it could work."

"But you still don't have your second briefcase, or at least any way of matching the original that makes sense."

"Granted, it needs some finessing."

"I'll say."

I breathed heavily into the telephone receiver. "You know, these are not the easy words of encouragement I was seeking."

"Well guess what, you didn't give me the complete solution I was seeking, either. So it appears we're both disappointed."

"Hmm."

"Although I am glad to hear from you. I've been worried."

"Sweet."

"It's true. Tell me, how are things?"

"Thieving things?"

"What else?"

"Well, they're interesting, I guess. Or complicated, depending on your perspective."

"Enlighten me."

And so I did. I told Victoria about my visit from Inspector Burggrave of the Dutch police, about my conversations with Marieke and Pierre, and what I'd learned about the American. In fact, I breezed through it all as if it was a familiar pitch for a new novel I'd been plotting out and when I was done she said, "So he's a burglar too. It's odd that he hired you."

"Isn't it?"

"You really think his nerve had gone?"

"I'm not sure," I said. "What do you think?"

"Well, it's difficult without meeting him, of course."

"Of course."

"But it does seem odd that he had enough nerve to plan a theft but not enough to carry it through."

"My thoughts exactly. And he killed a man, Victoria. If he'd had some kind of conversion in prison, maybe I could believe it, but a born again convict doesn't get out and start planning a new job."

"I don't like that at all, the fact he killed a man. Put that with the gun you found in the apartment and you've, well, you've got a handful of people who are capable of really hurting someone."

"By breaking fingers and beating skulls, you mean?"

"Quite. So what about the *blonde*," she said, layering the word with contempt. "What does she have to say?"

"Her name's Marieke, as well you know. And to be honest I don't think she told me everything she could have."

"They never do."

"Blondes?"

"Femme fatales, Charlie."

"She's hardly that!"

"She's the nearest thing you've got. It all makes you wonder, doesn't it, what Faulks might do in your situation?"

"Faulks wouldn't be in my situation. At this rate, I'd rewrite the opening chapters to give him some more clues to go on. Think about it: the man who knows everything is in a coma, the femme fatale, as you call her, is holding out on me."

"In every conceivable way."

"Funny. What else? Oh yes, Pierre, who got me into this mess in the first place, knows just about as much as I do, maybe even less. And then there's the rogue intruder, who I don't have a hope of tracking down."

"Plus the wide man and the thin man. Who sound more like a comedy duo every minute, by the way."

"And finally the monkeys."

"About which you don't have a monkeys."

"Ba-da-boom."

"That was one of the thin man's best lines."

"From their successful Blackpool season?"

"No doubt." She sighed. "So what are you going to do?"

"Sorry?"

"What's the next step to solving all this?"

"Who said anything about solving anything?"

"Nobody did. I just thought you might want to look into what happened. Honour among thieves and all that."

"Right. The thing is, I need to look out for myself here, Vic. And it strikes me the absolute best thing I can do right now is keep my name out of this mess. So I'm going to finish my book and then I'm going to work out where I'm off to next and that's it."

"You are thinking of moving on then?"

"Once the book is done, yes."

"Well, have you considered London? We could have a conversation in person for once."

"And remove my air of mystery? Let you put a face to my name?"

"Charlie," Victoria said, as if I was a touch slow, "I've seen your jacket photo a hundred times, remember?"

"Oh yes," I told her. "I forgot."

ELEVEN

After I was through talking to Victoria, I played around with some more plot ideas for a while but I didn't come up with anything new to solve the briefcase problem, at least nothing sensible. The truth was I was forcing things, trying to complete a book that wasn't ready to be finished just yet. Somewhere, deep in my subconscious, my mind was toying with the puzzle I'd set it and in time, though I had no idea when, the brilliant solution would surely come racing through the channels in my mind, like a kid running to show his parents the jigsaw he's just completed. Until then, though, I would just have to wait.

So I dropped my pencil and booted up my laptop and connected to the Internet and gave into my curiosity. Once I was online, I called up Wikipedia and typed in the words "Three Wise Monkeys". I clicked on "search" and soon found the content I was after.

"The three wise monkeys are a pictorial maxim. Together they embody the proverbial principle "to see no evil, hear no evil and to speak no evil." The three monkeys are Mizaru, covering his eyes, who sees no evil; Kikazaru, covering his ears, who hears no evil; and Iwazaru, covering his mouth, who speaks no evil.

The source that popularised this pictorial maxim is a 17th century carving over a door of the famous Tosho-gu shrine in Nikko, Japan. The maxim, however, probably originally came to Japan with a Tendai-Buddhist legend possibly from India via China in the 8th century (Yamato Period). Though the teaching most probably had nothing to do with the monkeys, the concept of the three mon-

keys originated from a word play on the fact that zaru in Japanese,
which denotes the negative form of a verb, sounds like saru, mon-
key.

The idea behind the proverb was part of the teaching of god
Vadjra, that if we do not hear, see or talk evil, we ourselves shall be
spared all evil. This is similarly reflected in the English proverb
"Talk of the devil – and the devil appears"."

All of which, to paraphrase, seemed to be saying that the message
the monkeys had been intended to convey was that you should stay
out of things as much as possible. And who could argue with that?
Not me, for one. So I powered down my laptop and I put on my
coat and then I left my apartment with the intention of taking a
stroll around the neighbourhood before finding a local brown bar
where I could drink a few beers, get something to eat and maybe
strike up a conversation or two.

It was a fine plan, a great one even, but it fell apart the moment
I opened the front door of my building to find Inspector Burggrave
at the bottom of my steps. A uniformed colleague was stood beside
him and a marked police car was parked just behind.

"Mr. Howard, you are under arrest," he told me.

"But Inspector," I said, "I didn't even whisper your name."

*

Handcuffed in the rear of the police car, speeding through the back
streets of Amsterdam with strangers gawping at me, I wondered if
perhaps I should correct Burggrave. I hadn't been *under arrest*. I
couldn't be, not until he had *placed* me under arrest in the first
place. But on reflection, I decided that now was not the time to
quibble over English usage with a man who seemed to have taken
quite a severe disliking to me. Now was the time to keep my own
counsel.

It was just as well I had some counsel to fall back on, because
Burggrave did everything in his power to prevent me contacting a
lawyer and when, at last, one finally arrived at the police station I
was taken to, his English was very nearly as poor as my Dutch. To

begin with the three of us sat around an interview table in a sparsely furnished room, arguing in Dutch and then somewhat more and
somewhat less broken English, about when I would be allowed my
first refreshment break. After ten minutes or so of this nonsense, I
finally made myself face Burggrave directly and said, in a measured
way, that I'd decided for the time being I would let myself be interviewed without my lawyer present. And at that point, we paused for
a refreshment break.

When we resumed, Burggrave was accompanied by the same uniformed officer who had been present at my arrest. He also had a
paperback book in his hand. Burggrave threw the book down onto
the table in front of me and I picked it up and fanned the pages, as
if I was deciding whether or not to devote the next two hours of my
life to reading it. I already knew what happened, though, because it
was my first mystery novel, *The Thief and the Five Fingers*, written
by Charles E. Howard and available at all good book shops.

"Who should I make the dedication out to?" I asked, motioning
for Burggrave's companion to lend me his biro. "My favourite
Dutchman, perhaps?"

Burggrave snatched the biro from his colleague's outstretched
hand and glared at him. Then he sat down in the plastic chair that
was facing me from across the interview table.

"Your picture," Burggrave said, opening the inside back cover of
the book, "it is not you."

"You're right."

"Why is this?"

"Women readers like a handsome author," I said, shrugging.
"This guy was a catalogue model, I believe."

"But you use your real name."

"It's a paradox, alright."

"You write books about criminals."

"A burglar, yes."

He raised an eyebrow. "And you are a criminal."

"Well now," I said, scratching my head, "I can only assume
you're referring to an incident from when I was a much younger
man."

"You were convicted for theft."

"Actually, for giving, though I admit there was a little stealing before that. I was sentenced to a short spell of community service. What of it?"

Burggrave chewed his lip and leaned back in his chair. "It is interesting, I think, that you are a criminal, and that you write books about a criminal, and that you lie about meeting a criminal."

"Well," I said, "I don't class myself as a criminal. And as for lying, I'm afraid I don't know what you're talking about."

Burggrave made a show of shaking his head, as though he was mystified by my response, and then he removed his gleaming spectacles to buff them unnecessarily with his handkerchief. When he was done, he put his spectacles back on and blinked at me, as if he was seeing me for the first time, almost as though the glasses had suddenly afforded him a rare form of super-sight that enabled him to see clean through my lies.

"You told me you did not meet Mr. Park."

"Did I? I have to admit I don't remember the finer details of our conversation."

"You said you did not meet him. But I have witnesses. Three men who saw you in Café de Brug on Wednesday evening."

"Well how can that be?" I asked. "I hope you didn't show them the picture from the back of my novel. That could be most misleading."

"They described you."

"They must have very vivid powers of description."

"I can arrange an identity line, if you wish."

I thought about it. There seemed little point in goading him further.

"I don't think that will be necessary," I said.

"So you admit you were there, that you lied to me before?"

"I met with Mr. Park, yes. But as I say, I'm afraid I don't remember exactly what was said in our previous conversation. I know I wasn't under caution then."

Burggrave made a growling noise deep in his throat.

"Why did you meet?" he snapped.

"I'd really rather not say."

"You are under arrest now," he said, pointing his finger at me.

"You must answer my questions. This man is in hospital."

"I'm not responsible for that."

"Prove this."

"How?"

"Answer my questions!"

"I'm not sure you'll believe me. I think you have a closed mind, Inspector." I turned to his wordless companion. "Is he often this way?" I asked.

The officer looked at me dumbly, then shook his head in a self-conscious fashion. He was using his biro to make notes on a pad of yellow writing paper. I couldn't read what he was writing because it was all in Dutch. Perhaps it was a book report on my novel.

"Tell me why you met him," Burggrave demanded.

"Alright," I said. "I will. He wanted me to write a book."

"A book?"

"His memoirs. He mentioned that he'd been in prison, for theft I believe. I understand he even killed a man. He had the idea I could write his story for him, given that I write books about burglary. I told him that wasn't possible. I'm a fiction writer, not a biographer."

"This you expect me to believe?"

"Believe what you like," I told him. "It's the truth. And I didn't tell you before because as far as I'm concerned a man's past is his own business. What difference would it make?"

Burggrave gave a testy shake of his head, then gestured for his colleague to note down what was about to be said. "You left at what time?"

"Nine o'clock, maybe."

"Did you meet him the next night?"

"No."

"Where were you when he was attacked?"

"I have no idea when that was."

"Thursday night."

"I was writing," I said. "Finishing my latest book."

"And you did not leave your apartment?"

Something about his tone put me on my guard.

"Let me see, I may have gone out for a quick stroll. Yes, I think I remember now. Not long after ten o'clock or so."

"Where?"

"Just around the neighbourhood."

"To St. Jacobsstraat?"

"Possibly. I don't remember too clearly."

"Try Mr. Howard. I think you had better try much harder."

He stood up and said something to his colleague in Dutch.

"He will take you to your cell," he told me. "You will eat."

"You're not letting me go?"

"You are under arrest. Do not forget this."

*

How could I forget? Give the Dutch their due, they know how to put a police cell together. The walls that imprisoned me were painted two-tone, deep beige on the bottom and a lighter beige above. Against one wall there was a hard plastic bed with a thin, stained mattress resting on it, and on the opposing wall was a metal toilet and basin. I had no window to gaze longingly out of – the only light in the room came from an overhead strip light that was housed in one of the ceiling panels above me, beside a heating vent. The door to my cell was made of some kind of reinforced metal, with a slot a little bigger than a letterbox in it, and it was through this slot that my food tray had been passed and where, every hour on the hour, an officer would peer inside to check I hadn't conspired to dig an escape tunnel through the concrete floor with my plastic cutlery. They may have done something clever to the walls, too, because I couldn't hear anything from my fellow inmates. Assuming I had fellow inmates, that is, because there was always the very slim possibility I was the only individual currently detained in Amsterdam on suspicion of committing a crime.

It was all a far cry from the only other police cell I'd ever known, back in England, when I'd first been arrested for burglary. That had been in Bristol city centre, late on a Saturday afternoon, and the place had given me a life-long lesson in just how oppressive a confined space can feel. It didn't help that the holding area was full of drunken football hooligans, swearing and raging and singing Rovers and City chants, kicking the bars and the few pieces of metal furniture, snarling and spitting at one another and spoiling for one more fight. It had made me feel very young and vulnerable at the time, which was not altogether surprising, because I was only just sixteen. And I was a posh kid, way out of my depth, and truth be told, I was scared witless.

I'm pretty sure it's not too fashionable to admit this, but thieving, for me, began at boarding school. You see, on weekends, when a lot of the other kids would go home to visit their parents, I'd wander along the empty school corridors, sometimes trying the odd door here and there. Most of the classrooms would be locked but every once in a while I'd find one that had been left open and I'd walk inside and pace the room and sit down and listen to the silence or to the distorted noises of other kids out on the playing fields. It was enough, to begin with, to be somewhere I wasn't meant to be, without anybody knowing about it. It was my thing, in a world without privacy.

Soon, of course, just being in a classroom wasn't quite the thrill it had been and I started to find myself looking for things to take. I wasn't looking for any one thing in particular, but every desk drawer and every supply cupboard held a secret and I was the type of kid who wanted to know what those secrets were, even if they turned out to be as mundane as pens and paper. It was nearly always pens and paper. And part of me was disappointed by that.

So I began to look around the boys' dorms. I'd wait until they were empty, which wasn't all that difficult, and then I'd approach a bed and open a drawer or two beside it and see what I could see. I found letters from parents, medicines, books, walkmans, cash. Very occasionally, I took something insignificant that the boy wouldn't miss, perhaps an eraser or an old birthday card, and then invariably I put it back the following weekend. Once, I found a condom.

The condom was a precious thing and I put it in the locked drawer beside my bed. We all had locked drawers beside our beds. It occurred to me then that everyone kept their most prized possessions in these drawers. Some drawers were never locked and their contents were generally quite dull. But it was the locked ones that intrigued me and I soon began to ask myself how I could get inside them?

The answer, of course, was to pick the locks. The fact I had no idea how to pick locks wasn't the kind of barrier to stand in my way back then. Pretty soon, I'd equipped myself with a small screwdriver from the technology classroom and a metal implement with a long spike on it from a science lab. And I practised. For hours. In fact, I must have spent just about every spare moment I could find probing at the lock on my own drawer, teasing the pins, trying to force the cylinder to turn. It took me weeks, perhaps an entire half-term, of experimenting. And then one day the thing just opened, simple as that. I locked it with my key and tried again and I was just as successful the second time around. I got quicker, more skilled. Days later, I tried unlocking the drawer of the boy who slept next to me. It was no different. On a whim, I tried my key and discovered that it fitted his lock too! It turned out my key fitted roughly one in every eight locks. Using my key was quicker than picking my way inside so I stuck with that method of snooping. But I remembered what I'd learned.

And then the Easter holidays came around and I found myself at home again in Clifton. Home with my parent's place to myself for much of the day and too much time on my hands. And one morning, bored out of my skull, I got a familiar itch in my fingers and dragged my school trunk out from beneath my bed and rooted around in it until I found my screwdriver and my pick. Then I went downstairs and tackled the Yale lock on my parent's front door. To my surprise, the Yale lock worked on much the same principles as the drawer locks at school and it proved only a little harder to open. I locked and unlocked the door a few times and then I decided to take things up a level.

Our neighbours, the Baileys, were away at their holiday villa in Spain. I'd been in their house on a couple of occasions before but never by myself and I decided that was going to change. After a quick recce, I flicked back the snap lock on their back door with one of my parents' cheque guarantee cards, then spent around an hour familiarising myself with their dead-bolt. It snuck back, eventually, as something inside me had known it would, and after that I had only to turn the handle and walk inside.

Inside to a place that made me feel two hundred feet tall – a space

where I made my own rules. I went to their bedroom first, naturally, since I was of an age where bedroom cabinets usually delivered
some kind of titillation. Those particular cabinets didn't disappoint.
At the back of one of them was a large rubber dildo, along with
some lube. I examined the dildo for a while and then I returned it
and took a tour of the rest of the house – the avocado bathroom
suite, the chintzy spare bedrooms, Mr. Bailey's study, Mrs. Bailey's
exercise room, downstairs to the kitchen-diner, the lounge and the
cloakroom. Pretty soon, I found I was hungry and returned to the
kitchen to see if there was something I could snack on. I stuck my
hand in the biscuit tin and discovered almost fifty pounds in cash. I
put the money back, helped myself to a packet of salt and vinegar
crisps from a nearby cupboard and then I left, re-engaging the snap
lock behind me.

Over the following week or so I broke into a number of our
neighbours' homes, always through the back door, where there was
often just a single snap lock that never tended to delay me. Few of
the homes held anything of special interest – just being inside them
was more than enough to give me the thrill I was after. But I did get
into the habit of always taking something to eat, even if I wasn't
especially peckish, and on one or two occasions, when I heard a
noise out on the street and had to wait nervously for it to pass, or
when a fridge shuddered or a water pipe knocked, I found I had an
urge to find someplace to hide and, once, had to make immediate
use of the toilet facilities.

At nights, I replayed my adventures over in my mind, carrying
out an inventory of all the rooms and the possessions I'd seen, of the
locks I'd opened and the private places I'd accessed. Before long, my
thoughts turned back to that fifty pounds in the Baileys' biscuit jar.
It was just sat there, no use to anyone until the Baileys returned
from Spain, and if it was gone by the time they got back, they might
not even notice, might very well just assume that they'd spent it
before they left. I became convinced that had to be right and so one
Saturday morning not too long afterwards I found myself flicking
back the snap lock on their back door, helping myself to another
packet of salt and vinegar crisps and pocketing the cash from the
biscuit tin. This time, I primed both locks when I left since I had no

intention of returning, but instead of going home, I walked a couple of streets away to the nearest council estate. It took me a little while, walking along the thin, litter-strewn back alleys, to find the kind of place I was looking for, but once I had it, I knew it was just what I was after. It was a small terraced property with rotting, single-glazed windows and a scattering of children's toys in the muddy back yard. I let myself in through the rear gate and peered through the unwashed glass of the patio door. There were no lights on inside and no signs of life. I pulled my burglar tools out of my pocket and probed at the by-now simple cylinder lock. The bolt snapped back in no time at all and I walked inside.

The tour didn't take me long. There were only two bedrooms upstairs, a laundry cupboard and a cramped bathroom. Downstairs there was a lounge that the front door opened into directly and an open-plan kitchen. I found myself some Wagon Wheels in the kitchen and returned to the lounge to find a good place to leave the money. I thought about leaving a note too but then I decided that was a stupid idea. Better to just get out of there. And that was precisely what I was about to do when all of a sudden the patio door flew open and two policemen rushed in, rugby-tackled me to the floor and pinned me to the ground. They were community officers, it turned out, and I'd made the mistake of casing for a likely target in a Neighbourhood Watch Area with a high break-in rate. Needless to say the police had no interest in my Robin Hood credentials and after handcuffing me and throwing me into the back of a waiting panda car, they drove me to the city centre police station, where I spent the longest afternoon and evening of my life before my father arrived to post bail and offer me the most distressed look I've ever had the misfortune to experience.

Come to think of it, I suppose those of you who've read my second Faulks novel, *The Thief in the Theatre*, might recognise much of this, the reason being I used it as back story to explain how Faulks became a burglar in the first place. There were differences, of course. For starters, there was no mention of boarding school, because Faulks is an everyman kind of guy my readers can identify with. And Faulks took more than just the money, he was also trying to deliver some new toys for the kid in the council house. And, of course, Faulks didn't blub like a child in front of the officer who arrested him. But one thing was as true for me as it was for Faulks – from that day on, I vowed always to keep the things I stole for myself.

The clock above the door to my cell read ten o'clock and I knew by now that I wasn't going to be spending the night in my own bed. I was tired and I was feeling low and suddenly all I wanted to do was shut my eyes and block out the beige walls for a while. So I took off my shoes and I lay down on the plastic-coated mattress and pulled the single, coarse sheet over my head, trying to think of nothing but how slowly I could breathe. I didn't ask for the lights in my cell to be turned off, though, because I knew there wasn't the slightest chance I would sleep.

TWELVE

I was in the middle of pushing some processed scrambled egg around my plate the following morning when the locks turned in my cell door and the door swung inwards to reveal Burggrave stood in the threshold with the duty officer by his side.

"The American is dead," he announced.

"You'd better get me a lawyer then," I told him. "One who speaks English, preferably."

When he arrived, it turned out my lawyer actually was English. He told me his name was Henry Rutherford and that he'd been sent on behalf of the British Embassy. Rutherford was short with a large, beach-ball gut and a chipmunk-like face, all swollen cheeks and fatty jowls. His balding head had just a few thickets of fair hair on it and his shirt collar, which seemed at least a size too small, bit into the loose, rolling skin of his neck. He extended a clammy hand to shake, and after I'd given him a brief summary of my arrest and a tailored version of what had led to it, he asked me a more important question.

"Where did you school, dear boy?"

I told him Kings' and we had the usual kind of conversation about it. Then he got around to the task at hand and asked me if I'd received any legal advice since my arrest.

"They gave me someone Dutch before," I told him. "He barely spoke English."

"Good," he said, and when I looked at him for an explanation, added, "It could help us. Unreasonable here in The Netherlands, you see. I say, how much money do you have?"

"On me? I had around six thousand euros when I was arrested."

"Six thousand! My, that's an awful lot to carry around. But I'm talking about bail, dear boy."

"Oh. Enough, probably. Though it might take me some time to get it together."

"That's fine. I dare say we should discuss tactics next. Tell me, have you told them much?"

"Only what I just told you. They didn't care for it."

"Bloody nuisance," he said, pressing a chequered handkerchief against his glistening forehead. "Is there more?"

I just looked at him.

"Very well, you don't have to tell me. You don't look or sound like a killer – any fool can see that. But not answering their questions, that could create problems."

"Can't I take the fifth, or something like it?"

"Of course you can. But you have to ask yourself how that will help your cause. Your aim is to convince them you didn't slay this American, surely."

"But if they can't build a case …"

"Yes, yes, but why antagonise them?" he asked, flapping his hand. "This Burggrave, he's a real career man. Made his reputation on cases just like this, you know."

"You're saying he won't let go."

"I'm saying you should think carefully about what you might be able to tell him. And about what you might not have told him so far."

"Let him interview me again, you mean?"

"Oh you'll have to do that, young man. He'll insist on it, in fact. The real issue is what you might be willing to say."

*

Not a great deal, as it happened. In my experience, one of the most convenient things about legal advice is that you don't have to take it. So for a number of hours Rutherford sat rather stiffly beside me in the interview room, making notes on his legal pad with a quite beautiful turquoise fountain pen, and all the while Burggrave tried everything he knew to get me to talk. Threats, lies, promises – they all came my way. And with each question I ignored or each facile response I gave him, his expression became darker, his brow more twisted. Occasionally, Rutherford would interrupt a line of questioning with a timely interjection and Burggrave would clench his right hand into a fist, dig his nails into the flesh of his palm, count to ten (or even *tien*) and try something else. None of it got him anywhere, though, and the effect this had on him was quite something to behold.

"Tell me the truth," he demanded at one point, grinding his fist down into the surface of the interview table. "Answer me."

"I'm not sure what truth you want to hear," I replied.

He glared at me and I glared back. Then Rutherford suggested that it was about time we took a break. Burggrave paused for long enough to contort his face into an expression of mild loathing, then stood abruptly and left the room without a backward glance. I got up from my chair too and stretched my arms and rolled my shoulders and my neck until it cracked. I wasn't smelling so great. The sweaty fug that comes from spending the night fully dressed was all about me. I turned to look at Rutherford and found him leaning back in his chair and scratching his temple with the end of his fountain pen.

"How much longer do you think this is going to go on for?" I asked.

"Oh, a while yet. Persistent, isn't he?"

"You might say."

"You're certain you don't want to tell him the whole story? We could have a statement drawn up and be out of here in an hour."

"You have a lunch date?"

"Just thinking of you, dear boy."

"No doubt. How do I get to the men's room in here?"

It turned out I had to be accompanied by a duty officer. The officer stood uncomfortably, shifting the weight between his feet, as he listened to the splash and flow of my urine, and then he practised his elevator staring-into-space expression as I washed my face and underarms at one of the grubby washbasins. When I got back to the interview room, Burggrave was already in there, glaring at Rutherford over the rim of a plastic coffee cup.

"I hope you didn't put sugar in mine," I said, and got a glare of my own.

The coffee was not so bad, considering. I nursed my cup while Burggrave repeated the same questions he'd asked me in the previous session. Why did I really meet Michael Park? What was discussed? What were my exact movements on the night he was killed?

I wanted to yell at him to stop being so bloody stupid. Marieke had told him about the thin man and the wide man herself, so why wasn't he following that up? Surely my minor criminal record and the small matter of my lying about meeting the American wasn't enough to distract him from the cold, hard fact that the last two people to be seen with the American had virtually frog-marched him to his apartment? He didn't know about the monkey figurines, that was fair enough, but he seemed to be wilfully closing his mind to the obvious.

I thought of ways I could bring this up but I couldn't see how I could do it without making it apparent that I knew more than I was letting on. I could imagine the sequence of questions I'd trigger and the awkward responses I'd have to come up with: How did I know of the two men? *Because Marieke told me.* Why were you speaking to Marieke and what were you discussing? *Life in the twenty first century.* Why didn't you mention the two men before? *It only just occurred to me.* What is the connection between the two men and Michael Park? *Search me.*

Soon, the futility of what Burggrave was doing began to affect my concentration and, as I moved into a phase where I blankly ignored everything he said, my mind began to wander to other things and I started thinking about what I would do when I got out. I probably wouldn't be able to leave Amsterdam right away, I supposed, but where would I go when I did? Italy, was my current thinking. Away from the constant drizzle and the gnawing breeze, into brilliant winter sunshine and grand open spaces and terraced cafés selling fine, dark espresso. Rome was one option I liked. I could see myself strolling around the Coliseum in the afternoons, eating near the Tivoli Fountains in the early evenings. Florence was another contender, and so was Venice. I wasn't sure about the canals, though – I might have had enough of canals for the time being. And Florence had so much art and culture, so many paintings and artefacts that might very well end up lining my pockets with lira. Or rather euros. But then again, perhaps Italy wasn't the answer. Perhaps I should open my mind to other possibilities. Perhaps –

The door to the interview room opened, breaking my focus, and a woman in a navy blue trouser suit marched in. Her hair was greying and cut in a functional bob and her jaw was set with determination. She nodded briefly at Rutherford, then leaned towards Burggrave's ear and whispered something in a no-nonsense way. As she spoke, Burggrave's expression passed through a spectrum of displeasure, then resolved into a look of aggrieved resignation, at which point he stood and followed the woman out into the corridor.

"You understand what she said to him?" I asked Rutherford.

"Couldn't hear a thing, I'm afraid."

"She didn't look happy. Maybe they've caught the real killer."

"You never know."

"It'd be nice to stop answering these same questions."

"I wasn't aware that you'd answered any."

"Well, I was thinking about it. If only to make him shut up."

"I'm not sure that would have the desired effect."

"Probably not." I glanced at Rutherford's legal pad. "You made many notes?"

Rutherford lifted his fountain pen and showed me the top sheet of paper. It was covered in doodles, elaborate swirls and cross-hatching.

"How much am I paying you again?"

"All courtesy of Her Majesty's Government," he replied.

We sat in silence for a time and I watched Rutherford add to his collection of doodles. I wouldn't have minded a pen and a piece of paper myself. Especially a nice pen like Rutherford's. Perhaps I could draw some doodles and we could get Burggrave to judge our efforts when he returned. Maybe the winning artist would get a fruit lollipop and the chance to go home.

I stood from the table and stretched my legs and my arms, and after that I paced the edge of the room. The room turned out to be square. Twelve paces on each side. I was going to try it with fairy steps next, just to be sure, but the door opened before I had chance and Burggrave and the woman walked back in.

"Mr. Howard," the woman began, planting her hands on her hips, "I am Detective Inspector Riemer. Miss Van Kleef has just given us a written statement. In it, she has sworn that you were with her at Café de Brug on Thursday evening. She says that you were with her there all evening. Is this true?"

Burggrave started to say something but the Detective Inspector cut him off with a wave of her hand. She turned back to me for my answer. I considered it for a moment and then nodded carefully.

"Then you may go," she said. "The Amsterdam-Amstelland police force wishes to thank you for your co-operation."

*

Outside in the car park, Rutherford and I shook hands and made our farewells.

"Just for my own edification," Rutherford asked, straightening his jacket and tie, "who is Miss Van Kleef?"

"Damned if I know."

"But – "

"Don't worry about it," I told him, patting his shoulder and removing a shred of lint from his jacket. "You did a great job for me in there, Rutherford. A real credit to your profession."

"I'm glad you think so."

"I do. In fact, I'd like to give you a little something as a token of my appreciation."

I reached inside my coat pocket and removed the brown envelope the duty officer had returned to me. I pulled the six thousand euros in cash out of the envelope and placed the bundle of notes in his hand.

"Well there's really no need," he said, eyeing the cash greedily. "You know, I didn't do a great deal."

"Nonsense," I said, closing his hand around it. "You did more than enough. But if you feel a little queer about it, how about we call it a retainer? I have a feeling I might need to call on your services again."

Rutherford ran his tongue over his fleshy lips. "Well, I can always use a little extra cash, dear boy. But you must promise to call if you need me. You have my number?"

"I do. You have a good day Rutherford."

"You too, dear boy. You too."

THIRTEEN

Since I hadn't slept at all the previous night, the first thing I did after parting company with Rutherford was to find the nearest tobacco shop and buy a fresh packet of cigarettes. I lit up immediately and smoked first one, and then a second cigarette right down to the filter. After that, I went back inside the newsagents and bought a strip of tram tickets. There was a tram stop right outside the shop and I waited there for just a handful of minutes until a three carriage street tram arrived. I boarded the tram and stamped two of my ticket coupons and then I rode the short distance to Leidseplein. From Leidseplein I walked east, past the crowded tourist bars and restaurants and the canal-side casino, into the entranceway to Vondelpark.

Even though it was a weekday afternoon in winter, the park was still busy. People on rollerblades and rusting bicycles zipped past me, couples strolled along arm-in-arm, groups of backpackers sat together on rucksacks, smoking candy-smelling joints, and the occasional freak show walked by – one girl had her face pierced with countless metal rivets and the man she was with wore nothing more to protect himself from the cold than a pair of fishnet stockings and a leather jockstrap.

I dragged my weary bones as far as the Blue Tea House, where I took an outside table, settled into a rubber-strung chair and ordered a Koffie Verkeerd. I smoked some more of my cigarettes and drank my coffee, letting the caffeine and the nicotine and the icy breeze battle against my fatigue and the sore ache in my eyes. Then I ordered a second coffee and sat there drinking it and smoking another cigarette until finally the chill and the nicotine became too much for me and I buried my hands in my pockets and continued my walk.

I walked right around the perimeter of the park and it took me close to an hour. By that time my toes were feeling the cold too and my nose had started to numb. My mind felt clearer, though, and I seemed about as awake as I was likely to get. So I made my way directly to a side exit from the park and after that another tram stop, where I punched two more coupons on my ticket and rode the tram as close to Café de Brug as it would take me.

Marieke didn't appear surprised to see me. Without uttering a word, she left the bar under the control of a middle aged woman she was working with and led me to her upstairs apartment. Once there, she settled on her wicker couch and lit a hand-rolled cigarette. The cigarette turned out to be a joint. She offered me a hit and when I waved my hand no, she vented a long stream of marijuana smoke towards my face. I blinked it away, inhaling just a little.

She was wearing a pair of low slung jeans with no belt and a hot-pink sweater. Her tanned stomach was exposed and from the way the sweater gripped to the rather lovely contours of her breasts, I could tell she wasn't wearing a bra. I waited for her to wrap her lips back around the joint and take another draw and once she had a mouthful of the smoke I got down to it.

"You took one hell of a risk with your statement," I said. "Say I'd already told them the truth?"

"I did not think you would tell them anything," she said, exhaling halos of blue smoke along with her words. "Like you told me when we found Michael."

"That was different. It was a spur of the moment thing."

Marieke watched me for a moment and, even in that short period of time, her pupils seemed to dilate just a shade and her features began to soften.

"So what if it was a risk?" she asked, in a faint drawl. "You did not kill Michael. I know it."

"I'm sorry he's dead."

She nodded and toked on the joint once more. "He liked you," she managed, her voice sounding pinched.

"We only had one conversation."

"Even so," she went on, croaking. "He told me you were smart."

"Not smart enough to avoid getting arrested."

"But you did not tell them about what Michael asked you to do. The stealing?"

I shook my head. "I told them Michael wanted me to write a book about him. That was all."

"They believed this?"

"No. But then you made your statement and they had to let me go. Burggrave didn't like it, not one bit."

She took another hit on the joint. She seemed to be enjoying it. The tension in her face eased yet again and her eyes became unfocused, dreamy even. I wondered how much she'd smoked since Michael had died. I wondered just how together she'd been when she made her statement.

"You told them what, we were smoking weed together?"

"I told them we were lovers," she said, in a matter-of-fact way, and tapped a fragment of ash into a mug on the coffee table.

"But they knew you were in a relationship with Michael."

"Yes, but it is not so hard to believe that I might have slept with you too," she said, straightening her back. "Or that you would not want to tell the police about this."

I forced my eyes away from her breasts and onto her face.

"I could have told them once he was dead."

She frowned. "But I told them this yesterday."

"Yesterday? What time?"

"It was quite late, perhaps eleven o'clock," she said, pouting. "I came to the police station when the woman called me. Riemer, ja?"

"But Burggrave kept me in until this afternoon," I said, half to myself. "No wonder she was pissed with him."

"I did not know."

"No," I said, turning back to her, "that's what he was relying on. I get the impression he doesn't believe either of us."

Marieke lowered the joint and searched my face, her movements languid. "But it is over now, yes?"

"I don't know," I said, shrugging. "Maybe. The two men Michael met, do they know about you?"

"No. We were careful."

"And you really don't know their names?"

She shook her head, then looked up abruptly. "But you know where they live. You have been there, yes?"

"And?"

"We can tell the police!"

"I don't see how," I told her. "Not without it being clear we've been lying."

Marieke took another contemplative drag. Then she nodded, as if to confirm the idea that had formed in her mind.

"We will say that we found some papers, that Michael left their names here where I could find them."

"But we don't know their names."

"Their addresses then."

"It might work. I'm not sure. You want them caught?"

"Of course."

"But we don't know for certain they killed him."

"Who else could it be?"

"Well," I said, "now there's the question."

I leaned back in my chair and threw up my hands, as if I was open to suggestions. Marieke watched me, her face quite severe. I didn't shy from her gaze. I just looked back at her, simple as that. From nowhere, she giggled. It just slipped out, as if she'd had no idea it was coming, and a plume of hashish smoke came with it. Wide-eyed, she smothered the laugh, doubled over with her body jiggling. Then she righted herself and took a deep breath and held it and fought to regain her composure. She arched her back and inhaled through her nose and her breasts swelled against the pink sweater in a way I gave up trying to ignore. I looked back to her face, where a druggy smile played around the corners of her mouth, and she looked away from me, towards the corner of the ceiling. She struggled to make her face serious again, one more smile slipping through the net. Then she waved it away, wafting it from her face with both hands, sighed, took her deepest drag so far, ground the joint into the ash tray on the low table between us and stood and crossed the short distance towards me. She paused for just a moment by my feet, and then, as if she'd finally resolved herself to it, she straddled me, lowered her face towards my own and pressed her lips against mine. She parted my mouth with her tongue and exhaled gently and, as we kissed, the reefer smoke floated up around us, catching in her sweet smelling hair and scratching at the back of my throat.

*

Afterwards, we lay on Marieke's bed while she lit a fresh joint that we smoked together. I watched the smoke drift up from my mouth and hang in the air above me, meanwhile teasing a strand of her hair between my fingers. She rested her hand on my chest and crossed her leg over my waist. Then, when I was sucking on the last of the joint, she finally asked me what she'd wanted to know all along.

"Charlie, will you give me the two monkeys?"

"But you don't have the third one," I said, exhaling.

She shook her head against my chest.

"So what's the use?"

"For me. Please. I would like the two you took."

I made a show of thinking about it.

"Do you have the twenty thousand?"

"Michael made me keep it here."

"Then we should go to my apartment."

FOURTEEN

In all honesty, I knew the moment we reached my apartment that someone else had been inside. Call it a burglar's intuition. Call it the small things I'd learned during my years of breaking and entering. Call it the fact my door had been smashed clean off its hinges and was lying flat on my living room floor.

As soon as I saw the door, I told Marieke to wait out in the hall-way and stepped cautiously inside. I didn't expect to disturb anyone but I didn't want to take unnecessary risks either. Checking the place didn't take long. I only had the living room, the kitchen, the bathroom and my bedroom to search. Once I'd confirmed there was nobody inside, I went back to the doorway and told Marieke to join me.

"Excuse the mess," I told her.

"But this is ridiculous," she said. "Charlie, it is terrible."

It was pretty terrible, even for a self-confessed burglar. My every possession was scattered across the floor – books, manuscripts, notes, CDs, photographs, even my laptop. The few soft furnishings in the living room had been sliced open and their stuffing exposed and much the same thing had happened in the bedroom to my clothes, my sheets and the mattress I slept on. In the bathroom, the side-panel along the bath had been unscrewed and my burglar tools had been removed from their hiding place there and discarded in the bath itself. In the kitchen, all the cupboard doors had been opened and the food and household sundries the cupboards had contained had been dumped in a big, soggy pile on the floor. The freezer door was ajar too and a pool of water had formed around its base, then spread to touch the edge of the grocery pile and form a stinking toxic sludge.

I led Marieke away from the kitchen and back to the living room, where I approached my desk, picking up the broken desk drawer from the floor on my way towards it. I set the drawer to one side, dropped to my knees and felt around in the space where the drawer had been. My fingers searched right around the drawer cavity but no matter how hard I searched, the figurines weren't there. My shoulders dropped and I turned to her and shook my head.

"They're gone."

"No," she said, through gritted teeth, like a teenager trying to deny the obvious.

"I'm sorry," I told her. "I thought they'd be safe here. I had good locks fitted to that door. And I didn't think anyone would know I was involved."

"Who could know?"

"Perhaps my arrest was in the paper. That would connect me with Michael and it would be easy enough to find out where I live. Anyway, it's obvious, isn't it? The second intruder, the man who broke into the apartment in the Jordaan while I was still there, he did this."

Marieke frowned at me. "It is obvious why?" she asked.

"Because I saw what he did to that apartment, remember? He's done the same thing here. All the ripping and the slicing. Forcing his way inside by breaking the door. Leaving everything in a mess. And it wasn't a random burglary. My laptop would be gone if that was the case."

"But who is this man?"

"You tell me."

"But I do not know. How could I know?"

"Because I think Michael hired him. And because I think he would have told you about it."

"I told you he didn't," she said, swatting the air with her hand and then pointing at me. "Do not say these things. They are not true."

Marieke stamped her foot on the floor and then she started to scream and yelp. I could have told her to quieten down, that she might disturb the neighbours, but then I remembered that the noise of my door being smashed through and my apartment being torn apart hadn't upset them, so I let her scream all she wanted. She was so good at it that part of me was tempted to join in. Eventually, though, she stopped and glared at me, looking for all the world as if I was the only reason for her present troubles in life.

"You told me they were safe," she said, pointing again. "You are an idiot. You kept them in your desk. This is stupid. It is the first place I would look."

"Well it wasn't the first place he looked, or he wouldn't have gone to the trouble of carving open a perfectly respectable couch. That's my damage deposit gone, right there."

"You joke? You think you can make me laugh? I will not laugh. You are stupid. The monkeys are gone. You are a stupid, stupid man. And to think I ... I ... with you," she spat. "For what? For this?"

"You mean you faked it," I asked, batting my eyelids.

"Stupid," she yelled, flapping her hands in the air. "Stupid!"

She kicked at the broken couch, then kicked it some more. When she was through kicking the furniture, she stamped her foot once again. Then she shrieked, eyeballed me with more contempt than I would have cared for, and finally stormed out of my apartment.

After she'd gone, I dropped onto my backside and looked around longingly for the well-ordered room I used to know and love. If I focused hard enough, I could almost picture it, but I soon gave up trying because the gulf between the image in my mind and the one that presently confronted me was so depressing. True enough, my own thieving is a pretty sizeable character flaw, but I'd never do anything like this to somebody's home. It was going to take me hours to clean up and probably hours more to explain to the letting company what had happened and to convince them there was really no reason to report it to the police. And I would have to pay to replace the door and the couch and the bedding, plus any incidental damage I happened to come across as I tidied. All things considered, it was turning into something of a costly day, especially if you included the six thousand euros I'd given Rutherford and the twenty thousand I'd missed out on from Marieke.

I was still slumped on the floor almost half an hour later, trying to muster the will to get started on the clean-up process and fighting the tiredness that was beginning to afflict me yet again, when my telephone rang from somewhere beneath the pile of scattered books by my side. I searched through the pile until I found the plastic telephone receiver and then I snatched it to my ear.

"Charlie," Pierre began warmly, as if he was greeting me after an interlude of many years, "where have you been? I have been calling since yesterday and you never answer. I am beginning to think you leave Amsterdam."

"I'm starting to think I should, Pierre. Tell me, what have you found out?"

"About these monkeys, it is not so good news, I am sorry. If they were very old, made from ivory maybe, they could be worth a little. Otherwise, non."

"I think they're made from a modern material. Plaster, perhaps."

"Then they are worthless."

"That's what I was afraid you'd say. There's no market for them at all?"

"A few collectors. One in Switzerland I spoke with. Mais, the price, it is not good. Sometimes, he collect metal monkeys, gold say, but usually these come from Japan. He did not sound interested in your monkeys. I am sorry Charlie."

"No, that's okay. I sort of expected it. And, well, there's something I have to tell you Pierre. It's bad news I'm afraid."

And at that point I did my best to explain that Michael was dead without blurting the news out insensitively or humming and hawing for no good reason. I told him when it had happened and I shared my condolences and then I shut up and waited for Pierre to react in whichever way he cared. He was silent for a few moments and then, in a slightly hollow voice, he thanked me for telling him and muttered a short blessing.

"You want me to try and find out if there's going to be a service?" I asked.

"No, thank you."

"He struck me as a good man," I offered.

"Oui. And an excellent thief."

"I'm sure." I paused for a moment, then cleared my throat. "Pierre, I don't mean to be crass but there's something I need to ask you. When Michael spoke to you about what he needed, did you recommend anyone else to him?"

"In Amsterdam? Non. Only you Charlie."

"So where would he have gone if he wanted to hire a second burglar?"

"This I do not know. Why would he do it?"

"Exactly what I've been asking myself," I said. "But not to worry. You've already been a help."

"If you say so Charlie. But please, take care, oui? It does not seem so safe for burglars in Amsterdam just now."

I couldn't agree with him more. Setting the phone down, I rubbed at my eyes and groaned rather indulgently and then I got up from the floor and made my way back into the kitchen. It was all just as I had left it, a sorry jumble in the middle of the floor. I stepped over the puddle of melted water from the freezer and kicked a cereal box and some kitchen paper to one side so that I had somewhere to put my feet. Then I rooted through the sticky, sodden detritus until I found the box of washing detergent I was looking for. I wiped my hand dry on my trousers, reached inside the box and delved into the citrus scented powder and felt around until I found what I was after. I checked the room for any prying eyes and then I pulled the two monkey figurines out from where I'd hidden them at the bottom of the box. I dusted the soap granules off of them, then held them before my eyes and asked myself for what seemed like the hundredth time what could possibly be so special about them.

Fifteen

I was up early the next morning, which might have surprised me given the lack of sleep I'd had during my night in police custody, if it wasn't for my mattress being somewhat less comfortable now that it had been sliced and torn apart. My early start was a blessing in some ways, though, because it meant I'd completed the bulk of the cleaning and tidying before the chore could impact on too much of my day. By nine, I was able to call a joiner to come and fit a replacement door to my apartment and afterwards the two of us worked together to secure my old locks to the new door. I could have changed the locks, of course, but it would have cost me a tidy sum and there seemed little point while they still functioned. It wasn't as if I'd left a spare set of keys lying around and besides, whoever had broken in was more than willing to bypass a good set of locks anyway.

Once I'd settled up with the joiner and seen him outside, I telephoned Henry Rutherford and asked if I could buy him breakfast. He said he'd be delighted to join me and we arranged to meet at a café-restaurant on Westermarkt, not far from the Westerkerk and the Anne Frank House. I arrived before him and bagged us a window table and when he showed up we made small talk over plates of fried egg and ham and mugs of strong black coffee until I asked him if he could possibly spare me an hour or so and accompany me to the city library. Rutherford agreed readily enough, as men who enjoy hard cash are prone to do, and so I led him down the Prinsengracht canal in a pleasant morning sunshine that reflected off the canal water and bathed the colourful Dutch barges and prestigious brown-brick townhouses lining the canal banks in a pleasant glow. At the Centrale Bibliotheek, Rutherford did the talking and I listened as, in fluent Dutch, he arranged with the girl on the counter for us to be given access to a micro-fiche machine and a series of slides containing back issues of De Telegraaf and NRC Handelsblad from roughly twelve years ago. The girl led us, carrying the slides, to a small private room where Rutherford hung his jacket over the back of a chair and rolled up his shirt sleeves while I fetched a second chair so that I could sit beside him and offer what help I was able to provide.

Together in front of the antique-looking machine, the two of us passed three of what were quite possibly the most tedious hours of my life, speeding through reams of Dutch headlines that rarely made even the vaguest sense to me. To his credit, Rutherford never complained, and though I apologised for the nature of the task I'd set him more than once, he proved the very definition of studious dedication. As the hours ticked by, it reached the stage where I could close my eyes and still see the sepia newspaper files rotating on the back of my eyelids, and had we not got lucky when we did, I'm sure it wouldn't have been long before I'd have called time on the entire endeavour and told Rutherford he could give it a rest. As it happened, though, Rutherford suddenly gave a self-satisfied gasp of delight and showed me exactly what it was we were looking for on the front page of an October 1995 edition of De Telegraaf.

At that stage, Rutherford made some hasty notes and afterwards we moved to a brown bar just a short distance further along the canal. There I ordered us a brace of toasted ham sandwiches and a couple of glasses of Heineken and, once we'd filled our stomachs with the food, Rutherford unfolded the sheet of paper he'd scrawled on and told me what I wanted to know.

"It was a botched robbery, by all accounts," he began, blotting his greasy lips with a paper napkin. "The article we found was the court report from the trial of your American friend. It seems he tried to carry off one of the biggest diamond heists in Amsterdam's history."

"Really?"

"Oh yes. There was quite a sizeable trading company back then called Van Zandt's. Have you heard of it?"

"It doesn't ring a bell."

"No reason why it should, of course." He drained some of his Heineken, meanwhile circling his hand to let me know he was set to continue. "Must be five, six years since they were bought out," he said, gasping. "By a South African multi-national I believe. Back in the day, though, they were a major company in the Netherlands. Every Dutch person would have heard of them."

"And their business was diamonds?"

He set his beer glass to one side, bobbing his head. "Precious jewels, I suppose you'd say, though diamonds were the heart of it. Like a lot of the Dutch jewellery merchants, they imported mined stones from the former Dutch colonies and cut them here in Amsterdam. They had a facility bordering the Oosterdok with quite a number of warehouses, if I remember correctly." He raised his eyes to the ceiling, as if the answer was etched into the Aertex above us. "Yes, that's right, they had their name plastered along the side of the buildings."

"So they were a big deal."

"Indeed they were. As were the diamonds they traded. Some of the world's finest gems, without question."

"And Michael stole some?"

"Well, yes, though how many is open to debate. The article isn't terribly clear on it. Apparently some jewels were recovered from his home, that's what they got him on, but there was speculation that a great deal more jewels were stolen. Van Zandt, though, denied this out of hand."

"A cover up?"

"That seems to be the implication. No doubt it would have been against their interests to let people know their security was anything but airtight."

I nodded, ignoring the way Rutherford was eyeing the last of my sandwich. "So Michael faced trial for burglary?"

"Aggravated burglary, with manslaughter. That's what they got him on in the end."

"Yes, he killed a guard."

"A security guard who worked for the company," Rutherford said, consulting his notes. "A Robert Wolkers, age 44. It seems Mr.

Wolkers disturbed the American while he was trying to access the main diamond storage facility. The American shot him."

"He was carrying a gun?" I asked, slipping the last morsel of ham and toast into my mouth.

"So it would seem," Rutherford said, through pinched lips.

"I've never heard of a professional burglar carrying a gun before."

Rutherford shrugged, no small gesture for a man of his size. "Well, your American did. The prosecution theory was he shot the guard but was so thrown by the whole incident he fled the warehouse before he got the jewels he was after. The ones he took weren't worth very much, you understand."

"According to Van Zandt."

"Yes, according to them. But the American would never confirm it either way."

"He was what, arrested some time later?"

"One day," Rutherford said, raising his index finger.

"Which would have given him time to hide the really valuable jewels, if he did have them."

"Arguably."

I chased the last of my sandwich with some beer, swilling it around my mouth to clear the toast from my teeth. "So what happened at the trial?" I asked, working my tongue around my molars. "Did Michael plead guilty?"

"Guilty to the robbery charge. There was enough circumstantial evidence to prove that, not least because of the diamonds they found in his home. But he denied the manslaughter charge."

"Interesting. On what grounds?"

"He said he'd never even seen a guard."

"There was only one on duty?"

"No, as it happens," Rutherford said, glancing at his papers. "There were two, though the other guard was in an altogether different part of the building when the robbery occurred. Didn't hear a thing, apparently, although he was the one who discovered the body. I wrote his name down somewhere. Is it important?"

"I'm not sure," I told him. "Probably not."

"Well it's here someplace. Ah yes, Louis Rijker."

"Riker? As in 'striker'?"

"Almost. There's a 'j' in there too. Silent, of course."

"Of course."

I paused and thought about what Rutherford had told me for a moment. As a burglar myself, there was a fair amount I didn't buy to begin with, but even then, some of the facts simply didn't gel.

"So why did he flee, I wonder?"

"Excuse me?"

"If he never saw a guard, as he claimed, why did he leave without the diamonds?"

"Ah, well that's the point, isn't it?" Rutherford said, leaning back in his chair and opening his arms in an expansive gesture, as if he was willing to give the entire café a hug. "One would assume that if the American never saw the guard, he got away with all the jewels he could care for."

"Yes, I suppose one would. But I take it the jury saw it otherwise."

"Well, yes. He put himself at the scene, after all, gave himself motive, had no credible alibi."

I sighed and put my face in my hands. "It's all pretty confusing Rutherford."

"Well, it was only one newspaper article. We could go back and find more. Only," he said, wincing a little, "I really do have to get back to the office this afternoon."

"That's okay," I said, peering out from behind splayed fingers. "I'm not sure it would help a great deal anyway. The trial report must have contained most of the information on the case."

"You're probably right. But there is one more thing I haven't told you yet."

I lowered my hands. "Oh?"

"The police officer who arrested the American. Guess who?"

"Not Burggrave?"

Rutherford nodded, a playful grin spreading across his face. "Oh yes," he said, rising from his chair. "Your favourite Dutchman."

SIXTEEN

"What does that mean?" Victoria asked me, when I telephoned her later. "This Burggrave being the arresting officer?"

"I'm not sure," I said. "Probably just a coincidence."

"You don't believe that."

"Don't I?"

"No. The lead character never does. He tells everyone it's just a coincidence but really he thinks it means something. And that's how he solves the case."

"Well, not this time," I said, smiling. "This Burggrave is a good officer. I might not like the man a great deal, but he knows what he's doing. And it's not so unusual that he arrested Michael back then. Somebody had to."

"And that somebody just happens to be investigating his murder too?"

"Well, try it this way: say he took the murder assignment *because* of his history with Michael. Or maybe he was *put* on the case because of it. That's very possible. It's not as if his bosses wouldn't know about the connection."

"I suppose. But still."

"But still." I glanced out of my window, above the uppermost branches of the tree outside my building to the low, grey clouds that had begun to form, pregnant with rain. "You know," I said, in an offhand way, "I'm beginning to think you read too much crime fiction."

"Well, duh. It is my job."

"Sometimes I worry it's a bit more than that though." I craned my neck and looked to the west, where the blue sky of earlier in the day was drifting away. "Tell me, when was the last time you went on a date?"

"You mean a real one? Not imaginary?"

"Seriously."

"Last night, as it happens."

I whipped my head back around. "Oh."

"But you needn't worry. It was a complete disaster. He was the brother of one of my friends."

"Compromising?" I asked, dropping into my desk chair.

"Potentially. But that wasn't the problem. He had false teeth."

"Really? How old was this guy?"

"Thirty-two," she said, primly. "Same as me."

"And he had false teeth?"

"Almost a complete set. He even took them out and showed me them."

"Am I that out of touch? I didn't realise poor dental hygiene was such an aphrodisiac these days."

"Ha ha. I actually felt quite sorry for him. It was an accident, the poor sod. He works back-stage at one of the theatre companies, you see, and a winch he was using hadn't been tied back properly and, well, it swung down and caught him square in the face."

"Ouch."

"Yes, ouch."

"And then you compounded things by freaking out about it," I said, laughing.

"They were yellow, though! Not canary yellow, but still, you could tell. And I couldn't stop looking. So he took them out, to put my mind at rest."

"Only it didn't."

"No, it bloody didn't. The thing is, when he took them out, he kept talking. And I happened to look up from his teeth to his gums. And they were ... horrid Charlie."

"He might have been a nice guy."

"He *was* a nice guy. But imagine waking up to those gums every morning. Urgh. It was too much for me. But you see, I do have a real life. It's just sometimes it's more fantastical than the books I read."

"I'll say."

"But even then it's nothing compared to what you're caught up in. It's exciting, don't you think?"

I sighed. "It's more worrying than anything else. These people have been inside my home now. And I've been inside a police cell. I'm wondering what else can happen."

"Maybe you've caught something from the blonde."

"Vic!"

"It's possible."

"Be serious though, it is all quite a mess."

"You'll figure it out, I'm sure."

"Will I? I still don't know if I even want to."

"Ah, but do you have a choice? Events seem to be conspiring against you."

"Jesus."

"It's true. Really Charlie, you're going to have to solve this thing if you want any peace."

"From you at least. But listen, how about I leave it to Burggrave?"

"The genius who arrested you?"

"It wasn't necessarily a bad move. I was lying to him, after all."

"But you're not the killer."

"No."

"So who is?"

"Got me." I heard a gentle tapping against my window and looked up to see the first drops of rain striking the glass. The beads of water began to cluster, then slide down the pane. "And to be honest," I went on, "I'm still more interested in these monkeys. Pierre says they're not worth a thing but then you look at all the trouble they're causing. The lengths people will go to just to get their hands on them."

"The blonde being a case in point."

"Thanks."

"So the monkeys are the key?"

"I guess so," I said, as the clouds really let go and the rain fell in sheets for the first time, the branches of the tree outside my window bowing under the onslaught.

"Either them or the second intruder," Victoria said.

"What's that?"

"You said he was the one who broke into your apartment."

"Yes," I replied, returning my attention to the telephone while the rain beat against the glass just to my side. "I did say that, didn't I?"

"But now you're not so sure."

"Tell you the truth, I never was." I turned in my chair and scanned my room, as if to jog my memory. "The break-in I had was similar to the one in the wide-man's apartment, granted. But there were differences too. Ignore all the mess, the slicing and everything. The thing that gets me is my door."

"The one you found on your floor."

"Exactly. Whoever broke into my apartment drilled the hinges and then kicked it through. But the second intruder used a mallet or something similar to break through the door in the Jordaan apartment. It was messy, but it worked."

"Is there really such a big difference?"

"I think so. Drilling the hinges was cleaner but it would have taken a little longer. And why would the second intruder try something different if the mallet worked for him before?"

"Maybe your door was sturdier."

"I don't think so. My door wouldn't have withstood a mallet attack."

"So," Victoria said slowly, as if to gather her thoughts. "If it wasn't the second intruder, who the hell was it?"

"Well, ask yourself something – what were they after?"

"The monkeys."

"Yes. And why would they want them?"

"We don't know that. We're going round in circles."

"Not if we make an assumption."

"What kind of an assumption?"

"That whoever broke into my apartment already has the third monkey."

I waited. It didn't take long for the cogs to mesh in Victoria's brain.

"Ah. And they want the complete set."

"Naturally."

"So it was the wide-man and the thin-man?"

"That's my guess. We can rule the second intruder out – the break-in didn't match his style and even if it did, I have no way of tracing him."

"Right. He's banished from my mind. So what now?"

"I find out what's so important about these damn monkeys."

"And how do you plan on doing that?"

"I have a few ideas."

"Oh, no. You can't be like that. Tell me."

"Not just yet. Things might not pan out."

"Not fair, Charlie. You know, I'm beginning to think you write too much crime fiction."

"Ha," I said, looking glumly towards my desk. "No danger of that at the moment. I still haven't solved my briefcase problem."

"I did wonder. I wasn't sure if I should ask or not."

"I have been kind of busy with other things, you know."

"I do. I guess I just thought with all that thinking time in your police cell ..."

"Didn't happen. I tried but I didn't come up with anything. How about you?"

"You're the writer, Charlie."

"Oh sure, I forget, that's why they pay me the big bucks, right?"

SEVENTEEN

He was waiting for me outside of my apartment building. I had walked down the front steps, still slick from the recent rain shower, fixed the headphones of my walkman into my ears beneath my beanie hat, and turned west, barely registering the noise of the car engine turning over or the sensation of the car trundling along the wet cobbled street just behind my shoulder. It was only when the car pulled level with me and I caught a glimpse of him leaning across the vast front passenger seat of the old Mercedes that I realised he was beckoning to me. I removed my headphones and lowered my head towards his open window.

"Inspector Burggrave," I said, as pleasantly as I could. "Just passing were you?"

He gave me a hard look, in no mood for my games.

"Get in the car," he said, speaking in a flat, robotic tone.

I cocked my head on an angle and studied him. His face was pitted with stubble and his clothes looked rumpled. His eyes were red-tinged behind his angular glasses and dried spittle was encrusted on his lips and at the corners of his mouth. He looked as if he'd been up all night but I couldn't quite bring myself to believe he'd spent the night in his car waiting for me to emerge. A man like Burggrave would have just called up to my apartment.

"Get in," he said again.

"Am I under arrest?"

"Just get in the car."

"So this is a social call. I'm afraid I have plans this morning. Perhaps we could do this another time?"

His hand tightened around the steering wheel, the flesh of his knuckles beginning to whiten. He took a deep breath and then prised his fingers away from the steering wheel and gestured at the world beyond his rain-streaked windscreen.

"Let us just go for a drive."

"No, not today," I said, and began walking again.

Burggrave engaged his clutch and crawled along the road beside me, his wheels splashing through the puddles. He didn't speak for a moment and I got the sense he was trying to order his thoughts. Either that or he was fighting to control his temper.

"You did not kill the American," he said at last, as if explaining events to a child. "I know this now. But you were with him that night, in St. Jacobsstraat."

I met his eyes. He certainly looked as if he believed it.

"Does Detective Inspector Riemer know you're here?" I asked.

Burggrave made a growling noise, deep in his throat.

"You were in St. Jacobsstraat," he repeated, fighting to keep his voice under control.

"And you know about the wide-man and the thin-man," I said. "The two men who made Michael go back to his apartment? Marieke told you about them."

He waited for me to go on, eyes wary.

"But you arrested me instead of investigating them. And ever since I've been wondering why."

"You lied to me."

"People lie to police officers every day. They don't usually spend a night in custody because of it."

The hint of a smile tugged at his features. He liked that he'd bothered me and that bothered me a little more. I stopped walking and he halted the Mercedes beside me.

"I don't know what you want from me," I said.

He didn't speak. We just measured each other, trying to gauge something indiscriminate from one another's eyes, the large engine of his car idling between us. There was something there, though I didn't know what it was.

"Is there something you have to say to me Inspector? Because I'm waiting to hear all sorts of things. Anything, in fact, you'd care to share. I have more questions than answers, you understand."

He thought about it. I could tell from the way his expression softened that he was considering taking a chance on me. But then, in the
next instant, his face clouded over and he set his jaw and re-gripped
the steering wheel. He shook his head, as if resolving himself to
some new course of action, and then, looking away from me, he
squeezed on the accelerator and the car slipped forward and moved
off along the sodden street.

*

I wondered at first if I should have done as he asked and climbed
into his car. I asked myself if he would have told me the things he'd
almost said. Perhaps he'd believed he would, if we got out of
Amsterdam for a while, but I wasn't so sure he could bring himself
to do it. He didn't trust me, and for good reason, so why should he
tell me more than I needed to know? And what did he want me to
tell him in return?

Somehow, the way the conversation had played out felt unsatis-
factory to me. I had the nagging sensation I'd missed an opportunity, though I had no idea what that opportunity was. And maybe, in
the end, I'd really saved myself from something. Maybe Burggrave
had planned to go all renegade on me. Maybe he'd intended to drive
me to a remote spot and beat the information about the monkey figurines out of me. Maybes. There were too many of them, too many
unanswered questions, all of them fogging my brain and preventing
me thinking clearly.

I walked on from my street the short distance to the
Oosterdokskade Bridge, at one end of the Oosterdok. To my left
was the grand red-brick façade of Centraal Station, nexus of the
Dutch train system and home to raggedy-clothed vagabonds and
glassy-eyed druggies, hookers who couldn't afford the overheads of
a lighted glass booth and western students bent-double with the
weight of the ruck-sacks on their backs. To my right was the bleak
expanse of the eastern dock area, rain drops ticking onto the surface
of the water from the bridge railings I was leaning against. The
dark, petroleum-laced currents undulated listlessly, nudging the flot-
sam of discarded city litter against the concrete edges of the dock.

Commercial vessels were moored all around – tugs, transporters, sightseeing barges and even a dated cruise ship that had been transformed into a floating youth hostel. A few decrepit houseboats awaiting refits or the scrap yard were dotted here and there, along with the odd rubber dinghy.

The edges of the dock were bordered by anonymous pre-fab warehouses where nameless industrial processes were undertaken or complex chemicals stored. Between the warehouses I saw bare concrete yards, with stacks of wooden palettes and mini forklift trucks parked beside the gleaming BMWs and Mercedes of the factory owners. Occasional manual workers, dressed in faded boiler suits and heavy duty work boots, smoked cigarettes or talked into two-way radios beneath plastic hard hats.

The docks were a large, open area and the biting wind that had followed the storm showers swooped across the surface of the water unhindered, cutting into me, seemingly passing right through the fabric of my overcoat and woollen hat and gloves. I blew warm air onto my hands and rubbed them together as I walked, pulled my chin down against my chest to stop the wind getting at my bare neck, and battled the cold for quite some time before I found the buildings I was looking for.

The complex of stone-built warehouses lined the curved area near the mouth of the harbour, at the point at which the dockland water met with the expanse of tidal water that separated central Amsterdam from its northernmost district. There were three warehouses in all, linked by raised walkways positioned on the fourth floor of the six storey buildings. All of the warehouses were empty and looked as if they'd been that way for a number of years. Most of the single-glazed panels in the windows fronting the dock had been smashed or blown through and on closer inspection, the bottom floor of each building was nothing more than a vast concrete carcass, while the yards that adjoined them were filled only with wild-grass and abandoned metal cages and the burnt-out remains of a Renault 19. Painted alongside the front fascia of the middle warehouse, in stylised, faded white lettering, were the words *Van Zandt*, just as Rutherford had said.

I'm not sure what I was hoping to find, really. Some grizzled old

employee of Van Zandt's, perhaps. A factory hand who'd worked
there twelve years ago and had fallen on hard times since, warming
his gloved hands over a burning oil drum, just itching to talk with
me and bestow a nugget of information every bit as valuable in its
way as the jewels the American may, or may not, have stolen. But it
wasn't to be. The truth was there was nothing there except dead air
and vacated space; the shell of a memory of a place that used to
exist.

EIGHTEEN

When I got back to my apartment I fixed myself a mug of hot tea and some toast and then I fished around in my wallet until I found Henry Rutherford's business card. I dialled his number from my desk phone and was transferred directly to an answering machine. A tinny-sounding Rutherford invited me to leave a message and I obliged him with the shortest one I could devise.

Once I'd returned the telephone receiver to its cradle, I leaned back in my chair, rested my feet on my desk and formed my fingers into a pyramid beneath my chin. I sat like that for a while, looking, I imagined, as if I was thinking about a whole bunch of terribly complicated things. As it happened, I was thinking of nothing very much at all. Sometimes it's just comforting to sit that way, to rest one's chin on one's finger tips, to balance one's weight over the hind legs of one's chair, and to stare aimlessly at the opposite side of a room. And before very long, I got caught up in a kind of game with myself, easing the chair just a shade beyond its natural balancing point, taunting myself with the possibility of falling and then catching myself with my heels before I toppled right over. I could have stayed that way for hours, at least until the room became fully dark around me, but before dusk had given serious consideration to settling my telephone rang and I answered it to be confronted by a good deal of huffing and wheezing.

"Charlie," Rutherford gasped. "You called and left me a message."

"I did," I agreed. "Are you alright? You don't sound too well."

"I just walked up four flights of stairs to my office. Damn elevator was broken again. I swear they do it on purpose to keep us all on our toes."

"You ever wonder if it could be counter-productive?"

"Oh, I'll be fine," he said, uncertainly. "Just give me a moment and the old ticker will be back to normal. You want to tell me what you need? How I can help?"

"This Van Zandt company you were telling me about," I said, "the one Michael robbed. I was thinking – you mentioned it was a family firm?"

"That's right."

"Well are any of these Van Zandt's still around, do you know?"

"There's one," Rutherford said. "Lives near the Museum District, I believe. A recluse by all accounts."

"You have his address?"

"I could get you it. But I doubt it would do you any good."

"I'd like to try," I said. "See if he'll talk to me, at least. There's no harm in that, I don't think."

"Only the risk of a wasted trip. Should I come along? I know a fine restaurant nearby and ... "

"That's okay," I cut in. "No need for you to tackle those stairs anymore than you need to. If you could just find me the address, though, I'd appreciate it."

"I'll have my secretary look into it. She'll call you as soon as she can."

True to his word, I received a phone call not ten minutes later from an efficient sounding Dutch woman who gave me the address and contact number for a Mr. Niels Van Zandt without even pausing to confirm who it was she was speaking to. I would have thanked her for her trouble but she rang off before I had chance. It's curious – the Dutch will tell you they're direct, but never rude. Why bother to embroider what you're saying with politeness, they'll ask? Just say what you need to. But the odd thing is, while the rational part of me can't fail to agree with this approach, my emotional side struggles every time I experience it. This occasion was no different and I shook my head in wonder as I replaced the telephone receiver. Actually, it was still bugging me when I gathered my coat and walked towards Centraal Station to catch a tram to Museum Plein.

It was already dark by the time I reached the castle-like Rijksmuseum and as I strolled through the archway running through the centre of the building, my path was lit by a series of ornamental lamps. I emerged from beneath the museum to find myself stood at the threshold of a thin reflecting pool shrouded in mist. A bar-café was open nearby, spilling neon light and music out into the gloomy space, but I turned from it and walked north in search of the Van Zandt residence.

The house was not what you might typically think of as imposing, but it was impressive by Amsterdam standards, largely because it was a detached property with a genuine front lawn. The lawn looked to be well tended and it was in remarkably good health considering the amount of rain the city had endured over the past few months. The lush grass was illuminated by two security lamps at the front of the property and the ambient light escaping the windows of the rooms on the ground floor. Directly ahead of me, two parallel lines of conical-shaped topiary plants bordered a pea-gravel pathway that led to right up to the giant double doors at the front of the house. I would have liked to follow that route directly to the ornamental brass knocker if I could, but a pair of gilded security gates barred my entrance. There was an intercom just by my elbow and I pressed the call button and lowered my face to the speaker.

I heard the burr and crackle of feedback and then a female voice answered with a simple, "Ja?"

"Hello," I began. "Is Mr. Van Zandt in?"

"Who is this?"

"My name is Charlie Howard. I'd like to speak to Mr. Van Zandt."

"You do not have an appointment?"

"No," I confessed. "But I'd appreciate it if he could give me five minutes of his time."

"This is not possible without an appointment."

"Can I make an appointment?"

"You must telephone in the morning."

"Can't I make one now?"

"It is too late."

And with that she cut the intercom connection. More directness, and this time I handled it about as well as I had done earlier. The childish portion of my psyche was all set for a bout of knock-knock ginger, but the dull, adult portion soon won out. I poked my face through the gates and looked longingly at the house. Part of me was tempted to climb up over the security fence and let myself in through a window, just to see if Van Zandt might talk to me if I could bypass whoever it was that had answered the intercom. Chances were, though, he'd call the police. And given recent events, it didn't strike me as a master plan.

Reluctantly, I began walking off along the street. There were several more houses of a similar style, though not many of them had security gates. A few welcome lamps tripped on as I passed but I got the impression they were there to aid house guests rather than deter burglars. On another night, that might have led me to consider whether the area was full of soft targets but my mind was on other matters anyway and with Burggrave on my case it wasn't the right time for me to contemplate any casual thievery.

I got as far as the end of the road, then turned left and left again, until I found myself stood opposite the entrance to the Van Gogh museum. It was closing time and the last visitors were wandering down the concrete steps at the front of the building, many of them carrying poster tubes. No doubt most of the tubes contained yet more prints of those damn sunflowers. They seem to be in every tourist shop window in the city. The image is available on postcards, on T-shirts, on tea towels and on coffee mugs. You can buy it on mouse-mats or baseball caps or as a jigsaw puzzle. It's a wonder the average visitor knows that Van Gogh painted anything else.

The tram stop I was after was just down the street from the Van Gogh building and when I reached it I found that I was stood opposite the Costers Diamond House. Now I'm not usually one to believe in symbols or fate or cosmic balance or any of that stuff, but quite honestly, it was one hell of a coincidence. And coincidence aside, maybe all I needed was an excuse to try my luck at Van Zandt's place one more time. Just leaving it alone was bugging me and in my experience persistence usually leads to some kind of resolution, however welcome. And if I was never going to get an opportunity to speak to Van Zandt himself, it seemed to me I might as well find out right away rather than waste my time waiting to telephone in the morning.

So, with my mind made up, I re-crossed the tram tracks embedded in the tarmac roadway and headed around the block to Jan Luijken Straat once more. And, wouldn't you know it, just as I was approaching from the end of the street I saw those self same gates open and a well-dressed woman emerge. The woman wore a beige raincoat and sheer tights and high-heel shoes, and she carried a compact satchel in one hand. Her hair was tied up in a tight bun and there was a business-like expression on her face. I watched her secure the gate behind her and then I waited for her to walk off along the street, feeling certain that the woman I had spoken to on the intercom had just concluded her daily duties. I waited until she turned at the end of the road and then I approached the intercom and pressed the call button for a second time.

On this occasion, there was no immediate answer. I gazed at the lighted downstairs windows for some indication of movement but I couldn't discern anything at all. Perhaps the house was empty altogether, though I doubted it somehow. The woman I had spoken to hadn't confirmed Van Zandt was home but I'd got the impression he was there. From what Rutherford said, he rarely left, and while the average householder might leave on the odd light to deter burglars, it was an unusual type indeed who left on as many lights as this.

I was just about to press the call button again when my patience was rewarded. This time, there was no voice on the speaker, only a short buzzing noise before the gate was released from its catch. I admit I was surprised, but not being one to shy away from a bit of good fortune, I eased the gate open and stepped inside, then made my way up the short pathway to the front doors, the pea-gravel crunching beneath my feet like a thousand tiny bugs. When I reached the door, I even tried something novel and lifted the brass knocker and used it to rap on the woodwork.

Silence.

I waited a moment and knocked again. This time, I heard shouting. Now my Dutch was still basic at best, but I got the distinct impression I was being cursed. What on earth was going on here? Did the guy want me to use my picks and make my own way in?

I knocked for a third time and the shouting drew nearer. It

seemed to become more vehement the closer it got, as though the person doing the shouting was approaching very slowly and their irritation was increasing with each new step. Before long, the voice was coming from just the other side of the door and, at last, I heard the deadlock snick back and then a face with the potential to knock me clean off my feet appeared in the gap between door and frame.

The thing is, coming completely clean here, sometimes in my novels I've based characters on people I've met in real life. I can even think of at least two occasions when I've lifted entire physical descriptions and personalities from acquaintances I've made. More often, though, my characters are an amalgam of two or more people. An older relative perhaps, mixed with a dash of a train conductor from the previous day and finished off with a television newsreader. Other times, I've based physical descriptions on a person from a magazine and invested them with character traits from a historical figure I've read about, or afflicted them with an illness I've been researching. But never before had I been confronted with the real-life incarnation of a character who'd only ever previously existed in the world of my imagination. For incredible as it seemed, stood before me now was the very image of Arthur the butler, and the likeness was so striking that I can do no better in describing him than by repeating the very first lines devoted to him in the pages of my book.

The old man had skin that had worked hard for its living. It was shrivelled and puckered and folded into fine lines all across his forehead and at the corners of his eyes. Where it was stretched, across the bridge of his nose for example, it looked gossamer thin, while at his neck it had braided itself together into what looked like frayed lengths of old string. The hair on his head was thinning and as white and downy as pillow feathers, and on either side of his head two sprigs of it poked out of his over-sized ears like the pads of cotton wool you used to find in pill jar lids. His eyes were grey and watery, like pebbles on a seashore, and he seemed to look clean through me with them, almost as if he was blind. His shoulders were rounded and his back bowed and he walked with the aid of a dark wooden cane. Hanging from his bony frame was a black butler's suit, finished off with a white shirt that was yellowing at the collar and a dickie bow that had probably last been tied at about the time the Titanic went down.

So okay, the man who faced me wasn't wearing a butler's outfit, but in every other way the similarity was enough to make me jump. Oddly enough, he did the same thing, and then he clutched at his heart with the hand that was holding his walking stick. He steadied himself against the door frame, lips opening and closing wordlessly, like those of a beached fish. Then he looked up at me and shook his head ruefully, his teeth clenched together and eyes glowering out. All at once, he began yammering away in confrontational Dutch once more.

"Hang on," I said, holding up my hands. "I'm English, I'm afraid. And I didn't mean to startle you."

He paused, mid-tirade, then switched to words I could understand.

"Who are you?" he asked, eyes narrowing.

"My name's Charlie Howard. Are you Mr. Van Zandt? I'd like to talk with you, if so."

"You do not have an appointment?"

"No."

"Then you must leave. This was a mistake. I thought you were my housekeeper. I thought she had forgotten her keys."

"She just left."

"Then she makes you a good example."

He started to swing the door closed. Before I could think better of it, I stuck my foot in the jamb and pressed back against the door with my palm. Alarm flashed in his eyes. His cheeks trembled. For a moment, I was pretty sure he thought I was going to attack him.

"I just want to talk," I said. "Please. It's important."

He shook his head wilfully and pushed against the door again. He was a strong old goat and if I hadn't had my foot stuck in the way he would have caught me out. As it happened, the door bounced back off of my shoe.

"Move your foot," he told me, shoulders quaking.

"It won't take more than a few moments."

"I will call the police."

"Listen, it's about Michael Park."

The name carried impact. All of a sudden, the force he was exerting against the door began to ease. He glanced up with a certain wariness and I knew then what it was I needed to say.

"He's dead, Mr. Van Zandt. That's what I came here to tell you."

Nineteen

Niels Van Zandt directed me into what looked to be his library. There were floor to ceiling shelves of books on every wall, many of them leather bound, almost fake looking, like those dumb book-shaped VHS cassette holders from the eighties. It was always possible he'd bought the entire collection just to fill the room and make himself appear intellectual but I didn't think so. I got the impression this was a room where he spent a great deal of his time. The large reading table over by the front window was covered in piles of books that had been removed from the shelves, for instance, and several note pads and a typewriter were positioned among them. If what Rutherford had said about Van Zandt being a homebody was true, this was how he occupied himself.

I guess it didn't hurt that he had a drinks cabinet too and while he ushered me into a fabric armchair positioned just away from the imposing central fireplace, he set about fixing us both a bourbon. He didn't ask me if bourbon was something I drank – it was an assumption he made, like trusting me that Michael really was dead. The news had certainly affected him and I was fairly sure the palsied tremble in his hand as he grappled with the ice tongs was not simply because of his age.

"How did he die?" he asked, casting me a hawk-like glare as he held a couple of ice cubes above one of the glasses.

"He was killed," I said. "Beaten."

Van Zandt's brows hitched up, though not in surprise. It was more as if he was acknowledging that another of his assumptions had been confirmed.

"This was in prison?"

"No," I said. "Amsterdam. He was released just over a week ago."
Van Zandt dropped the ice cubes into the glass and pursed his lips.
"I was not told."

"By the police? That doesn't surprise me. They don't seem as switched on as they might be."

"Most of them are fools. Have they caught his killer?"

"Not yet."

"Do they know who it is?"

"You're asking the wrong person."

Van Zandt limped over to me with the aid of his cane and handed me my drink. I nursed it for a time, reluctant to take a sip in case the burn was more than I could handle. Spirits are not my thing. Beer, yes. Wine on the right occasion. But whiskey? Bourbon? I'd never developed the taste for it. I could drink the stuff, sure, but I had yet to learn to appreciate it.

Very carefully, Van Zandt settled himself in a chair across from my own and then he reached to the side and grabbed for a fresh log to toss onto the fire. The lit coal in the grate fizzed with the impact and a few embers spiralled up into the chimney. He leaned back in his chair and sipped from his glass.

"You're probably wondering why I'm here," I said.

He looked at me blankly, the flames from the fire catching the light in his drink.

"The truth is I'm a writer," I went on. "Michael Park wanted to hire me."

"Hire you?"

"To write a kind of memoir about him. There's a market for that sort of thing nowadays. True crime is a big seller in Europe and the States. He wanted me to tell his story."

Van Zandt lowered his drink to his lap and tilted his head on one side, his stony eyes narrowing.

"It is your habit to write books for murderers?"

"Well, there's the thing," I said. "He claimed he was innocent."

Van Zandt laughed, but not in a genuine way. It was a showy kind of laugh, more like a bark really. He wanted me to know how perverse he found what I'd just said, as if I'd just uttered one of the oldest and most widely known lies in the universe.

"Innocent," he said, as though the word was doused in vinegar. "He was a killer."

"With respect Sir, I didn't get that impression."

"But of course," he said, waving his free hand. "He was a thief, yes? A liar. He shot one of our guards. And for what? A few cheap diamonds? The drink you hold in your hands is worth more. This glass is worth more."

I took a mouthful of the bourbon. It sounded like good stuff and if I was ever to educate my palette, I figured I might as well start at the top. It stung, like a hundred pin-pricks on my tongue. I swallowed cautiously and stifled a cough.

"There was talk," I said, hoarsely, "speculation that he got more than a few cheap jewels."

"It is not so," Van Zandt said, stiffening his shoulders. "If he told you this it is just another lie."

"Actually, I read it in the papers. After he was attacked. I was intrigued, you see."

"Journalists," Van Zandt said, with more pantomime distaste.

"It was in a number of papers."

"And?"

"And if the speculation was false, I thought maybe you could tell me the truth."

"You are still writing your book?" he asked, brow raised.

"I'm thinking of it," I told him. "And the reality is I can go about it in two ways. I can write with all the facts to hand, or I can go on what I know right now. It might not be accurate, but I can only work with what I have."

Something flickered in Van Zandt's eyes. A brief smile played about his lips.

"You appeal to my thirst for truth?"

"To your love of books," I said, gesturing around me. "To the written word."

"Ha. This book of yours will not be Shakespeare, I am thinking."

I shrugged. "Granted, it'll have to be a little more accessible to the modern reader."

"It will be trash."

"It could be. Without your help."

Van Zandt drained some more of his bourbon, his withered throat working overtime as he swallowed. When he refocused on me, there was something new in his eyes. It looked like mirth, as though I was amusing him greatly. He had the air of a predator toying with some hapless prey.

"It is not Van Zandt company policy to discuss security matters. I know this, because I was the director of security."

"There's no longer a Van Zandt company. No longer a policy."

He turned that one over, debating where to go next. The thing was, I could tell he wanted to talk about it. That's the problem with things that should be left unsaid – it's always so tempting to say them.

"Put the diamonds aside," I tried. "Leave all that to speculation. What I'm interested in is the mechanics of what happened on the night Robert Wolkers was killed. That's what my readers will want to know. How the raid went down."

"And how the killing happened?"

"Perhaps. But why don't we start with the simple stuff. There's no harm in that, surely? Having met you now, I'm certain you would have overseen a sophisticated security system. Would you describe it for me?"

I reached inside my coat pocket and removed a spiral-bound notepad and a pen. Van Zandt eyed my props carefully, sucking on his cheeks.

"We had the best security system in Amsterdam," he declared.

"I don't doubt it."

"It was a point of principle to me. I made sure that we invested heavily. This is why we had so few ... incidents."

"I understand. But how did it work? You had a safe or something similar?"

Van Zandt bobbed his head non-committaly, as if I was working along the right lines but not quite there yet.

"A strong room?"

He smiled and rattled the ice in his glass.

"I commissioned it myself," he said. "Very good steel. The walls were twenty centimetres thick."

He held his unsteady hands a short distance apart, as if to demonstrate the metric system to me.

"And that's unusual, right?" I said, playing along.

"The door contained five steel bolts. There were at least three locks."

"Really? Three?"

He grinned. "It is good for your book, no?"

I smiled. "Yes," I said, meanwhile jotting down on my pad a note to the effect that there was probably one lock, at most two. "Where was this strong room located?"

"In the factory."

"Whereabouts in the factory?"

"The centre," he said, straightening in his chair.

"Really? You didn't want to conceal it?"

He beamed at me, as if I'd asked just the question he'd hoped for. "It was very secure. We wanted people to know this. At the end of each day, all of the diamonds were placed inside."

"Every single one? That sounds a bit risky."

"There was no risk," he said. "The concrete floor was many feet in depth. A cement wall was poured around the strong room. There was a cage also."

"A cage?"

"With thick steel rods. Like this," he said, forming his hand into a tube and peering through it at me

"Could the rods be cut?"

He shook his head confidently.

"What about a blow torch?"

"It would take many hours."

"Really. Wouldn't the lock be the weak point?"

"Which one?"

"So there were several again."

"Write five," he said, gesturing to my pad with a little more enthusiasm.

"And that was it?"

"It was enough," he said, puffing his chest.

"Along with the guards, I suppose it would be. How many on duty by the way?"

Van Zandt made a performance out of deciding whether to tell me or not. He twisted the glass in his hand and sucked on his lips. At last, he said, "There were four in the daytime. Two at night."

"Always?"

"Always."

"Do you remember the name of the guard who was working with Robert Wolkers on the night he was killed?"

Van Zandt hesitated. "I do not remember."

"You're sure?"

"It was a long time ago."

"But a significant night. You really don't remember?"

"I do not," he said, shaking his head determinedly.

I held his gaze but his eyes were placid as a mountain lake. Lowering my head, I looked over the notes I'd made, reviewing where the conversation had taken us. It was a good job I was only playing the role of a biographer. My questioning had shown no clear structure whatsoever and I felt sure we'd got off track somewhere along the way. Van Zandt was telling me more than I'd expected, but it was still only the things he was willing to share. In my head, I wondered if it would be better to move away from facts and appeal to his emotional side. Perhaps it would lead him to open up.

"Tell me," I said, "what was your opinion of Michael Park?"

"He was a killer."

"Yes, but how did you feel about what he did?"

Van Zandt shrugged and lifted his cane from the floor. "How does this matter? He shot a man, yes? A man with a family. A wife. One daughter. I felt what anyone would feel."

"Yes, but what is that? Anger?"

He pouted.

"Hatred?"

He shook his head earnestly.

"Even when he took your diamonds?"

Van Zandt wagged his finger at me and clucked his tongue.

"You insult me?" he asked. "For what? For this American? What is he to you? He is nothing. He is this," he said, picking up one of the cubes of ice melting in the base of his glass.

"He said he was innocent."

"He was a thief."

"And he admitted as much. Why not confess to being a killer too?"

Van Zandt blew a raspberry. "And spend his life in prison?"

"It's not so different from how he ended up."

"That is not my concern. My concern was my guard. The family he had. My concern was the safety of all my employees."

"And that's noble."

Van Zandt nodded, then drained the dregs from his glass, tilting his head right back so that I could see his Adam's apple plummet and rise. He motioned towards my own drink.

"You do not like?"

"I do," I said, and managed another sip. This time the sting was less severe, as though the first mouthful had dulled my taste buds. The burn was still there at the back of my throat, but now I was prepared for it, and it wasn't such a shock. I swallowed, tried another question.

"I wonder, if Michael Park had already killed the guard, why didn't he take all the jewels? He'd crossed a line by then, so it seems to me he might as well have made the most of it."

"But he could not get into the strong room."

"A professional burglar?"

"It was secure."

"But these locks? Who had the keys or the combinations to them? Was it you?"

"It was combinations. Changed every day. I knew them."

"And the guards too?"

Van Zandt shook his head.

"So it's not possible that Michael made Robert Wolkers give him the code before he killed him?"

"There is no chance of this at all."

Van Zandt dismissed the notion in a cool tone and then levered himself up from his chair and crossed to his drinks cabinet once more. He began fixing himself a second bourbon, not bothering to offer me a refill. I had the sense I'd taken things as far as I probably could and that unless I stopped antagonising him I would soon outstay my welcome.

"I'd be interested," I said, resigning myself to what I was about to do, "to hear a little about the history of the Van Zandt company. I'm certain some background information would be fascinating for my readers. Could you possibly oblige?"

TWENTY

Later that night, after Van Zandt had finally grown tired of droning on about the wonders of his family's business empire, I let myself back into my apartment and drew myself a bath. Once the water was hot enough to scald flesh, I added a little cold and then I climbed into the tub and lay flat amid the steaming water, staring blankly at the white bathroom tiles on the opposite wall. Every now and again, I allowed my backside to slip on the porcelain and my head to ease beneath the waterline. Submerged there, I could hear a kind of metallic echo in my ears and I could feel my hair floating above my head like fine seaweed. Slowly, I'd resurface, spitting water from my mouth and feeling the skin of my face prickle against the damp air.

Van Zandt had lied to me, of course, though I was unsure how much. There was always the chance that his memory was not what it used to be but I was certain some of it was deliberate. I couldn't take offence, since I'd lied to him myself, and in any case it was nothing personal because he'd been spinning the same tale for more than a decade already. The funny thing was how weak the central deceit happened to be. As Van Zandt had said himself, the company line had always been that no more than a handful of cheap stones were taken on the night Robert Wolkers was killed, those jewels being the exact same ones that were found in Michael's home when he was arrested. I'd been confident for some time that was nonsense but something Van Zandt had said had made me surer than ever before. There was just one strong room, he'd told me, and at the end of each day all of the jewels on the cutting floor were returned to it. Well now, that being the case, how could the American have got his hands on those worthless chunks of zircon unless he'd also got inside the strong room where every other stone was kept?

The contradiction was enough to get me thinking and pretty soon I was stepping out of the bath and patting myself down with a towel and wrapping the towel about my waist and making my way over to my writing desk. I picked up the telephone when I got there and I called Rutherford's office number again, and while I waited for the machine to pick up I looked out through the dark picture window at the semi-naked reflection of myself suspended in mid-air above the uppermost leaves of the tree that grew on the canal bank just in front of my building. My reflection looked gaunt and hollow-eyed, like some form of gormless refugee from the spirit world. It raised its hand to me, spreading its fingers wide open, and waved half-heartedly, as if it was uncertain whether I was really there. I smiled thinly and was about to mouth something back when the message tone on Rutherford's machine interrupted my thoughts and I broke away from my double to leave a few words.

Rutherford's call the next morning woke me from a deep sleep, one in which I'd been dreaming that every last one of my teeth had fallen out and the only thing I had to put my teeth inside to transport them to the dentist with was a glass of coca cola. When the telephone rang, I was in the middle of a mad dash to the dentist's office, my way barred by countless zombie-like commuters, and all the while my teeth were fizzing and dissolving away into nothing in the glass of pop I held in my hands. The ringing wormed its way into my dream and I found myself struggling to answer a mobile telephone while pushing through the crowds of people. Then, mercifully, the ringing made abrupt sense to the hard wiring in my brain and I woke with a start and grabbed for the telephone receiver.

"Hello?" I managed, before running my tongue over my teeth to check they really were all still there.

"Rutherford here," said Rutherford. "Got your message. Not too early to call, I trust."

"Not at all," I said, pushing myself up on my elbows and rubbing my face with my hand. "I was just reworking a chapter that's been bugging me. How can I help?"

"Isn't that for me to ask? You said to call as soon as I got your message."

"Ah, yes." I scratched my head and stifled a yawn. "So I did. Sorry Rutherford, I'm just a little caught up in the scene, I guess. How are you fixed for later this morning?"

"One moment," he said, and I could picture him consulting his schedule. "I could make myself available for a little while, I think. What do you have in mind?"

"Another favour," I told him. "It's maybe something your secretary could help out with for starters, but I was also hoping you might be able to come along and meet someone with me."

"You mean Niels Van Zandt?"

"No, as it happens. I'm thinking of the guard that was on duty with Robert Wolkers the night he was killed. Rijker, I think you said his name was."

"You have an address?"

"That's where your secretary comes in. He's not in my phone book."

"Well, let me see what I can find out. I'll be in touch."

And he was, within the hour. But the news wasn't what I'd hoped for. It turned out neither one of us would be talking to Louis Rijker in the near future because according to Rutherford's secretary, he'd been dead at least two years, something that went a long way to explaining why I'd been unable to find an entry for him in the city telephone directory. It was a blow, alright, because he was just about the only other person I could think of who'd been anywhere near the Van Zandt factory at the time of the robbery. There was, though, a silver lining. Rutherford had an address for his mother.

"She lives on Apollolaan. In the Old South district," he told me.

"Any chance you could come along?"

"Every chance," he said, with all the eagerness that six grand in used notes can buy.

The property I met Rutherford outside of was a one-storey, red-brick bungalow with double-glazed windows that had been blocked out with an opaque film on the lower panes. The film was there, I presumed, to frustrate prowling eyes, although the rationale was lost on me to some extent once I saw the cat flap that had been fitted into the base of the U-PVC front door. The contraption put me in mind of a moggy about the size of your average Alsatian. The opening, to be clear, was huge, and anyone of below average build, including yours truly, would have no trouble at all poking their head and arm through and grasping for the plastic door handle from the inside. And chances were if it was locked, the keys would be hanging conveniently nearby, just waiting to do the very job they were designed for.

Not that any of that really mattered, of course, because the most daring thing I intended to do for the time being was to step forward and press the doorbell. And wait. And then wait some more.

I looked at Rutherford. "You're sure this is the right address?"

"Of course. But perhaps we should have telephoned first?"

"Perhaps so," I said, and turned back to face the door and tap my feet on the concrete stoop.

"Why don't you ring the bell again?" Rutherford asked.

"You don't think that's rude?"

"Why would it be rude? She might not have heard."

I bobbed my head, conceding the point.

"You're right," I told him. "I'll risk it."

And so I did. And this time, I pressed the doorbell for longer than before, making quite certain that the ringing couldn't be missed. Once I let go, the silence felt strangely inappropriate and I was almost tempted to ring the bell some more, just to fill the sudden void. Instead, I linked my hands together behind my back and rocked on my heels, then looked down at the damn cat flap again. Even Rutherford could get in through it, I'd bet, and there could be no more telling indictment of the device than that. The man had a head the size of a weather balloon, after all.

"Perhaps we should come back," he said, lifting his rounded shoulders.

"Perhaps you're right."

Only he wasn't. Because just as we were turning to leave, a shadow passed over the panels of bubble glass on either side of the front door and then I heard the noise of a key in the lock. Moments later, the door opened and I found myself looking at a middle-aged woman holding a plate of food in one hand and a congealed fork in the other. The woman wore a colourful plastic apron and her coarse, greying hair was pulled back from her face in a functional, if less than stylish, ponytail.

"So," she said, drawing the word out and letting the 'o' hang before us for an eternity.

"Sooooo," I mimicked, then looked to Rutherford for assistance.

"Goedemorgen," he began, brightly, and continued from there in much the same tone, though the details of what he was saying were lost to me until I heard the name Louis Rijker, after which Rutherford gestured at me, explained we were "Engels" and finally asked if she happened to speak our language.

"Yes," she said, in a matter of fact tone. "But I am not Mrs. Rijker. I am her nurse."

"You are?"

She nodded.

"May we speak to Mrs. Rijker?"

The woman inhaled deeply and held both hands up to us, raising the fork and the dinner plate until they were level with her shoulders and framing an expression that seemed to be saying our guess was as good as hers.

"You may try, of course," she explained. "But she does not speak English, I do not think."

"My friend can translate," I said, pointing to Rutherford.

The woman gave another helpless shrug of her shoulders and then backed away from the door and ushered us inside with a wave of her fork.

"Please," she said. "Come in."

I glanced at Rutherford and then stepped inside the threshold ahead of him, my feet sinking right into the downy fibres of a dark-red carpet. As soon as I was inside, my eyes began to sting like I'd just snorted lemon juice. The smell of cat was incredibly strong. The thing is, I'm allergic to cats at the best of times, but in this place the scent wasn't just air-born, it was in the very fabric of the building. Cat pee and cat hair in the carpet, cat odour in the wallpaper, cat food in a tray by my feet. Everywhere, CAT. But nowhere could I see the little blighter responsible for it all.

I sneezed, and snatched my hand to my face, wafting a fresh

dose of the feline miasma towards my nostrils so that I sneezed again.

"Alright, dear boy?" Rutherford enquired, while wiping his feet behind me.

"Uh huh," I nodded, holding my finger beneath my nose and squeezing my eyes tight shut.

"You are allergic to cats?" the nurse asked, perceptively.

"Some cats," I said, and just managed to stifle a second sneeze before it took hold of me.

"Here," she said, placing her fork onto the plate and then gripping me by the bridge of my nose with her spare hand, pinching hard between her forefinger and thumb.

I winced, then almost sneezed again, but found I couldn't while she was holding me in that way. Maybe it was just the pain distracting me, because she was squeezing pretty damn hard.

"Better?" she asked.

I nodded, carefully, but before I could extract myself from her grip she led me by the nose into a dimly lit room on our left. I stumbled after her, nose aloft, unable to tell if there were any obstacles in my way.

"Here," she said again, and this time I heard her set the plate down before guiding my own fingers to my nostrils. "You try."

"D'alright," I managed.

"Sit. Please."

She pushed me down and I fell onto a soft couch covered with a woollen throw that might as well have been weaved from cat hair. Rutherford gave me an apologetic look and then dropped his considerable backside next to me, creating an instant allergy-cloud that made matters much worse. I whipped out my hanky and got it in front of my nose just in time for another sneeze and then I held it there and bit hard on my tongue until I was able to regain some composure, at which point I looked up and noticed for the first time that we were not alone.

Across the room from us sat a woman who was well beyond retirement age. She was overweight, with swollen wrists and ankles, perhaps eighty years old. She wore a blue floral housecoat, or some kind of velour dressing gown, and several blankets across her lap.

On top of the blankets was the direct cause of all my discomfort, a giant marmalade cat with a torso so distended it looked as if a tear-away teen had got hold of it on its last venture out from the bunga-low and force fed it helium. The creature barely lifted its head to survey us before burying its nose back into its forepaws and closing its eyes, content to just lie there and emit as many pollutants as it could conjure without moving a single muscle.

I lowered my hanky and managed to manipulate my face into something approximating a smile, though my efforts seemed to have no effect on the old dear and I began to wonder if she could even see us. Her eyes were pinhead-small, like tiny emerald studs that had dulled over the years. They seemed to be focused, quite randomly, on a point on the wall a few feet above Rutherford's forehead. I glanced up and Rutherford did the same but neither of us could see what was there to hold her attention besides a featureless square of wallpaper. After trading a look, the two of us returned our attention to the nurse.

"Karine," the nurse ventured, in a singsong voice, calling to the old woman as if she were hoping to coax a shy child into socialis-ing. "Karine," she repeated, and then looked at us with a pained expression, wringing her hands.

I looked back at the old lady. She was absently clenching and kneading at a roll of cat flesh in her fingers. Did she know we were there? I got the impression I could pop a crisp bag right next to her ear and she wouldn't flinch.

"Is she deaf?" I asked.

The nurse shook her head.

"Does she ever talk?"

"Sometimes." The nurse forced a smile. "She does not have so many visitors, I think."

I thought so too. She clung to the cat as if it was her sole com-panion in the entire cosmos, and looked grimly ahead of her, lips puckered, as though her chair was approaching the tipping off point of a giant rollercoaster.

"Have you worked here long?" Rutherford asked the nurse, test-ing a different approach.

"A month only," she said, and shrugged.

"Do you know anything about her son? Does she talk about him?"

"Yes. This is him," she said, pleased to help at last, and reached for a teak occasional table set beside the wall where a single photograph frame was positioned. She handed the frame to Rutherford and the two of us contemplated the man pictured in it.

The Louis Rijker in the photograph was of a similar age and build to Rutherford, although he had more hair, with just a small coin-shaped patch of it beginning to thin on top of his head. He had a dark, bushy mono-brow and his teeth were crooked and gapped. Like his mother, though, what struck me most about him were his eyes. In the photograph, he was looking straight to camera, but you got the sense there was something missing. To be blunt, Louis Rijker didn't look like the smartest Dutchman who ever lived.

"Does she have other family?" I asked.

"I do not think so," the nurse said, and cast a mournful glance towards her patient.

"Is she ill?"

"A little. Her heart," she said, and patted her own chest.

"And her mind?" I asked, twirling my finger at my temple.

"It is okay. She talks sometimes."

"About her son?"

"No. The weather maybe. Or Annabelle."

"Annabelle?"

"The cat."

I sniffed, as though just the mention of the creature had stirred something in my nasal passages.

"Maybe if you came back tomorrow she would talk," the nurse suggested.

"Yes," I agreed, nodding and regaining my feet. "You could be right."

I smiled reassuringly to the nurse, waiting for Rutherford to stand too. We were just on our way out when one last thought occurred to me. Holding up a hand to the nurse, I unzipped my coat pocket and removed one of the two monkey figurines I was carrying. Then I stepped over towards the old lady and crouched down, doing my best not to recoil from the cat.

"Do you recognise this?" I asked softly, lifting the monkey into her line of sight and turning it before her eyes. "Did Louis ever have one of these?"

I started to wave the figurine from side to side in front of her, as if it was a hypnotist's pocket watch. Left to right, left to right. Gradually, the movement drew her under its spell and then, quite suddenly, like a television set tuning into a crystal clear signal for an instant, the old lady focused directly on the figurine. Her eyes brightened, irises opening like tiny flowers blooming, and she raised a quivering hand from the cat to reach for the monkey. She grasped at my fingers and went to take the figurine from me but just as I let go her grip failed her and the monkey fell to the floor. I reached down for it but when I looked up again her sightless gaze had returned.

"Do you want to hold it?" I asked, taking her hand and unpicking her clammy fingers, then placing the figurine in her palm. But her hand was limp. I tried to shape her fingers around the figurine but it was no use, there was no life in them at all.

"Does this mean something to you? Do you know what it is?"

There was no response. I may as well have been addressing a waxwork.

"Come on," Rutherford said from behind me, resting a hand on my shoulder. "It's no good."

"Perhaps tomorrow," the nurse suggested again.

"Yes," I managed. "Perhaps."

Outside on the street, away from the cat, I took a few deep breaths to clear my airways, then pocketed the monkey and raised my eyebrows to Rutherford.

"You think she even knew we were there?" I asked.

"I suspect not."

"I suspect not too." I inhaled another lungful of air and glanced about us, shaking my head disconsolately. "It looks like I've rather wasted your time."

"No, not at all," he assured me, placing an arm on my back. "I happen to know the perfect place for a spot of lunch."

TWENTY-ONE

After we'd eaten in a nearby patisserie, we parted company and I went in search of Marieke once more. I found her working behind the bar in Café de Brug, her hair tied up in a tortoise-shell clip and a white apron secured about her trim waist. She seemed skittish when I walked in, unsure how to react for perhaps the first time since we'd met. It took her a few moments to decide what attitude to adopt and in the end she reverted to what seemed to be her default setting – moody.

There was just one other customer inside the bar, an old man in a thick horsehair jacket who had a tailored woollen hat and a tot of rum on the table before him. We shared a nod when I walked in but he failed to focus his milky eyes upon me. He was licking his lips and staring at his rum, looking as if he might tempt himself with a sip for the entire afternoon.

"I'd like a beer," I told her. "And don't look at me that way. I'm not the worst mistake you ever made."

Wordlessly, she took down a small glass from the shelf above the bar and began to fill it from the pump. The beer formed a foaming head and she wiped the froth from the rim of the glass with a plastic spatula. I took a mouthful and watched her watching me. She hadn't expected this and I could tell she wasn't sure what to make of it. Was I just some dumb Englishman who'd become infatuated with her or was I here for something else?

"It's good beer," I said. "And the glass is clean and the service is impeccable. You should be proud of yourself."

That got a sneer. At least it broke up the scowl for a while.

"How many years do you figure you have ahead of yourself

here? Two or three, maybe, before you quit and let some rich guy with a hole for a brain marry you?"

A sneer *and* a scowl. Who'd have thought it.

"I mean, that has to be the plan, doesn't it? Assuming you really have missed out on these diamonds."

Amazing, isn't it, what just one word can do to a person's face? Marieke's turned utterly blank. The bitterness and distrust just evaporated, leaving her stunned, as if her face was re-booting while it waited for the next set of instructions to be transmitted to the network of muscles beneath her skin. She didn't stay that way for long, but it was enough to tell me I was on the right tracks.

"Michael got away with them, didn't he? The rumour was he stole a fortune all those years ago, so who knows what it's worth now, right?"

She pouted, and tried glancing out of the window in a carefree manner, not willing to commit just yet.

"What I don't get is how the monkeys fit into it all. Or why you need all three of them. You feel like sharing?"

"Why should I?"

"It could be in your interest."

"But you do not have the monkeys. You have nothing to interest me."

"You have to get high first, is that right?"

Her lip curled. I didn't mind. I could look at her lips all day long.

"These monkeys," I said. "I got them once. I can get them again."

"How would you do it?"

"Well, that's for me to figure out. Question is, how much is it worth to you? And before you even think it, the twenty thousand euros won't do. I want half the diamonds."

She cast a sudden look towards the old man, then focused back on me.

"Keep your voice down."

"By all means," I said. "But you haven't answered my question."

"I cannot give you half. They are nothing to do with you."

"But you're different? Listen, you might have been sleeping with Michael, but I don't picture it is a love affair."

"You do not know," she said.

"So tell me."

She stared at me peevishly and took a deep breath, blinking once or twice. Then she looked at the window once more, without focus this time, and exhaled with a faint sigh. She was crossing her fingers on the bar, I noticed, though whether it was a conscious gesture I wasn't sure. I didn't look at her fingers for long; it was her face that stole my attention. In profile she looked so elegant, like a young blue-blood monarch on a postage stamp. Wisps of blonde hair at her sun-kissed temples, a faint scattering of freckles on her cheeks. And those lips, delicate and upturned, just waiting to entrance any fool dumb enough to obsess over them.

"How did you meet Michael?" I asked. "He was out of prison, what, a handful of days?"

"He wrote me letters," she said, turning to me and speaking in a disarming monotone. "Sweet letters."

"And you wrote back?"

"Yes, why not?"

"He was a killer. Didn't it bother you?"

"We did not talk about that."

"Did you talk about the diamonds?"

She shook her head.

"Not in the letters. The guards read them."

"So you met in person?"

Marieke delayed for a moment. She reached up to the shelf above her head and fetched down another glass. She filled the glass with tap water from the bar sink and took a sip. Her hands weren't shaking, nothing like that, but the water seemed to calm her to some extent.

"It was where I worked," she said, finally.

"The prison?"

"For two years. In the kitchens."

"And what, he told you a piece of his story each time you dropped mashed potato onto his plate?"

"Stupid. You ask me how it happened and then you say these stupid things."

"It's a bad habit, you're right. Go on."

She took another sip from her water, then dabbed at her lips with her finger tips. I sat there waiting while she pinched her bottom lip between her fingers. Eventually, she continued.

"Michael was ... polite. And also he was different, an American in a Dutch prison. He liked to talk to the cooks and the guards, to people who lived outside of the building."

She paused, half expecting me to interrupt with something flippant, but I controlled myself.

"He would ask me anything – what had I done the day before? Where was I going at the weekend? What was the weather forecast to do? What car did I own? Did I visit Amsterdam often? Of course, we were not supposed to answer such questions. They told us it could be dangerous."

"If a prisoner learned too much about you?"

"Or if they liked you. They might ask you to do things for them, bring them things."

"Did Michael?"

"Never."

"But he wrote you letters."

"Not at first. When I worked there he would just ask me his questions. But then I lost my job."

"So how did he get in touch? Had you told him your address?"

"No," she said, shaking her head. "It was me."

"You?"

She shrugged. "After I left, I missed his questions. I missed telling him the things he asked. And I did not know if anyone else was answering him. It made me sad to think of it. So I went to see him again."

"And he just opened up?"

"He felt the same way. He had ... developed feelings for me."

"Useful."

"And this is when he told me about the diamonds."

"And I bet you looked surprised. Only, you already knew by then, didn't you? I mean, all you would have needed to do was ask someone at the prison what he was in for, or consult an old newspaper. Maybe you'd done that before he began talking to you. Like you said, an American inside a Dutch prison, it is kind of novel."

She waited me out, neither confirming nor denying it. She didn't have to. It made complete sense to me.

"He wouldn't have told you where they were, he was too careful for that. Twelve years can teach you a good deal of patience."

"He told me he had them." She lowered her voice and leaned towards me across the counter of the bar. "He said there were many diamonds," she whispered. "But they had not been finished."

"You mean cut?"

"Cut, yes."

"Which is why he wouldn't have been able to sell them immediately. He needed a fence. One in Paris, I'm thinking."

"Excuse me?"

"Nothing. Go on."

"There is not much else. After I visited him, he wrote me the letters and I wrote back to him. It was not so long before he was released by then."

"No. You wouldn't want to risk him losing interest."

"When he was released, he came to Amsterdam."

"And you gave him the homecoming he'd been waiting for. And afterwards, he whispered sweet nothings in your ear until he happened to mention that getting his hands on the diamonds wasn't as straightforward as you'd hoped. There were the monkey figurines to think about, and the other men who had them. That must have been crushing."

Her lips thinned. "It was not like this."

"Oh, I think it was. But you can stick to the Disney version if you like. The real question is the monkeys, though, isn't it? Did he tell you what they meant right then or did you have to work on him for a while?"

"He told me everything," she said, straightening. "More than he told you."

"No question. But then I was just the hired help. You were his one and only true love."

She adopted a prim expression. "You were supposed to bring him the monkeys. We were to leave Amsterdam."

"With the diamonds?"

"Of course."

"So they're still in the city."

She nodded, rolling her eyes as if that much was obvious.

"Where?"

Just then, the door to the café opened and the young man I'd seen working behind the bar earlier in the week walked in. He clocked me right away and paused, half way through unzipping his coat. He said something to Marieke in Dutch, his tone hostile, and it was enough to make the old man turn away from his rum and question me with his eyes. I didn't have to respond, though, because Marieke did it for me. And whatever she said seemed to set him straight because once he'd given me his best menacing stare he disappeared through the door at the back of the bar.

"You were saying?" I said, turning on my stool to face Marieke once again.

"Bring me the monkeys and I will tell you," she said, glancing towards the door her colleague had walked through. "Otherwise, how can I trust you?"

"You want to bring trust into our relationship? Don't you think it's a little late for that?"

"Not if you bring me the monkeys."

"You make it sound so straightforward."

She adopted a stern expression. "But if you get them, do not leave them in your apartment. Bring them here."

"We'll see," I told her. "You never know, I might figure this all out and keep the diamonds for myself."

She clamped her teeth together.

"What? You think I'm joking?"

I stood up from my stool at the bar and buttoned my coat. Then I slipped my hands into my pockets and bowed my head goodbye. It felt good, in a childish way, talking about the missing figurines and offering to try to find them while all the time I had two of them in my pocket, gripped between my fingers. It was almost tempting to pull them out and wave them at her with a grin on my face but I didn't do it. I still didn't know exactly how much she would take.

Outside of the café, twilight had begun to descend, lowering the temperature a few degrees and causing the canal-side streetlamps to power up. When I checked my watch, I saw that it was almost half past five, and because I didn't feel like being crushed in a tram full of commuters I looked around me for a nearby bicycle rack. There was one just a short distance away and I walked across to it and immediately selected a pale blue bike with fitted mud-caps and a wicker basket affixed to the handlebars. The metal chain that secured the front wheel to the bike rack was fastened with a modern padlock and I had my picks out and the lock undone before my fingers could begin to numb. I relocked the chain to the rack, freed the bike from the tangle of adjoining pedals and handle bars, and wheeled it to the side of the road where I prepared to hoist my leg over the saddle and ride away.

Before I could, though, a white panel van surged out of a nearby parking space and veered across the road towards me. The driver didn't straighten up. Instead, he stamped on his brakes and brought the van to a halt just in front of me, blocking my way. The front doors of the van flew open.

I knew all the clichés about white van drivers, sure, but the recklessness stunned me and it took me a moment to gather my senses and prepare to confront the driver. As it happened, though, the confrontation that followed was of a different order to the one I was expecting because the two men who jumped out of the van were wearing balaclavas and one of them had a baseball bat over his shoulder. I opened my mouth to speak but before I could get the words out the man whipped the bat forwards and buried the sweet spot deep in my solar plexus. The pain was immediate and disabling. It exploded from my chest out to my fingertips, making me let go of the bike and meanwhile robbing me of my breath. My legs buckled and I fell to my knees on the cobbled roadway as the bike toppled over beside me. I looked up, gasping for air, to find the masked man bringing the bat down once again. And this time, when he connected, I didn't feel a thing.

TWENTY-TWO

The briefcase wouldn't shut. I was pushing down hard on the lid, fumbling for the clasps, but I couldn't get them to engage. Something was in the way. I dropped the briefcase onto the floor and stamped on it. When the obstruction still wouldn't give, I jumped up and down on the lid with both feet. There was some flex but not enough. I decided to open the briefcase and try repositioning Arthur the butler's hand but when I threw back the lid there was no hand there at all – there was a man's head. The man was pleading with his eyes, his eyeballs almost crawling out of the slits in the balaclava he was wearing, and he was groaning. The man's groaning became more insistent and his head began to shake, as if he was trying to say something but couldn't. I reached down and pushed my fingers past his lips and felt around inside the moist cavity of his mouth until I touched something hard. I gripped the object as best I could and pulled. A monkey figurine slipped out of his mouth, slick with his drool. I raised the figurine to my nose and sniffed. A sweet, peppery smell crawled up my sinuses and clawed at my brain. Then my eyes snapped open and the man who was holding my head upright by my hair passed the smelling salts beneath my nose once again.

He slapped me for good measure and I mumbled something that my dry mouth and lips failed to articulate. I worked some saliva with my cheeks and swallowed and it was then that the nausea hit. Sudden and unstoppable, a wave of heat rushed from my chest to my scalp, turning my forehead into a hot plate. My ears popped and my throat spasmed. I doubled over and let go of a gut-full of vomit.

The man released my hair and jumped clear, grumbling as I spit the last threads of bile from my mouth. I longed to use my hand to clean my lips and wipe the sweat from my face and forehead but found that I couldn't because my hands were tied to the back of the plastic chair I was sat on. My feet were bound too, secured to the metal legs of the chair. The heat was unbearable. I wanted to be stripped and thrown into an icy pool, longed to be hosed down with gallons of freezing water. I turned groggily to the man and was about to ask him for help but as I parted my foul-tasting lips to shape the words my vision blurred and I found that I was looking into a long, unfocused tunnel that led only to unconsciousness.

*

The second time I woke the man was holding my head back and pouring water down my throat. I gagged and spluttered, nearly vomiting again. The man tried to give me more water but I shook my head, moaning, and butted the glass away. He moved back and studied me for a moment and then he called over his shoulder in Dutch until his companion walked into the room and joined him. Both men wore jeans and leather jackets and the hair of the thin man with the water glass was flattened and tangled from the balaclava he'd had on. The wide man had no hair. I may have only seen them once before, in the café with Michael, but I'd thought about them often enough since then and I knew right away who they were.

Something caught in my nostrils and I looked down to find that my vomit was still pooled on the floor in front of me. Lifting my eyes, I scanned the room they were keeping me in. I'd been here before too. The mattress and bedding were still torn and ruined, the wooden trunk was positioned just as it had been previously and the hatch to the attic was right where it should have been, immediately above the trunk. On the bare floor a short distance in front of my pooled stomach contents were the two monkey figurines.

The men saw me looking at the figurines and said something to one another. Then the thin man bent down and snatched them up, zipping them into the pocket of his leather jacket and giving me a wary look, as if I could somehow steal them from before his eyes. I wasn't sure how he expected me to manage it. Just the pull on my chest of having my arms tied behind me was enough to make me wince each time I breathed. My chest felt raw and tender where I'd been hit with the baseball bat and I was afraid that at least one of my ribs might be broken. In a sense, it was good that I couldn't move my arms because it meant I couldn't aggravate my injuries or raise my hand to discover just how bad a state the back of my skull was in. Even so, I'd had much better evenings.

"You are English," the wide man said, finally.

I nodded, then winced as the room lurched to one side.

"Do you know who we are?"

This time I shook my head very carefully.

"We know you. Mr. Charlie Howard. You are a writer."

"Yes," I managed.

"And a thief."

I met his eyes. They were deep-set and very dark. He pulled his head down into his bulky shoulders and breathed through flared nostrils, awaiting my response. The thin man looked between us, like an eager spectator at a blood sport event. I glanced at the floor, struggling to focus, and the wide man repeated himself.

"You are a thief. You stole from us."

"It was a mistake," I croaked.

"You say this now."

I glanced up. "Actually, I've been saying it for over a week. Ever since you killed Michael."

The thin man turned to the wide man, about to say something, but the wide man held up his hand and stopped him. He walked towards me and dropped to his haunches in front of my chair, his face just inches from my own. He hoisted his eyebrows and looked deep into my eyes, stroking his chin with his fingers like a golfer sizing up a tricky putt. For a moment, I thought he might strike me, but instead he just crouched there, wordless and breathing slow, trying to read something from my expression. I wasn't sure what he was looking for and I was too weak to put on any kind of an act so I let him read me in whichever way he chose. In time, he placed his hands on his thighs and stood upright once more.

"You sleep," he said, and with that he raised his booted foot into the air and kicked my chair so that it toppled over and I crashed down onto my side, a fresh spasm of pain blooming from my chest.

*

Somehow, I did sleep, though not for long. I was woken by a tingling sensation in my arm. The blood had drained right out of it and it had gone numb and had started to throb. I gritted my teeth and struggled against the stabs and twinges all around my chest as I tried to manoeuvre myself upright once again. But I couldn't do it. I was on too awkward an angle. I ground my forehead into the floor and tried to prise myself up a little to let the blood flow back into my arm. It helped a touch but I wanted badly to stretch and shake my arm out.

"Hey," I called, the note of panic in my voice surprising me. "Hey, my arm hurts. Please. It really hurts."

I heard feet shuffling towards me out in the hallway.

"Please," I went on. "At least help me upright. There's no blood getting to my arm."

I could see a shadow on the floor at the threshold of the room but it didn't come any closer.

"Please, I'm begging you. Untie my arms. Let me stretch them. Please."

There was more shuffling, though this time the shadow receded. Then the light in the hallway went out and not long after that I began to whimper and curse to myself. I could have let go at that point, could have really started to lose it, but instead I got angry. I swore and I gnashed my teeth and I began thrashing around on the chair, screaming each time I aggravated my injuries, which was often, until I somehow managed to throw myself right around so that I was lying on my other arm. And there I lay for God knows how long, face pressed against the dusty wooden floor, my breathing irregular, my chest pulsing sporadically and the gash on the back of my skull maturing into the mother of all headaches, until, at long last, the wide man and the thin man came back into the room and stood looming over me once again.

"Get up," the wide man ordered.

"I can't."

With great impatience, he motioned to the thin man and together they lifted me and set the chair back onto its feet. I had no idea what time it was although something made me think it was probably late at night or early in the morning. The thin man looked tired and drawn, so maybe that was what it was. In any case, it really made no difference.

"Tell us about the American," the wide man said.

I blinked, trying to gather my senses and put them in some form of order.

"His name was Michael Park," I began, working my jaw loose and wetting my lips. The vinegary, mucus taste still lingered. "He just got out of prison. He was convicted for –"

"Yes, yes. Tell us about how you know him."

"He hired me. To steal those monkeys from you. While you were meeting him for dinner."

"You lie," he said, drawing his arm back as if to hit me.

"No," I said, flinching. "It's the truth, really. He said you would trust him. But he arranged to meet you for a meal so that I could steal them. He told me where you lived and where you kept the monkeys."

He lowered his arm cautiously. "Why would he do this?"

"I don't know. But he was going to leave Amsterdam once I gave them to him."

"He told you this?"

"Yes. And I believed him."

The wide man thought about what I'd told him and the thin man watched him at it, his rat-like face twitching, spindly arms hanging limp by his side. I didn't like the thin man at all. The wide man I could talk to but I got the feeling the thin man didn't have a brain for me to reason with. He appeared jittery, always on edge, though I got the feeling that was his nature rather than any drugs he might be on.

"Anyway," I said, trying to keep the wide man talking, "what does it matter to you? Michael is dead and you have the three monkeys."

The wide man pulled his head down into his shoulders once

again, as if he was bracing himself for something, and this time I really thought he might step forward and strike me. He took a deep breath and his huge chest lifted up and out, while his hands balled into fists at his side. I could see him squeezing his fists, the skin around his knuckles whitening.

"Why do you say this about the monkeys?"

"It just seems obvious. You stole the figurine Michael had. That was why you beat him – so he'd tell you where it was. And now you have the two monkeys back that I stole from you."

"You said this before, that we killed him. It is not true."

The thin man shook his head fitfully.

"Well if you didn't kill him, who did?"

"You did," the wide man said. "This is why the police arrested you."

"That was a mistake."

"Another mistake." He twisted his head from side to side. "The policeman who arrested you, Burggrave, he does not make them."

"He did this time. Listen, the truth is I went to Michael's apartment after I stole the monkeys from you but he was already hurt by then. He was lying in the bath. His fingers were broken."

The wide man caught his breath sharply and turned his face away, as if shying from the image I was painting. The thin man's tongue flicked out of his mouth, like a lizard's.

"Did he speak?"

"No."

"He's lying," the thin man said, conclusively. "He is trying to trick us."

"I'm not," I said. "It's true. Believe me."

The wide man held up his hand, silencing us both.

"You do not have the final monkey?" he asked.

"Don't you?"

He looked me square in the eyes, trying to read me again. This time I did the same. Where was the third monkey? If I didn't have it and these two didn't have it, then who did? And were they really telling me the truth about not killing Michael? It was hard to tell, given they'd just beaten me with a baseball bat and bound me to a chair.

"How about," I went on, "you let me go and I get you the third monkey? I have an idea where it is."

"Where?"

"Somewhere I should have thought of in the first place. If you let me go, I'll find it and bring it back to you."

The wide man grinned then, showing me a mouthful of fillings. He even managed a chuckle.

"You lie. You will go to the police."

"Believe me, that's the last thing I'd do."

"But I do not believe you." He nodded towards the thin man. "And my friend says we should kill you. I am starting to agree."

"No, listen to me. I *know*."

"You know nothing."

He motioned to the thin man and the two of them walked out of the room, closing the door behind them.

*

As soon as they'd gone, I got right back to what I'd been up to before they came in. When you think about it, being a burglar is a lot like being an escapologist. All those locks, chains and bindings, they each work on the same principles. And while being a burglar is all about getting into confined spaces, being an escapologist is all about getting out of them. A recruitment consultant might say that the two professions have transferable skills. All of which is a round-a-bout way of saying that I'd finally managed to loosen the ropes that bound my wrists to the back of the chair.

The truth is I'd been working at the ropes since I'd first regained consciousness. It hurt my chest to do it and bending my wrists and contorting my fingers when my arms were already going numb was certainly painful, but it was a damn sight better than being killed. So I teased away at the rope and fumbled gamely with the knots and after several hours I finally got a break and managed to undo the first of them. And from there it was more of the same, only with a tiny bit more give on the ropes and a fraction more movement in my wrists, until I had the ropes all but ready to slip off of my hands. And slip them off was exactly what I did the moment the wide man and the thin man walked out of the room and left me to my own devices.

Of course, that was only the first step, and after I'd gingerly stretched my arms and assessed the burns on my wrists and shaken some life back into my hands, I had to repeat the same process with the ropes that were binding my feet. This time, though, I could see what I was doing and what I was up against, and once I had the crucial first knot loosened it was just a question of whether I had enough time to finish the job before one of them waltzed back in with the baseball bat to finish me.

Thoughts like that didn't help. In fact, thoughts like that positively hindered my progress by making me snatch at the ropes and rush things a little too much. Problem was, while I was aware of how it was slowing me down, I was so worried I'd miss my chance to escape that I kept going in the same fashion; all flailing fingers and thumbs. Then again, perhaps the terror helped in a way because it kept my mind off my injuries. And thinking of something other than the pain I was in was crucial when I'd finally freed myself completely and was able to stand woozily from the chair and begin preparing myself for the challenge of getting up into the roof space.

As it happened, hauling myself up into the hatch hurt like hell, and I'm not going to pretend otherwise. There's also a fair chance I did myself more harm than good by attempting it, given the way I had to strain my ribs, but the experience did make me think that maybe all that stuff about people summoning extra strength when they find themselves in extraordinary circumstances is true because I pulled myself up in spite of it all and I did it without screaming or yelping at the stabs of electric pain that showered my torso.

And because it was do or die, I suppose quite literally, it was one almighty relief when I finally hooked my elbow and my thigh over the edge of the hatch and then plunged my hand down below the scratchy loft insulation to find that the gun was still there, right where I'd hidden it, just as things always are when the planets are aligned just so and the Good Lord is in a gracious frame of mind.

Not that I had time to think of such things just then because I was far too concerned with feeling around the butt of the gun as quietly as possible until I found something that felt like a recessed button and, teeth clenched, depressed it. A cartridge of bullets fell out. Not what I'd intended. I fumbled the cartridge back into place, then located another lever, one that I hoped was the safety guard. I slipped the lever to one side, experienced nothing untoward, then lowered my leg back into the ceiling space of the room below and, bracing myself, dropped onto the lid of the trunk as deftly as I could.

With the gun held out before me like a particularly menacing torch, I walked to the edge of the room and paused, listening for any noises from the two men that might suggest I'd been heard. I listened hard but there was only silence and the sound of my breathing; shallow and ragged in my throat. Stepping into the hallway, I trained the gun onto the darkened space in front of me and followed the muzzle towards the second bedroom. The door was closed. I checked over my shoulder, then looked back to the door and thought about kicking it through. In the end, I reached out and turned the handle as slowly and as quietly as I could, easing the door open a crack and peeking inside.

The room was unlit. After a few anxious moments, my eyes adjusted and I could just make out the form of the thin man asleep on the single camp bed. By his side and resting on the floor was his leather jacket. I tiptoed towards the jacket and bent down, one eye on the thin man the whole time, and then I felt around the jacket until my fingers located the monkey figurines. They were in the zipped pocket still. I daren't risk opening the zip so I just took the coat and backed out of the room into the hallway where, it transpired, the wide man was waiting for me with the baseball bat above his shoulder.

He didn't expect the gun, though. If he had expected it, I guess he would have waited by the side of the door and smacked me over the head as soon as I emerged. Instead, he was facing me at the end of the hallway and when he flicked on the overhead bulb he must have thought that just the sight of the bat would be enough for me to submit. His eyes became very big when I straightened my arm and pointed the pistol in his direction. Then his eyes narrowed and a series of frown lines appeared on his forehead.

"But we searched you," he protested.

"Well, that'll teach you to leave guns lying around," I whispered back. "Anyone could find them."

"But ..."

"Drop it," I cut in, motioning to the bat. "And walk backwards. Now. Back up."

He hesitated. I jerked the gun at him. Slowly, the wide man set the bat down to his side, handle leaning against the wall.

"No, on the floor," I hissed.

The wide man began to kneel down. "Not you," I said. "The bat. Lay it on the floor."

He did as I told him.

"Good, now move away from it."

He shuffled backwards and I eyed the front door, noting that it had been crudely repaired instead of replaced. Just then, he yelled something in Dutch towards the second bedroom and an instant later, the thin man slurred a reply. I shook my head and this time the wide man said nothing further but it was already too late. I advanced down the hallway, then wheeled around as the thin man appeared behind me, bleary eyed, his jaw dropping to the floor the moment he saw me with his coat and the handgun.

"Where are the keys to your van?" I demanded, switching the gun between them.

The thin man was still too shocked to answer and the wide man delayed.

"Your keys," I shouted, jabbing the gun towards the thin man, gripping the trigger ever tighter. "Now."

Mutely, he motioned towards the jacket I was holding and I shook it until I heard the keys jangle.

"Okay," I went on, turning to the wide man again. "You open the door. Good. Now back away some more. Further, further. Good."

I checked on the thin man one last time, just to make sure he hadn't come any closer.

"If I hear either of you on the stairs before I get out of here, so help me I will shoot. Understand?"

The thin man stood there with his mouth open, looking furtively towards his partner, but the wide man nodded and placed his

I paused in my apartment for just long enough to stuff a few clothes and my passport into a holdall and to grab my burglar tools. I packed the gun into the holdall too and was just about to run out of the building when I thought to go into the bathroom and check on my injuries. I lifted my shirt in front of the mirror and saw that I had a deep purple bruise smack in the centre of my chest, as if somebody had painted a target on me. Then I lowered my head and prodded gently at the blood that had clotted in my hair. I ran the cold tap on the bath and soaked a towel and used the sodden rag to clear as much of the blood as I safely could without reopening the wound. Then I changed my top for an unbloodied sweatshirt, put on the thin man's leather jacket with the monkey figurines still zipped in the pocket and made my way back outside. There was no sign of the wide man and the thin man out on the street but I wasn't about to hang around for them. Instead, I paced through the Red Light District to St. Jacobsstraat and readied myself for something I should have done a long time before.

The front door of the building was just where it had been a little over a week ago, when Marieke had first led me through it. I glanced at the door and thought about picking my way inside, but I had my doubts. A garish crime scene notice had been pasted over the flyers at eye level and there was the remote possibility the door was under surveillance. And even if I did press ahead, there was a risk I might pass one of the building's other tenants on the short trip upstairs to Michael Park's bed-sit. I hovered nearby, thinking. Dance music pulsed out from the sex booth on one side of the building and some type of reggae ska was audible from the coffee house in the hands behind his back in a casual gesture. I edged towards the door, gun swinging between the two of them in a wavering arc, and then when I was through the threshold I just turned and bolted for the stairs, beginning a half-jump, half-stumble routine that took me to the bottom of the five flights as quickly as I could go in my condition. By the time I was on the final flight, my breathing was laboured, my head felt light and my heart seemed to be in real danger of beating its way clear out of my body, but I couldn't hear any footfall behind me. I reached the front door and grabbed for the snap lock, yanked the thing back and rushed out into the cold, dark night. Then I hurried away as best I could, meanwhile fumbling around in the pockets of the leather jacket until I found the van keys and veering towards the canal to toss them into the water. I thought about ditching the gun too but in the end I settled for wrapping the leather jacket around it, tucked the bundle beneath my arm and shuffled away in search of the nearest bike rack.

opposite direction. Faintly, I could hear the more distant noise of an emergency siren wailing elsewhere in the city.

On balance, I didn't feel comfortable going in through the front. There was every chance it would be fine but why go against my instincts? So I backed away from the door and walked off along St. Jacobsstraat again, then to the nearest cross street and afterwards to the rear of the building. Once there, I found a dark nook to stuff my holdall into and a large wheelie bin that I rolled across the alleyway until it was positioned beneath the roof overhang I was interested in.

I climbed up onto the wheelie bin and braced one foot against the side wall and, through a kind of leaping, springing motion that ripped into the very heart of the sore spot in my chest, managed to gain enough height to grab onto the curved, felted edge of the flat roof that extended from just below Michael's back window.

Without the stimulus of impending death, I made something of a meal of hauling myself up, swearing and groaning with abandon. Once the ordeal was over with, I laid flat on my back in complete silence and stared at the slate grey clouds in the night sky above me. The clouds were faintly iridescent in the glow of the city's sodium bleed, as if the sky was a dark and grisly sea, threaded with phosphorescent plankton. I took in the queer effect as I caught my breath, meanwhile fumbling in my pocket and removing a pair of disposable surgical gloves that I slipped onto my hands. Then I rolled onto my side and looked up at the bathroom window and steeled myself for one more effort.

Luckily, there was a cast iron drain pipe positioned just close enough to the window ledge to give me something to shinny up and for some reason, the shinnying motion wasn't as painful as I'd expected. After hoisting myself several feet into the air, I braced my right foot against one of the metal brackets securing the pipe to the wall and reached across for the window ledge. I pushed up from the ledge as best I could and, suspended diagonally, gripped one of the cross-slats on the sash window with my spare hand so that I could force the window slowly open. It took a minute or so until I had the window high enough to crawl through and by that stage my legs and arms were beginning to shake and my ribs felt like a rack of hot knives in my chest but I still somehow managed to push off from the pipe and grab the inside edge of the window frame and pull myself in through the window all in one largely fluid movement.

I dropped down onto the toilet cistern, then the bathroom floor. The room was in darkness and it took me a few moments of feeling my way around until I found the light cord and was able to turn on the low wattage bulb suspended from the ceiling. Right in front of me, dried blood and bits of hair and possibly skull matter were still smeared against the white porcelain of the bathtub, soaking into the yellowing tiles and dark grout on the wall. It was odd, in a way, that his body wasn't there too. Other than the bloody residue, there was no real reason to believe I was in the middle of a crime scene. I'm not sure what I expected – chalk marks or signs of a forensics examination perhaps – but it wasn't there. I wondered how long it would be before the landlord would be allowed to clean the bath and then I wondered if the landlord would even bother. Perhaps the bed-sit would become yet another Amsterdam squat.

Enough of that. I didn't think I would find what I was looking for in the bathroom and I didn't relish the prospect of searching it too thoroughly, but I did pause just long enough to lift the lid on the toilet cistern and peer inside. A clear plastic bag containing an ounce or so of white powder was floating in the stagnant water, like a listless jellyfish, but there was nothing else out of the ordinary. I replaced the porcelain lid and moved into the cramped living area, flicking on the main overhead light as I entered.

The living area was all just as it had been too, although Michael's suitcase was gone, and there was now a printed slip of yellow paper that looked like a police form on the foldaway kitchen table. I rested in the middle of the room, hands on my hips, and scanned the interior, asking myself where I should start and how long I should take. To some extent, I was trying to put myself in Michael's shoes, thinking what I would have done if I'd been confronted by the same space. What I'd realised I'd overlooked, you see, was that Michael was a burglar too. And if he was anything like me, he'd keep his valuables somewhere that most people, particularly opportunist thieves, wouldn't think to look. I'd hidden my burglar tools behind the side-panel of my bath and the two monkey figurines in a box of washing powder and my theory was that Michael could have done something similar. If he was as good as Pierre said, the third monkey might never have left his apartment, no matter how many thugs and police officers and forensic teams had been through it.

That was the theory. Now I was back in the bed-sit, though, it was difficult to imagine where his hiding place could be. It was such a confined space, with barely any furniture, that the possibilities were limited. I started with the obvious and slid the chest of drawers out from beside the bed and removed each of the drawers and searched the cavities behind them. Then I turned the chest upside down and checked the underside. There was nothing there besides clumps of dust and household debris so I put the drawers back and pulled the bed away from the wall. The bed had a metal frame and no apparent openings where anything could be hidden. I felt around the blanket and sheets and then I lifted the mattress up and searched below that. When I didn't find anything, I dropped the mattress, prodded it for a while, much like a surgeon feeling for a hernia, and then gave up and transferred my attentions to the kitchen area.

The foldaway kitchen table and chairs were no good but I shook the gas canister to check there was fuel in it and then I shone my pocket torch into the back of the single burner stove where I found a miniature world of burnt crumbs and blackened chunks of who knew what, but nothing of import. I straightened with my hands on my hips and looked at the aluminium sink. It was possible he'd hidden something in the plastic U-bend beneath it but that seemed unlikely and so I passed it over for the time being. Then I looked up above my head and spied the faux-marble light fitting. The fitting was made of an opaque material and there was a possibility there could be something inside of it so I moved one of the kitchen chairs and climbed onto it and was just about to unscrew the fitting when I heard the front door of the building open, then close, and afterwards the sound of footsteps on the main stairs below.

The footsteps were measured, as if the person they belonged to was in no hurry to get to where he or she was heading. I glanced around the room, wondering if I could put it back as I had found it in time, but I knew I couldn't without making a great deal of noise. Instead, I unscrewed the light fitting and untwisted the scalding bulb a fraction so that the room was plunged into darkness and the owner of the footsteps wouldn't see any light shining from beneath the front door of the bed-sit. As I blinked away the translucent hexagons that had formed in front of my eyes and tried to ignore the smell of burning plastic from my disposable gloves, I felt around blindly inside the casing of the light fitting until I was sure there was nothing there either.

Meanwhile, the footsteps came ever closer. It was unlikely anyone from the police would be checking on the apartment so late at night, I thought, but I couldn't be certain of that, and there was always the chance somebody was about to enter in less than strictly legal circumstances anyway. I tensed and readied myself to flee at the first sound of the lock being touched, my toes curled up inside my trainers and my mind already rehearsing my leap towards the bathroom. The footsteps came closer still and then I heard the squeak of a loose floorboard on the landing just in front of the door. There was silence for what seemed like an eternity. It was so quiet I could hear the creaking of my knee caps. My whole body went cold, then flushed hot the moment I became aware of it. I held my breath as best I could but I was afraid the thudding of my heart might just be loud enough to give me away. It was all getting a bit too much and I was on the brink of bolting for the window when finally, and to my considerable relief, the footsteps began again and I heard the sound of measured footfall on the next flight of stairs. Either the person the footsteps belonged to was drunk and weaving slowly upwards, or they were old and needed a rest, or they were simply curious enough to pause outside of a bed-sit where someone had recently been killed, but the upshot was they weren't about to walk in on me. I waited until the footsteps could no longer be heard and then I twisted the bulb back into its socket, looked away from the lighted element and screwed the light fitting into place once again.

I got down from the chair and removed my micro-screwdriver and immediately used it to unscrew the light switch on the wall. I checked the cavity behind the switch and then I did the same thing with the two power sockets positioned above the floor near the sink. They were no use either. I popped the screws back into position and tightened them and then I began to think about lifting the carpet and checking the floorboards. It didn't seem a likely scenario. If Michael needed to access the monkey in a hurry, the floorboards wouldn't work. It was still possible, of course, but I didn't like it, and I decided to leave it as a last resort. Much as I'd wanted to avoid it, the bathroom seemed a better bet.

As a first step, I checked the side-panel of the bath, just in case we really were on exactly the same wavelength. It proved a tricky panel to remove. One of the screw-heads was mangled and the panel had been forced in at an awkward angle so I had a real job to get it out and, quite typically, I needn't have bothered. All the panel concealed was the underside of the plastic tub and the metal pipe work and I wasn't about to start tackling the plumbing.

There was no towel rail or shower rail in the bathroom and even if there had been the monkey was probably too big to be fitted inside something like that. I checked the plastic toilet brush holder and found only a yellowy-brown sludge in the receptacle beneath. The light above my head was from a bare bulb and there was no medicine cabinet or laundry cupboard of any description.

I looked again at the bloody scene around the bath, at the discoloured porcelain and the tiles, and just then a jolt ran through me. It was only a small thing, but the metal cover of the overflow pipe seemed a touch proud. I reached for my screwdriver again and very carefully used it to prise the metal cover away from the bath, keeping my wrists and arms clear of the dried blood and pulped body tissue surrounding me. There was no rubber sealant holding the cover in place and it popped out into the palm of my hand with no trouble at all. Something else came with it. Taped to the back of the cover was the top of a small, clear plastic bag. I tugged on the bag and the rest of it came up and away from the overflow pipe all at once. The bag was bone dry, though it smelt pretty foul. I shook it out and opened it up and then I removed what was inside. It wasn't the missing monkey figurine – it was far more interesting than that.

TWENTY-FOUR

By the time I'd put everything back as I'd found it and slipped out of the bathroom window onto the flat roof once again, it was almost dawn and a faint, gauzy rain was beginning to fall. I collected my holdall from the nook where I'd hidden it and ditched my gloves in the waste bin, then rolled the bin back into position and went in search of a place where I could collect my thoughts.

I found a café nearby, a few streets over towards the Singel canal, where the owner who was opening up took one look at my pallid, sleep-deprived face and ushered me inside for the first coffee of the day. I drank it sat beside the etched-glass side window, warming my hands around my mug, thinking about the events that had transported me to where I was now. On the table in front of me was the single piece of paper I'd found folded up in Michael's overflow pipe. It was a photocopied document and the reproduction wasn't perfect but it was good enough to tell me what it had been intended to. I sipped on the coffee and waited for the caffeine to trickle into my grey cells and get me thinking around the implications of what I'd found, listening, in the meantime, to the clatter of crockery being removed from the dishwasher as the owner continued to prepare for the day.

A half-hour later, when he'd finished the donkey work and found time to drink a coffee himself, I asked the owner for some food and he nodded and disappeared into a back room while I went in search of the gents and tended some more to the bloody gash on the back of my skull. I emerged some minutes later, clutching a paper towel to my wound, to be presented with a plate of just about the best cold meat and cheese I had ever tasted. I chewed the food, along with my

he asked it. She could see the flint of disb
is face.

if they caught us like now, alone? What wou
hen?'

pose they would have to kill you.'

ughed and then cursed. 'What makes you

at they could?'

strike me as a man who could easily prot

ut if there were two of them, then, perhaps–

n't let her finish.

exactly are they?'

rvants,' she ventured. 'When I left Jamai

nd it would have been dangerous to tra

ey offered to accompany me to London.'

en they offered to follow you up here?'

Even to her ears the explanation sound

le.

u did not think to ask me to house them

the servants' quarters?'

ke their independence. Once they saw I w

ur house and that you were a gentleman–

rupted her. 'How do you contact them?'

signal of a candle at night.' She was hone

er, for he looked as if another lie might we

nger.

the window of your room?'

uld I worry that they may frisk Falder wi

ompetence than you have?'

is summation of the situation was so clo

---

her nipple once, he pulled back, watching the skin pucker and crinkle.

'At the dinner with the Bishop of Kingseat you did not wear undergarments and when you bent over...' He stopped, giving her the impression of a man only just holding on to some semblance of control. 'Suffice it to say that I have wanted to touch you here ever since then.' His thumb lightly skimmed the wet coldness of her nipple. 'And kiss you here.' His lips were warm against the small patch of freckles lying in her cleavage. 'I have wanted to know the taste of your sun-warmed skin and find the line where clothes have shielded you. His hand dipped lower. 'Have they, Emma? Shielded you? Here?'

She could not speak. She could only feel as hot drifts of longing assailed her and the rhythm of his breathing changed. Her eyes fell upon his lips. He had beautiful lips. Full and defined. The stubble on his jaw was light as her palm brushed against it and when he tipped her lips to his, the slick shattering passion spun her wild and heat took over.

Away. From everything. She was all woman. Open, alive, free. And he was the sun and the ocean and the warm solid earth.

Again.

For ever. Cast as she was from a storm into the safe harbour of his body. And needing refuge.

The heavy footfall of boots were suddenly heard above them on the deck.

'Hell.' He pulled away and helped her straighten herself, as a man came down the stairs.

'Duke, I thought I heard you…' The words petered out and stopped, uncertainty replacing the earlier hurry. 'I'm sorry.' The newcomer's voice held a strange quiver. Not sorry at all, she determined, but amused.

'This is Peter Drummond, an old friend of mine who is also the ship's captain. Peter, meet Lady Emma Seaton.'

'It is my pleasure,' he said softly, his glance falling to the crushed silk of her skirt. A definite question was in his eyes and the tone in his voice was puzzled.

'You got my note, then?'

'Note?' Asher shook his head.

'To meet here. I thought that was why…'

'I came for the plans to take up to London. Is there a problem?'

'There might be.'

Emerald could tell the man did not wish to say more in front of her, so excusing herself, she walked back up the steps and on to the moonlit deck. The quiet burr of voices from below was a backdrop to the frantic beat of her heart.

What had just happened? Again? If Peter Drummond had not come…?

She could not think of it. Did not want to think of it.

'I am the pirate's daughter,' she whispered to herself. *'The pirate's daughter. The pirate's daughter.'*

She remembered the taunts of the children on the dockside at Kingston Town, when the *Mariposa* had come into port, and the slanted glances of their parents.

Her father was a man who used fear to distance

himself from everyone. And
Just as she was not being h
With Asher.

The realisation made her
her she was hard-pressed to
cupied and angry and threa
been ten minutes earlier. Th
darker, the tan of his face s
velvet of his eyes.

He was beautiful.

She admitted this simpl

They had gone a good
a voice that sounded noth
heard him use.

'Who are the men car
'I am not certain wha
he interrupted her.

'The men you brough
that make my query an
'Who told you that?'
'Peter Drummond j
few days ago. His fath
and he remembers you
and an Arab, four ches
lot longer than it appe
'I see.' There was
grouped her defences
are here to see that I
'Protected again

even as
lief on
'And
happen
'I su
He la
certain t
'You
himself,
He di
'Who
'My s
for Engla
alone. Th
'And t
'Yes.'
implausib
'And y
Falder, in
'They li
safely at y
He inte
'By the
in her answ
incite his a
'Throug
'Yes.'
'And sh
even more
Because

to what she had just been thinking she blushed, giving him his answer.

'I see.' He ran his fingers through his hair. Or what was left of his fingers, she amended.

'It is not as you think,' she began.

'Then how is it, Emma? Explain to me exactly how it is.'

'I cannot,' she said simply and turned away. In the shimmering glass her reflection was barely visible, a thin reminder of the person she purported not to be.

'You cannot because the truth is that you are a liar, Lady Emma Seaton. A beautiful liar, but a liar none the less.'

'Yes.' She faced him directly and left it at that. Tonight the untruths just would not come and his kisses still burned on her lips and hands and neck.

Lady Liar.

Pirate's daughter.

There was some sort of symmetry of verse in the expressions and both left her with a completely groundless counter-argument.

She *was* a liar. And *would be* a thief if she could only find the damn map. Regret swamped her. All she wanted to feel again was the warmth of his lips against her own.

And know again the safety he offered.

She could not remember ever being truly safe. Not since her mother had left and not for a while before then too.

Blood.

And screaming.

The sounds of cold arguments on the warm winds of Jamaica. She tilted her head and tried to catch the glimpse of something elusive. But she couldn't, and when the Gravesons' house came into view she was pleased, for it released her from the close confines of the carriage.

Dinner was horrible.

Oh, granted, Annabelle Graveson had gone to an enormous amount of trouble and was the most gracious of hostesses, just as her son Rodney was the very epitome of excellent manners and careful conversation.

But Asher barely looked at Emerald and when he did she could see only a veneer of distrust in his eyes and a good amount of distance. She missed his banter. She missed his smile. She missed the breathless possibility that he might lean across and touch her and she would feel again the slow rise of passion and the quick burn of excitement.

What was she coming to? She was at dinner, for goodness' sake, with a widow woman and her son. With an effort she tried to listen to what it was that Rodney was talking to her about.

Guns. She'd never liked them.

'I can now hit a target at thirty feet. Sometimes more. We often hunt in the grounds of Falder.'

'We.'

'Carisbrook and I. He's teaching me.'

'The Duke of Carisbrook is teaching you?'

His eyes swivelled around at the mention of his name.

'Is there a problem with that, Lady Emma?' he asked in his frostiest voice. A voice that implied she thought he could barely hold a gun, let alone shoot it.

'Certainly not.'

'I am pleased to hear it,' he returned and his smile was strained.

Annabelle Graveson seemed oblivious to everything as she leaned forward and placed her hand on Emerald's. On the third finger of her left hand was a ring bearing a diamond the size of a large rock. The house. The jewellery. The clothes she wore. Annabelle Graveson had become a rich woman on the death of her husband.

'I would like to make you a gift of some gowns, Emma. Would you accept that from me?' Her voice quivered.

'Gowns?' She did not umderstand the reason for such an offer.

'For your Season in London.'

'Oh, no, Lady Annabelle.' She went to say more, but could not.

'Is it because I am a stranger to you? I am hoping we may change that.' The fingers on her forearm tightened.

He looked as puzzled as she felt.

'Lady Emma is staying with the Countess of Haversham, Annabelle, and is well looked after.'

'Yes, of course,' she replied, a semblance of calm once again in place. 'Of course she is. When is your birthday, my dear?'

The question was so unexpected it took Emerald by surprise. 'My birthday?'

Annabelle Graveson nodded.

'It's on the third of November.'

Tears filled Annabelle's eyes and she dabbed at them with her handkerchief and waved the attention of her son away. 'No, Rodney,' she said. 'I am quite all right. In fact I have never felt better.' And with that cryptic remark she bent over the pudding she had before her and demolished the lot.

'They are unusual people,' Emerald chanced into the silence as they wended their way home a few hours later. When she got no reply, she amended her observation. 'Nice and unusual, I meant.'

Still no reply. She was not daunted.

'Annabelle seems rather a nervous woman,' she continued.

'Whereas you, on the other hand, are not.'

'I wouldn't say that.'

'Name one thing that you afraid of.'

She was silent and unexpectedly he laughed. 'Thank you, at least, for not lying to me.'

'I did not lie about James.'

'I know.'

She held her breath and looked out of the window. The clouds against the moon reminded her of her little brother's curls as he had lain there asleep while she watched him.

Tonight he seemed close. Perhaps that was because it had been so long since she had spoken to anyone about him. And Asher Wellingham had been a good listener.

What else had he been? A would-be lover, a man whom she could trust and respect and like.

Like? Too tame for what now raced inside her and yet with the ghost of her father hanging so baldly between them nothing else could be possible.

Nothing.

She saw he kneaded his thigh with the fingers on his left hand and chanced the opening.

'Do you have a cane, your Grace?'

'A cane?'

'For your leg. Perhaps if you took your weight off it…'

He stopped rubbing immediately.

'My uncle had a cane once. A fine one, carved in ebony. He had hurt his knee at Waterloo and found the stick to be invaluable.'

God, how many more clues could she safely give him?

One more.

She took in a deep breath and spoke.

'Walking sticks are actually quite a passion of mine. I collect them, you know.'

She did not let the pained look on his face dissuade her.

'I have twenty from all parts of the world.'

'Fascinating.' The tone he used intimated that he found the subject anything but.

'Indeed, your Grace, it is.' She was grateful for the dark and for the movement of the coach. 'If you had any at Falder, I would be pleased to look at them for you to give you some idea of their value.' She felt the thick beat of duplicity in her throat when he did not answer and the look in his eyes was one of singular calculation.

She should not have gambled on his intellect. Already she could see the wheels of his brain turning and so she was not surprised by his next question.

'Would it be a cane by chance that you are looking for at Falder?'

'No.' She met his question directly as the lights of his home came into view. As the carriage began to slow he lifted her gloved fingers into his.

'What happened to your hands? Are they also a part of the mystery of Emma Seaton?'

'I don't understand.'

'Do you not?' he chided, the soft light in his eyes hard and flat. 'If I looked into the records of the Haversham family, where exactly would you be placed in relation to Miriam?'

Taking a breath, she pulled her hand away and tried to rally. Lord, if he was to do that...

'I am her niece, as I believe you already know.'

'I see,' he returned as the lights of Falder flooded the carriage. All around there now stood servants, waiting. Emerald was pleased when the first footman seemed to take her smile as a signal and moved forward to open the door.

An escape.

Gathering the skirts of her gown, she hurried from the coach. The ruse was up. She knew it. When Asher backtracked into the depths of her family history, he would have his suspicions confirmed that there was no cousin called Liam Kingston. And he would also know that Miriam's only brother was Beauvedere Sandford Louden. It would take him but a moment to work out the rest.

She would have to forgo her searching and be gone from Falder at the first possible opportunity. The map offered riches, but discovery could mean prison. She had failed in her quest and now there was little else to do but return home.

A tight feeling of absolute uncertainty engulfed her.

Ruby and Miriam.

How on earth could she protect them?

Asher roamed the hills above the ocean, cursing the note in his pocket, the note he had found beneath his door when he had returned to his room in the hours after dawn. Emma Seaton was gone.

Back to London.

Back to Jamaica.

Back to God knew where.

The horse beneath him whickered and pranced and he stilled her with a quiet whisper, hating the way his mind kept replaying the feel of Emma's skin beneath his hands.

He wanted her. That much was plain. He wanted her like he had never wanted any woman before. Even with Melanie he had not experienced this white-hot flash of passion, this desperate uneasiness. And the way she responded to him...

'Stop it.' He said the words out loud, surprised by

the gut-tearing anger in them. Emma Seaton was a thief and a liar and a threat to his family. He had given her a chance to trust him, after all. More than a chance. If it had been anyone else, she would have been thrown out after the night he had seen her dressed in the lad's clothes in front of his dead wife's picture.

Why had he not, then?

He knew the answer even as he posed the question.

Because he admired her. She was so unlike any other woman who had ever made his acquaintance that she threw him somewhat and he doused down the urge to place his hands around her neck and strangle the truth out of her.

Why would she not trust him?

What had she to hide?

He swore into the gathering wind and turned his horse for home.

Lucinda met him in the front portico and she did not look pleased.

'Emmie is gone.'

'Emmie?' He had not heard her called that before.

'She was my friend. She told me her friends called her Emmie. She said that I could too and now she has gone.'

'Did she tell you why she went?' He could barely keep the irritation from his voice.

'No, she did not have time, though she did leave this note for me.' She handed him a small piece of paper to read.

Miriam and I need to return to London. Thank you for letting me borrow the clothes and jewellery.

'I do not think she went of her own free will, Asher. I think you were cross with her. I think she reminds you of a time when you used to laugh and enjoy life and so you frightened her off somehow…'

'That's enough.' The whiplash of his words shook Lucinda visibly and she turned towards the stairs, but not before snatching her note back.

'She may be gone from Falder, Asher, but you can't forbid me to see her in London, for I like her, even though you are determined not to.'

He watched her as she flounced up the stairs, the letter tightly held in her hand and the promise of rebellion in the staunch set of her shoulders. Life had not burdened her yet, he thought as he made for the library, all her hopes and dreams still intact and possible.

So unlike his own.

Taris sat in the armchair by the window. Today he looked tired, and when he removed his glasses to clean them Asher saw that his right eye was strangely opaque.

'Emma Seaton has gone?' His brother's tone had the same ring to it as Lucinda's. Tired of defending his actions, Asher reached down and took a cigar from a box on the desk near the fireplace. Cutting it, he breathed in deeply before sitting on the leather sofa opposite his brother.

'When Father died he made me promise on his death bed that I should never compromise Falder because a thousand years after our demise this pile of stones and mortar will still be here, and a thousand years past that thousand too. Custody. Tradition. Responsibility. Call it what you will, but I listened.'

'Lord, you actually believe that she would compromise Falder? In what way?'

'Rifling through the silverware at midnight would be one way I could mention.'

'And did she steal anything?'

Asher shook his head. 'Nothing I could determine, but I think there was something specific that she was after and she has not yet found it.'

'Specific. Like what?'

'God knows, for I don't. Money, perhaps. Jewels. The combination lock on my safe had been tampered with.'

'She had the skills to try to break open your safe? Who sent her, do you think?'

'She wouldn't say. I did ask.'

A moment went by as he watched Taris play with the tassel of a burgundy bookmark left on an open copy of Webster's *Duchess of Malfi*.

'She's in trouble, Asher. You said as much yourself.'

'And you think that it concerns me?'

'I can hear it in your voice that you admire her, which leads me to conclude that, if you have any hopes of an heir to enjoy these hallowed halls, now might be the time to take action.'

Asher swore to himself and did not answer. Could not answer. Whatever it was that Emma Seaton inspired in him was irrelevant. Lust? Like? Love?

thoughts, for close to an hour and then I made my way to a pay-phone at the rear of the café and dialled the number on the business card Rutherford had given me. I was expecting to leave a message on his machine but to my surprise Rutherford picked up, sounding groggy.

"Sleeping at your desk?" I asked, once we'd exchanged greetings.

"Telephone's on divert," he explained, then yawned. "I wondered if you might be in touch."

"Considerate of you," I told him. "Thing is, I need another favour."

"Not in the clink again are you, dear boy?"

"Not just yet. But I am in a tight spot Rutherford and the truth is I was wondering if you might be able to put me up for a day or two. I could go to a hotel, only ..."

"Wouldn't dream of it," he interrupted. "Truly. You're familiar with the Oosterpark?"

I told him I was.

"Very good. I live on the western side. You have a pen?"

"And a napkin."

"Good man," he said, and then he told me the address and asked me if I thought I could find it.

"I'm sure I can," I told him. "Is it okay to come on over?"

"Of course. I'll fix us some tea."

I thanked him again and hung up, then paid the café owner, leaving a few extra euros on his tip tray before bidding him farewell and walking off in the direction I'd come from earlier that morning. The chill air was raw against the cut on my head and I was shivering. I pulled the thin man's leather jacket tight around my body for warmth, slipped one hand in my trouser pocket and drew the hand that was carrying my holdall up inside the jacket sleeve.

From St. Jacobsstraat, I crossed the tourist strip of the Damrak and walked past the Oude Kerk into the very heart of the Red Light District. The scene was drearily familiar. Here and there, hung-over revellers stumbled out of whore booths and twenty-four hour sex clubs, their clothes unkempt and their movements limp and aimless. Meantime, clusters of working girls, their arms linked together, walked away from the area in plastic overcoats and knee-high PVC boots, heading for Centraal Station and whichever homely suburb they hailed from. In their place, other girls were arriving to begin the less lucrative day shift, layers of heavy make-up giving their faces an expression of forced optimism.

I lowered my head and avoided their eyes, looking instead at my feet on the grubby concrete, tuning out of the half-hearted rugby song a handful of my compatriots were slurring. Soon, I was nearing the Nieuwmarkt, passing from the fringes of the Red Light District into an off-shoot of China Town. East Asian grocery stores and butchers and restaurants began to surround me in a splash of bright yellows and reds and a world of symbols and signs I couldn't decipher. The rapid-fire yammer of Chinese conversation filled my ears and strange, meat-based scents caught in my nostrils.

I strolled down Zeedijk street, and was just passing a newsagents when the owner of the store tottered out into the street carrying a postcard display unit in front of his face. Because of all the postcards, he couldn't see where he was going and he bumped right into me. The display unit fell from his hands and crashed to the floor, scattering postcards and pocket-sized maps across the street. I stooped to pick the goods up, not sure if the man was cursing himself or me, and while I was reaching for a handful of the loose cards something in a first floor window above the newsagents caught my eye. I hesitated, and stared at the window, and by now I knew that the man was cursing me but I no longer cared. Adhered to the glass was a familiar motif, no more than a couple of feet in height, and above it were more Chinese symbols. I couldn't read the symbols but the motif was as clear as day. Three monkeys – one covering his ears, the next covering his mouth and the final one covering his eyes.

Wordlessly, I found my feet and pressed some of the cards into the man's hands. Already, I was walking beyond him towards the glass and aluminium-framed door beside his shop. There were several buzzers positioned next to the door but I didn't delay myself with them. Instead, I opened the door and walked into an unheated entrance hall where my breath instantly condensed in the still air before me.

Ahead was a darkened storage area and a lighted staircase lined with a threadbare red carpet. I climbed the stairs, walking in a vaguely dazed fashion like a man who has been hypnotized, and at the top of the stairs I faced up to a second door with a bubble glass insert that again contained the monkey insignia, though this time the insignia was smaller. I tried the handle. It was unlocked. I opened the door and walked inside.

The room I found myself in was cramped and cheaply furnished. It was dominated by a waist-high plywood counter that faced three plastic chairs only a few feet away. The walls were bare and painted in an off-white colour. The only items on top of the counter were a cordless telephone and a small brass service bell. I hovered for a few moments and when nobody appeared I stepped up and rang the bell.

Let me tell you, I wish there were more bells just like it because the woman who appeared to answer the chime was just about the most beautiful creature I've ever seen. Perhaps five feet tall, she was dainty as air and she wore a lustrous, peacock-blue kimono that complimented the dark, glossy hair tied atop her head. Her face was painted in an almost geisha style and she bowed her head in the Oriental fashion as she approached.

I bowed my head too but when I looked up the charmed smile I'd adopted slipped from my face in an instant. Flanking her were two huge men, with shoulders like boulders and no necks to speak of. They wore suit jackets and dark shirts but they would have looked more at home in a sumo ring. Waxed hair scraped back on their heads, they walked in an odd kind of shuffle, throwing their considerable weight from one foot to the next, as if their ability to move depended entirely on a complex form of perpetual motion, like one of those executive toys with the rows of silver ball bearings knocking endlessly together.

The Asian goddess waited at the counter, smiling sweetly, until the two giants were hovering behind her shoulders in a queer visual echo of the three monkeys. I focused on her dewy eyes and she nodded in discrete encouragement.

"Hi," I began, rather brilliantly. "Do you sell monkeys here?"

The woman shook her head minutely, as if it genuinely troubled her that she didn't quite understand.

"Monkeys, like those ones?" I asked, pointing over my shoulder towards the motif etched into the bubble glass on the door.

She shook her head again and then lowered her eyes, focussing on a point of unfathomable interest on the bare wooden counter. Very slowly, one of the goons behind her rolled his neck around his massive shoulders and I heard the crunch and crackle of his load-bearing vertebrae as clearly as if I was eating cereal. His twin inhaled deeply through his nose, looking as if he might vacuum every last molecule of oxygen from the room just for the thrill of seeing me pass out.

I got the impression they weren't in the habit of having their time wasted, so I fumbled in the pocket of the thin man's leather jacket until I found the two monkey figurines and then I placed the figurines onto the counter in front of me. They lay there haphazardly, the one covering his ears and the other covering his mouth, somehow appearing to cower under the quiet gaze of the beautiful girl. To my great relief, the girl raised her head and smiled at me easily and the two men either side of her allowed their massive shoulders to relax just a fraction.

"Do you recognise these?" I asked. "Were they made here?"

The girl just blinked at me, as if waiting for me to rid my system of such trivial questions.

"I don't have the third one. Are you able to make it? Or would you like to buy these?" I asked, gently sliding them across the counter towards her. "How much would you pay?"

This time, the girl nodded, as if she understood my wishes completely. Then she reached below the counter for what I imagined would be some money or a ledger. I was wrong. Her hand emerged holding a small metal hammer. The hammer was rendered in some dull, lead-like material, but unlike a normal hammer, both ends of the striking head were shaped into a point so that, side-on, it looked like a flattened hexagon.

She reached below the counter a second time and fetched a shammy cloth and spread it flat across the surface of the counter. Then she picked up my two monkey figurines and positioned them carefully on the shammy and, before I could stop her, raised the little hammer in the air and bought it down hard onto each figurine with a sharp, deadly tap that instantly reduced the monkeys to a fine and irretrievable rubble of plaster and dust.

I gasped and reached out, mouth agape, but as my eyes scanned the destruction properly for the first time my sense of horror was suddenly replaced by the first glimmerings of understanding. There, shining amid the mess of plaster debris, was a small metal object. I stepped closer and brushed the plaster chunks aside with my fingers and picked it up. The object was a key, no bigger than the kind that would fit a suitcase, and there was a second one just like it amid the remnants of the other figurine. Both keys had an identical Chinese symbol etched into them. I picked the keys up in my hand and studied them in my palm. So it was true – the monkeys were worthless – it was what had been inside of them that had been worth killing for.

As I held the keys aloft and marvelled at how clean and shiny they were in spite of the plaster they had been housed in, the girl raised a hatch in the plywood counter and motioned for me to walk through and join her. I did as she suggested and then she bowed once more before stepping aside and inviting one of the tailored sumos to relieve me of my bag and search it while his partner patted me down. The one who was patting me down didn't find anything of interest but his friend who was searching the bag pulled the handgun out and showed it to him. They studied me carefully, as if from a new perspective, and I shrugged, as casually as I could, and then watched as they deftly emptied the cartridge of bullets, put the gun back inside my holdall and kicked the holdall to one side. When they were done, the girl motioned for me to follow her towards a plain white door at the back of the room. I did just that and the two heavies fell into line behind us so that we walked towards the door in group formation, looking, I imagined, a lot like a bizarre delegation from a far flung planet in a television Sci-Fi series.

On the other side of the white door was a small vestibule and beyond it was a substantial metal door with a circular wheel fixed to it. The metal door was wider and taller than a normal door and looked to be made of a highly polished steel. It was the kind of door you might expect to find in Fort Knox or at the entrance to a top-flight nuclear bunker. To the side of the door was a flat, electronic screen and I watched, soundlessly, as the girl pressed her palm against the screen and the screen flashed a blinding light against her delicate palm, almost like a photocopier. There followed a solid clunk and then the door dropped on its hinges just a shade. The girl nodded to the sumo on my right and he stepped forwards and turned the wheel on the front of the door, then heaved the thing wide open.

What I saw beyond the door was enough to take my breath away. Here, on the first floor of an ordinary looking building in Amsterdam, was the kind of security facility that a first rate bank would be proud of. Row upon row of safety deposit boxes stretched for the entire length of the room, forming a corridor that was illuminated by the flickering light from a series of suspended fluorescent tubes. The safety deposit boxes were made of a similar metal to the door and they gleamed in the light as if they had never been touched. There were perhaps three hundred in all, stacked side by side, and there was nothing else beside the boxes and the lights in the room, not even a window. I turned to look at the girl and she gently took the keys from my hand and led me into the heart of the metallic corridor ahead of us.

A little over halfway down the corridor the girl paused and consulted the Chinese symbol on the front of both keys, then matched it to one of the safety deposit boxes beside her hip. She gestured to the box and I saw that it had three locks on the front of it. The girl inserted the keys she was holding into two of the locks and then waited for me to produce the third key. I couldn't, of course, because the third key was inside the final monkey, wherever that might be.

"I don't have it," I said, and showed her my palms and shrugged my shoulders by way of explanation.

She pointed to the third lock and said something in Chinese, then acted out inserting the final key and turning all three locks and opening the box.

"I know," I told her. "But I don't have the third key. Do you have a copy?" I asked, pointing at the third lock and then the girl with a hopeful look on my face.

The girl glanced anxiously over my shoulder towards one of the sumos and he motioned towards the door we had come in from. She nodded minutely, then began to remove the two keys she'd inserted.

"A copy?" I asked. "Don't you have a copy?"

But it was no good. The girl placed both keys in my hand, rather dismissively I thought, and then bowed ever so slightly before walking away in the direction of the door. I didn't follow her immediately and the delay was enough for the sumo nearest to me to place his sizeable palm on my shoulder and usher me after her with a no-nonsense shove. When we got back to the reception area, the girl peeled off into a side annex where I glimpsed a low table and a leather couch and a television set, while the two sumos accompanied me to the bubble-glass door, handed me my holdall and watched me climb down the stairs until I was out on the street.

Normally, I might have consoled myself by planning to break back in at some point in the future but I didn't rate my chances. I had no idea how to bypass a fingerprint scanner like the one that guarded the room and I didn't possess the kind of high-tech gear that might enable me to get through the steel door without it. And that was not to mention that safety deposit boxes are notoriously difficult to open or that the two sumos could tear me apart like a sheet of origami paper if I happened to get caught. And I thought there was a reasonable likelihood of that happening because I was pretty sure they manned the place on a twenty-four hour basis. That kind of accessibility would be a major draw to the type of clientele I guessed they catered for but, more to the point, Michael had told me he'd planned to leave Amsterdam right after I'd given him the two monkeys. The building I was stood outside was just a five-minute stroll from Centraal Station so it didn't take a genius to work out where he was headed before leaving the city. It didn't take a genius to work out what was inside the deposit box, either, but knowing where the diamonds were didn't mean a thing without the third key. I groaned and shook my head. I was tired and beaten up and in need of a rest, and I wasn't keen to hang around outside a building that I assumed the thin man and the wide man knew all about. With each passing moment, Rutherford's apartment was becoming an ever more appealing place to be.

TWENTY-FIVE

Rutherford's apartment was on the third floor of a grand old mansion building with an imposing stone façade. The floor-to-ceiling windows of the sitting room looked out over the Oosterpark and the distant outskirts of the city and I imagined Rutherford had spent many an hour absorbing the expansive view. The décor was English traditionalist, heavy on the floral patterns and antique furniture and watercolours. Some of the paintings were originals and had probably cost him a fair sum. His family money must have been pretty substantial, I supposed, because the whole shebang would have dwarfed his government salary.

"Dear boy," he said, when I walked into the sitting room for the first time and he caught sight of my head wound. "What on earth happened?"

"I was jumped," I told him. "By two of the American's associates."

"The killers?"

"I don't think so. But they certainly know how to swing a baseball bat."

"Sit down," he said, patting a nearby chair. "I'll fetch something."

He returned a few moments later with a bottle of iodine and some cotton pads and began to clean my wound, making me wince each time he applied the iodine to a sore spot or caught an area that had clotted with my hair. I could smell the musty odour of his underarms as he reached for my head, pressing his large stomach up against me. He was wearing his suit trousers and a work shirt with the sleeves rolled up and every now and then he would pass me a bloodied pad to hold onto. By the time he was finished, I had quite a collection of the discoloured rags and Rutherford fetched a waste bin for me to drop them into.

"You look drained," he told me.

"I feel it. I haven't slept at all and I've had a busy night. I'm not sure I needed to impose on you though, Rutherford. I could have checked into a hotel under a false name, I suppose."

"And who would have cleaned your wound? The maid? I think you may need stitches, incidentally."

"Terrific."

"You have health insurance?"

I nodded, then yawned.

"Well, I've made up the bed in the spare room," he went on. "You're welcome to stay as long as you like, naturally, though I'm afraid I have to leave for the office shortly. Unless," he said, raising a finger to his lips, "I call in and delay for a while. I suppose I could. Are you concussed at all?"

"I imagine so. In fact, it would explain a hell of a lot. But you should go. The main thing I need right now is sleep."

"Very well, let me show you the bed. I'll fetch you some night clothes too."

I didn't use the night clothes, as it happened. They were more than a couple of sizes too big for me anyway and as soon as I saw the neatly made bed all I wanted to do was fall down onto it and shut my bleary eyes. And once Rutherford had left me to my own devices, I removed my shoes but left my clothes on and did just that, collapsing on top of the covers and plummeting into a deep and fitful sleep.

*

When I woke, many hours later, my head was stuck to the pillow. I must have twisted and turned a fair bit in my sleep and that seemed to have aggravated my wound and started it bleeding some more. The blood had clotted, binding my hair to the pillow fabric and making the procedure of lifting my head away a tricky one. Once I'd negotiated it and I was upright again, I looked down at the crusted

stain on the pillowcase and decided it was a right off. I turned the
pillow over and hid it for the time being.

I hadn't had time to draw the thick velveteen drapes in my room
before sleep took hold of me and I was relieved to see it was still
light outside when I glanced at the window. Knuckling my gummy
eyes, I checked the bedside clock and saw that it was coming up to
three o'clock in the afternoon. I hadn't heard any noises in the rest
of the apartment and so I assumed that Rutherford was still at
work. Standing feebly from the bed, I gently tested the area around
my head wound with my fingertips and decided that I would risk a
shower.

The bathroom was ostentatious by Dutch standards, with the
shower positioned over the centre of a claw-foot bath. I shed my
clothes and stepped into the bath and then I positioned the shower-
head so that the hot water hit me on the neck and shoulders rather
than the back of my head. The steamy water sluiced over the dark-
ening bruise on my ribs and I carefully soaped my chest and let the
suds rinse away. I cupped the water to my face and eased some of
the soreness from my eyes and then I reached down as best I could
to clean the rest of me. When I was done, I dried myself in one of
Rutherford's soft, downy bath towels and then I tiptoed back to my
bedroom to find a clean change of clothes in my holdall. The gun
was still there when I opened the holdall, resting amid the clothes
I'd managed to grab, but I didn't pick it up or investigate it at all. It
had done as much of a job as I'd needed it to in order to get me out
of the wide man's apartment and for that and the fact I hadn't needed to fire it I would be forever grateful. But it didn't change my mind
about owning a gun and I wondered how long I would have to wait
before I could ditch it safely.

Beside the gun was my passport, and since I wasn't a spy, it happened to be my real passport, with my real name and my real date
of birth in the back of it. I didn't pick it up either – it was just reassuring to know it was there.

I dressed and made my bed, then stood still for a moment, making a pretence of deciding what to do next before quickly giving in
to the urge to look around Rutherford's apartment. It was a new
space, after all, and it would have been remiss of me not to famil-

iarise myself with the layout – imagine the fire risks!

I left the bedroom and faced up to the closed door positioned next to the sitting room I'd been in earlier. Closed doors are never quite satisfying enough for me so I tried the handle and found myself inside a dining room with an oval-shaped, teak dining table and eight elaborately carved dining chairs. The windows shared the same park view as the sitting room, and the walls displayed another pair of quality watercolours that in my non-law abiding moments I might well have been tempted to snatch.

Interesting.

I moved on through a door on the far wall of the room and found myself in a functional galley-style kitchen that I paused in just long enough to find a packet of crisps to eat. The kitchen led back to the main hallway and the bathroom I'd showered in. Beside the bathroom was Rutherford's bedroom and I stuck my head inside for a quick peek. Almost inevitably, it was dominated by a four-poster bed, though no offence to Rutherford, you could tell he was a bachelor. The bed-set he'd chosen was of a dark-grey colour that did nothing for the room, while a spare pin-stripe suit and several clean work shirts were hanging from the wardrobe doors. I left the bedroom and entered the final room in the apartment, which was sandwiched between Rutherford's bedroom and my own. It was only a small room but it was the space I warmed to most of all – his study.

The walls of Rutherford's study were lined with row-upon-row of books, there was a comfy fabric arm chair with an ethnic-style throw in one corner, a matching rug on the floor and a large antique writing desk made of a deeply burnished oak across the way. The desk was covered in loose papers and correspondence and there was also a green-tinted reading lamp and a touch-tone telephone. I settled myself in the leather swivel chair that faced the desk and reached for the phone. While it rang, I idly sorted through the papers and knick-knacks on top of Rutherford's desk, not really paying any attention to what I was looking at.

"You're a genius," I said, when Victoria finally answered.

"Mr. President?"

"Close." I smiled, opening a small personal banking book and thumbing the pages. "How are you?"

"Just dandy. You?"

"Like a burglar with a sore head."

"I won't ask. But tell me, why am I a genius?"

"You don't know?"

"Well it could be anything, I suppose," she said, airily.

"Actually, it was something you said the last time we spoke."

"About you catching something from the blonde?"

"No," I told her, sounding more stern than I'd intended. "I'm going to rise above that one. See, I'm rising as we speak. I'm helium. I'm a hot air balloon. I'm a fresh loaf of bread."

"You're a writer running low on similes. Come on, what was it I said Charlie?"

I closed the banking book and began flicking through a loose-leaf pad of paper.

"You said, and I might be paraphrasing a bit here, but it was something like the monkeys were the key to everything."

"I did?"

"Yes. And do you know why that was so clever?"

"Surprise me."

"Because the monkeys *contained* keys. And that's what all the fuss has been about."

"Really? Just keys?"

I turned the pad over, then switched the reading lamp on and fanned a few pages of the Dutch-English dictionary that was open on Rutherford's desk. I lifted the dictionary by the spine and shook it in case anything interesting fell out but nothing did.

"Just keys to a safety deposit box," I told Victoria. "With the stolen diamonds inside of it."

"Aha."

"Aha indeed. There's just one problem."

"Which is?"

"The box needs three keys to open it."

"Oh. And you're still missing a monkey."

"Exactly. Although, now I think about it, I suppose being kidnapped last night was something of a problem too."

"Sorry?"

"Kidnapped. Beaten with a baseball bat. You know how it goes."

"No Charlie, I don't. I think you'd better fill me in."

And so I did. And while I brought Victoria up to speed, I turned my attention from the things on the top of Rutherford's desk to the contents of his desk drawers. There were seven drawers in all, three on either side of the desk, and one central drawer situated just above my knees. The central drawer was the only one that was locked and, as ever, it tweaked my curiosity. So as I talked, I wedged the telephone receiver between my neck and my ear, removed a paper clip from one of Rutherford's documents, unbent it, and began to pick at the lock.

"Charlie?" Victoria asked, a few moments later. "What are you doing?"

"Nothing."

"You're breathing rather heavily."

"Am I? Sorry. I'm just trying to open something while we talk."

"As long as that's all it is."

"How do you mean?" I asked, pausing.

"It doesn't matter," she said. "But the wide man and the thin man – you really believe they don't have the third key?"

"Or even the third monkey," I said, resuming my task. "If they did, they wouldn't have stayed in the apartment with me. They'd have gone and got the diamonds themselves."

"Unless they were bluffing."

"Why would they do that?"

"Why is anyone doing anything anymore? I don't know, maybe they wanted to make you think they didn't kill the American."

"But they didn't kill him. And why would they care what I think? To them, I'm just a burglar who happened to be in the wrong place at the wrong time. I'm not a threat. I'm an inconvenience."

"Only now you have their monkeys again."

"Actually, no. The monkeys are long gone. They're powder. Now all I have are their keys and a long-shot at a locker full of diamonds."

"Poor you."

"I will be if they catch up with me. Damn."

"What?"

"This bloody thing I'm trying to open. I just broke a paperclip."

"A paperclip? Why are you using a … Oh, Charlie, do I want to know about this?"

"It's just a desk drawer. Probably harmless."

"Is it your desk drawer?"

"Don't ask dumb questions, Victoria. You're a genius, remember?"

"A genius. Yes, of course. A genius who has no idea whodunnit."

"You're not the only one."

"But it doesn't bother you, does it? You're only interested in the diamonds, right?"

"Right," I said, distractedly.

"Charlie, what is it?"

"The drawer," I said, "is open."

"And?"

"And you'll never guess what I just found."

TWENTY-SIX

No, it wasn't the third monkey. But it wasn't so far off either. Perched on the top of a small collection of personal items was a Dutch passport, red in colour. I picked it out of the drawer and flicked to the back cover and what I saw there turned everything upside down. Why? Because it was the exact same document I'd found a photocopy of in the overflow pipe of Michael's bath. But what was it doing in Rutherford's apartment?

"I'll call you back," I told Victoria, then hung up the phone and stared at the photograph at the back of the passport for a long time, not really thinking of anything in particular, at least not on a conscious level. The photograph would have been around five years old, I guessed, but the likeness was still there. The hairstyle had changed and the glasses had been replaced with contact lenses, but there was no mistaking who it was. I read the name and address details for perhaps the twentieth time and then I put the passport down and picked up the telephone receiver.

The call I placed took no longer than a couple of minutes to complete and it told me what I'd suspected it would. Once it was over with, I had only to wait. It was gone four thirty already and I was expecting him to return some time after five o'clock. I occupied myself in the meantime by pacing his sitting room, occasionally glancing out of the picture windows at the cyclists and joggers circling the Oosterpark, at other times working out exactly what it was I was going to say. Of course, the moment I heard his key turn in the lock and his footsteps out in the hallway, all of it escaped me and I had to make do with whatever popped into my head.

"Wonderful, you're up," he said, meanwhile setting his plush overcoat down on the back of a Chesterfield and beaming at me. "Feeling better?"

"My head's begun to clear," I told him.

"Splendid news. And your appetite?"

"It can wait a while. I thought we might have a chat."

"Of course. Everything alright, dear boy?"

"You tell me, dear boy," I said, and with that I pulled the passport from my pocket and threw it at him. Rutherford fumbled it, then bent down to retrieve the document from the floor. He opened it up, then looked wide-eyed at me and shook his head as if he didn't understand what was happening.

"You can drop the act," I told him. "I called the British Embassy. They don't have a Henry Rutherford working for them."

He almost tried something else at that point. I could see him turning ideas over in his mind, probing new possibilities that might just work. But then he met my eyes and he seemed to see something there that told him whatever it was just wouldn't wash.

"Bollocks," he said, shoulders plummeting. "I arseing well knew I shouldn't have left you on your own. Didn't expect you to find this, mind."

"Dumb luck, I guess."

"No use complaining, I don't suppose?"

I looked hard at him.

"Yeah, I should probably just be grateful you didn't rob me blind. Plenty here that's worth a bob or two."

"Any of it yours?"

"In a round-a-bout way. You know how it is," he said, gesturing at me with the passport in a helpless way, as if everything that had happened was beyond his control.

"Tell me."

"What's to tell? We're the same, you and I."

I frowned. "You're a burglar too?"

"Nah," he said, casting his hand around his apartment in a vaguely fey manner. "Confidence man. But neither one of us exactly plays by the rules now, do we?"

Shaking my head, I dropped down into the wingback chair

across from him and gestured at the passport.

"What are you doing with that?"

"Mikey asked me to get it for him," he said, eyes blank.

"The American?"

"The one and same."

"So you knew him?"

He nodded. "We were inside together."

"In the Netherlands?"

"Not so far from the Hague, as it happens. I was doing some bird for a scam that turned sour. Dutch lady I went into partnership with got more suspicious than I bargained for when she checked into the company I'd set up."

"I don't think I need to know."

"You don't. Want a drink? I could do with a beer."

I shook my head and he left me for a moment, returning from the kitchen shortly afterwards with a lager can in his hand. He popped the lid on the can, loosened his tie and his shirt collar and began to drink greedily, his swollen throat working overtime.

"Name's not Rutherford, by the way," he offered, belching.

"I guessed as much."

"It's Stuart. Rutherford's just a persona I use. You get the right name, the right way of talking, the right clothes and the right apartment and, well," he said, drawing my attention to the room around him, "you can do okay by it."

"So long as you stay out of prison."

"Occupational hazard. You done much time?"

I shook my head. "I don't plan on it either."

"Nobody does, son. Mikey sure as hell didn't."

Stuart knocked back some more beer, then collapsed onto the Chesterfield, his stomach ballooning up and quivering in front of him like a moulded jelly on a plate

"Tell me about the passport," I said. "When did he ask you to get it?"

Stuart stuck out his bottom lip, thinking it over.

"Month ago, maybe. He called me from inside. Said there was this girl he wanted looking into."

"Marieke."

"Was the name she gave him, yeah," he said, nodding. "But he figured there was something up with it."

"So he asked you to steal her passport?"

"Nah." He ran his hand backwards over his glistening forehead. "He asked me to find out what I could. So what I did was I found where she worked and I spoke to some guy who works there too."

"The young barman? Has a good scowl?"

"Fella worked behind the bar. I guess he could be the one you're referring to. Anyhow, fact is barkeeps in Amsterdam are the same as any place else – they don't get paid so good."

"So you bribed him."

He rolled his eyes and showed me his clammy palms. "I asked him to have a quick shufty at some of her things, was all. He was the one brought me the passport."

"And you photocopied it and sent it to Michael."

"Now how'd you know that?" he asked, eyes narrowing.

I shook my head. "Never mind. What was his reaction when you sent it to him?"

"No idea," he said, casually. "I just posted it to him, inside a birthday card."

"The prison guard's didn't check?"

"Not the way I did it. I pasted the thing inside a cardboard flap in the card."

"Clever."

"Not really. Prison security is pretty slack over here. Doesn't take a lot to figure out ways around it. I mean, I doubt it was even his birthday."

I sat forward in my chair, elbows on my knees and my fingers pointing at him.

"Did her name mean anything to you?"

"The girl? Not until we were in that library. The minute we found that newspaper article, it started to make some sense."

I looked at him intently. "Kim Wolkers. Her surname is the same as the security guard Michael killed."

Stuart nodded. "Except he didn't kill nobody. Least, he always said he didn't. But you're right about the name. You figure she's his daughter?"

"That would be my guess."

"Mikey's too, I reckon. Fact, I have a suspicion he knew all along."

"What makes you say that?"

"Just a feeling I got. Something in his voice. I can't explain it."

"There's still a few things I don't get," I said.

"Only a few?"

I smiled, nursing my head in my hands. "One thing in particular – why did he get close to the girl once he knew who she was? He must have realised she was setting him up."

Stuart shrugged and slouched further down in his chair, balancing the lager can on his gut.

"Mikey was a peculiar fellow. He swore blind he'd never killed that guard but he was never your average prisoner either." He paused, face clouding over as his finger tapped absently on the side of the lager can. "Thing is, he had no beef with being inside. Me, I'd bitch about it just about every minute but with him, well, it was almost as if he welcomed it."

"Penance?"

"You might say."

"Though that doesn't add up if he didn't kill the guard."

"No."

"And it doesn't explain why he didn't blow her cover."

"Unless he did. In private, say."

I bobbed my head from side to side, as though mimicking a set of weighing scales.

"I didn't get that impression."

"Me either. But it's a theory."

Stuart threw up a hand in a helpless gesture, then imbibed from the lager can. He was sat in a very un-Rutherford way, gut hanging loose over his trousers, legs splayed open. The contrast made me aware of just what a performance he put on whenever he got into character and knowing that made me cautious. I very much doubted Stuart was his real name. It was probably years since he'd last used that.

"You're not a lawyer," I said.

"Nope."

"So just out of interest, how did you pull that off? Getting to represent me, I mean."

He grinned, like he was recalling a recent sexual conquest.

"Easier than you'd think. I kind of just waited around in the police station for a while that morning. Overheard a couple of uniforms saying you were refusing to talk until you had a lawyer there. So I waited until they'd gone and I presented myself to the duty sergeant, or whatever it is they call them over here."

"But didn't they want to check your papers?"

"Oh I have papers. Anyone can get them."

"I see. No, scratch that, I don't see. How did you even know to come to the police station?"

"Your arrest was in the papers," he said, sounding surprised I hadn't thought of it. "I came as soon as I saw. Thought I might pick something up that could be useful to me."

"About what?"

He shrugged.

"The diamonds," I prompted.

He nodded, slowly. Then he glanced up at me with doleful eyes. "Turned out better than I imagined."

"It was one hell of a trick."

"Well," he said, chin bobbing, "you do something for a living, it pays to be good at it. I'm guessing you don't just steal things as a hobby."

"You could say."

"You wait until something comes along that's worth your time, right?"

"And the risks."

"The risks are half of the fun."

"Not for me," I replied, shaking my head.

"Come on, you don't get a thrill when you break into someone's home? I don't buy it."

"It's maybe a side-effect of what I do."

"Sure."

"Really. I'm a writer first of all. It's just, every now and again, I might supplement my income a little."

"Reminds me," he said, poking a fat digit at my forehead. "Read one of your books the other day. Had the murderer sussed by chapter three."

"Maybe you just guessed right."

"Nah, I knew. Doesn't mean I didn't enjoy it, mind."

"We're getting off the point," I told him, finding my feet and walking around to the back of the wingback chair, gripping the fabric in my hands. "You said you knew about the diamonds from the start?"

Stuart nodded again, the fatty skin on his neck folding up like a thick roll-neck sweater as he pulled his chin towards his chest.

"Heard about them inside. Not a lot else to do other than talk, you know. And a man like Mikey, a whole bunch of myths can build up."

"How so?"

"Well, he was a quiet one, I guess," he said, peering down into the opening of his lager can and gently swirling the contents. "Most every con I ever met is willing to tell you what scam he's inside for, where it went wrong, how he'd do it different next time. But not Mikey. He wasn't like that at all. It gets to the masses. Everyone wants to know what the deal is. Every detail gets picked over."

"Like?"

"Like for instance the little monkey toy he kept in his cell. A queer little thing, right? He was always looking at it. Made people talk."

"And what did they say?"

"All kinds of things. Before long," he said, tapping his forehead sagely, "a man like Mikey can become a real topic of conversation."

"One of which was that he'd got away with a fortune in diamonds."

"Among others."

"Did you ever ask him about it?"

"Sure."

"And what did he say?"

"Nothing." He shook his lager can, drank a little more. "But that changed."

I waited a beat, trying not to rush things. "Oh?" I said, as casually as I could manage.

Stuart grinned, aware of what I was trying to do. "Listen," he said, "I'm putting some pieces together here myself, okay? But I'm assuming you're the English guy he asked to steal the two monkeys for him. I mean, who else, right?"

"Go on."

"And you said no. At least, that's what you said to begin with."

He paused, waiting for me to confirm it, but I didn't oblige him. It didn't seem to matter a great deal. A confidence man is a story-teller at heart and Stuart liked to tell a good story.

"It got Mikey," he went on. "For whatever reason, he needed those monkeys. And it was getting late on that Thursday and he began to think maybe you wouldn't go through with it. And then he called me."

"As back-up."

"Except he didn't know for sure it was back-up."

"Right. And you agreed to break into the houseboat and that apartment for him."

He made a whining noise deep in his throat, almost a whimper. "Not to begin with. Like I said, I'm a scam king, not a B&E merchant. But ..." He raised his eyes to the ceiling and nodded his head, as if to acknowledge his moral failings. "It was getting late in the day and it was important to him that he got the monkeys that night, okay? And I knew about the one he'd had inside with him, knew how important it always seemed to be. So I played him for a while, got him so he was almost begging me to help, but being careful, you know, not wanting to blow it. And I guess I couldn't have done it much better in the end because that was when he came clean about the diamonds."

"How much did he offer you?"

"Half," he said, then gulped some lager.

"You're lying."

A sly grin crept across Stuart's face. "What makes you so sure?"

"Your lips are moving."

"Jeez," he said, throwing a hand up, then letting it drop onto his belly. "That line's as old as my grandmother. And she's been dead almost twenty years."

"Even so, it's true, isn't it? I'd say it was more like ten per cent."

"Well guess away, buddy. All's you need to know is it was enough to get me on board."

"So you were the second intruder."

"Come again?"

"The guy who broke into both places after me."

"If you say so. It makes sense that way but I've never known for certain you were there."

"I was there," I said, folding my arms. "I was in the apartment in the Jordaan when you were searching it. You cut the mattress with a knife."

"Well, I'll be. Where were you hidden?"

"The attic." I glanced up, as if an identical hatch had appeared in Stuart's ceiling to help me explain. "There was a crawl space there. But I couldn't see you."

"Or else you'd have had me pegged the first time you saw me in the police station," he said, in an almost wistful tone.

"You were luckier than you realised."

"Although what could you have told them, I guess?"

"It's a conundrum."

"Isn't it?"

"You know," I said, scratching at the sore spot on my chest, "I happen to believe what you're telling me. I knew whoever broke into the apartment was a beginner. What did you use on the door, by the way?"

"Fire extinguisher. Found it on the street."

"I'd figured it was a mallet, though a fire extinguisher works I suppose."

"Sure worked for me," he said, grinning again.

"But why did you go to the apartment at all? You must have known I'd taken the first figurine from the houseboat."

Stuart shook his head. "Couldn't get into the safe, could I? I told Mikey I wouldn't be able to but I guess that shows how desperate he'd got. He wanted me to try."

"But when you got to the second apartment and the monkey wasn't there, you had to assume I'd been in before you?"

"There was no sign that anyone had broken in."

"Because I didn't break anything. I used my picks."

He pouted. "Except I didn't know that, did I? It was a possibility, sure, but equally the monkey could have been moved."

"So what did you do after you left?"

"Headed to the café the girl works in. That's where Mikey wanted to meet. But when I got there he was already leaving so I came here and waited for him to call."

"Was he with the wide man and the thin man?"

"There were two men, yeah."

"You think they're the ones who killed him?"

"Could be. Or it could have been the girl. Or maybe it was you." He peered at me, brow furrowed.

"Or you," I suggested.

"Well now," Stuart said, sitting up in the Chesterfield and spilling some of the beer on his shirt. "I know it wasn't me."

"Likewise," I told him, then reached up and probed at my head wound, picking away a flake of dried blood. "And after they put a baseball bat to my head, the wide man and the thin man said it wasn't them."

"So it was the girl then."

I leaned my head on an angle. "Perhaps. Although she would have had to wait until the wide man and the thin man had left him alone, then beaten him, then got back to the café to meet me. Which I don't see happening. Are you sure she wasn't with Michael and the two men?"

"Absolutely," he said, looking as serious as he had done at any time since he'd got home. "Although she could have already been in his apartment, maybe. I didn't go inside the café once I saw him leave but I didn't see her through the window either."

"It's possible."

"Or somebody is lying."

"Or somebody else killed him."

"Hell, maybe it was suicide."

I gave Stuart a look that told him that wasn't funny. He slumped a little on the sofa, then drained the rest of his lager.

"Was it you who broke into my apartment?" I asked.

He frowned, wiping his lips clean with the back of his hand. "I don't know anything about that. Matter of fact, I've been tying to find out where you live. So you got burgled, huh?"

"I'm not sure it's something I'm entitled to complain about."

"Did they get the monkeys?"

"I'm afraid so."

Stuart squinted at me, then gestured in my direction with his lager can.

"You know, you just looked away when you said that. It's a sure sign you're lying."

"I'm telling you the truth," I said, focussing on his eyes.

"Horseshit. You blinked."

I sighed, then rubbed the back of my neck and afterwards the stubble on my chin.

"What about your secretary, the one who called me?"

"Some bird in a bar. I gave her a few notes."

"She was kind of curt."

"No shit. You get what you pay for, I guess."

"And that whole library thing," I went on, throwing my hands up. "Why'd you go through all that? We were in there for hours."

"Well, I couldn't go finding what you were looking for right away now, could I?"

"But three hours!"

"Yeah," he said, smirking, "I sensed you were getting a bit restless. I could have gone another hour or so."

"There was no need."

"I was being thorough. Besides, you'd paid me well enough."

"The six thousand euros? I found it in the safe in the houseboat."

He shook his head, amused. "Easy come, eh?"

"Something like that. Truth is I figured it could be marked and I might as well get it laundered through your office account."

He whistled. "What did you think, you'd ask for some of it back after a while?"

"The thought had occurred to me."

"From a lawyer? Man, you're a born optimist."

I leaned forward against the chair and planted my hands on the backrest again.

"One final question," I said. "Marieke, Kim, whoever she is – you think she might have the third monkey?"

He chewed his lip, then nodded slowly. "I'd say the odds are pretty good. And I say that as somebody who knows you must already have been through my apartment."

"Hey," I told him, smiling, "you do something for a living, it pays to be good at it."

TWENTY-SEVEN

Café de Brug was busier than I'd ever seen it. All of the tables were occupied and a cigarette smog was suspended above the room. Both the girl and the young man were working the bar and because of the number of customers she didn't see me to begin with. I took a stool and lit a cigarette with a book of matches from a nearby ashtray, looking, I thought, a bit like Clint Eastwood in one of his Western movies. I'm pretty sure I don't want to know how I really looked.

When she finally saw me, I could tell she thought about not serving me and leaving it to her light-fingered friend. In the end, though, she thought better of it and fixed me a beer.

"Thanks Kim," I said, when she placed the beer in front of me.

Her hand didn't leave the glass. All that mattered right then was that she'd heard me say her real name.

"You might want to let go," I told her. "Otherwise, it's going to be pretty hard for me to drink."

When she still didn't move, I prised her fingers away from the glass and raised it to my lips, swallowing a mouthful of the icy liquid. Then I took another draw on my cigarette. My chest still hurt when I inhaled deeply, though I did my best not to show it. I vented the dry smoke through my nostrils, reached into my pocket and removed her passport. I slid it across the surface of the bar towards her.

"Let's take a walk," I said. "Tell your friend to earn his wage for a while."

I drank another mouthful of the beer and then got up from the bar and waited outside for her to join me. She emerged around five minutes later, having taken longer than I'd expected to put on a black puffa jacket and gloves. I led her towards the lighted canal bridge without saying anything and waited until we were in the middle of the bridge span before taking a last draw on my cigarette, then flicked the butt into the oily waters below and leaned against the brick balustrade.

"Michael knew," I began, looking down at the dark, curd-like surface. "I found a photocopy in his apartment."

My words were met with silence. Either she didn't know what to say or she was waiting to hear where I was going with it. The truth was I didn't really know where I was going with it but it seemed I had to say something more.

"It was in the overflow pipe in his bath. I happen to know he had the copy before he got out of prison. So he knew who you were. He knew it was your father he'd killed."

She pulled her hands out of the pockets of her jacket and wrapped her arms around herself. Then she kicked at the soot-coated brickwork with her foot, nodding her head, as if part of her had already known.

"He didn't tell you?" I asked, and she shook her head in a cheerless way. "You were sleeping with the man who killed your own father," I went on, the words sounding harsher than I'd intended.

Finally, she said, "Not me."

"Well," I replied, "unless you have a double I don't know about, I'm pretty sure it had to be."

"No. Marieke, maybe, but not me."

"I'm not sure that's a distinction you can make."

"You do not know how it is," she said, giving me a sharp look.

"I guess I don't. I guess I don't understand it at all."

She turned and leaned back against the balustrade beside me, resting her elbows on the stone plinth and looking up at the dark night sky. Her breath fogged in the air, obscuring her face, but I could see that the cold had given her skin a pinched look, somehow making her cheek bones more pronounced. With her blonde hair hanging loose on her shoulders and her eyes seeming to retreat into their sockets, she had a heroine-chic look about her, like a catwalk model from the nineties.

"I didn't mean to like him," she said, in a small voice, half to herself. "At first, I hated it. But it was true anyway. If we'd met by accident and I didn't know who he was, I would have been attracted to him."

"But you always knew who he was. What he'd done."

She closed her eyes, as if to block out my words and focus on her own. "When he told me for the first time that he was innocent, it was so shocking. Not because it made me angry." She turned to me. "Because I wanted to believe it was true."

"Maybe it was."

She bit down on her lip, draining the blood from it. "No," she said, and shook her head wilfully.

"It was something he told a lot of people, I hear."

"Not so many killers say they are guilty."

"Some must. Some even plead that way."

She inhaled deeply, composing herself. "I was nine years old when it happened. I saw his pictures in the papers. I saw his eyes and I knew it was him, even before the trial. But then, all of a sudden, it was over. He was in prison and I knew nothing about him. Did he think about me? Did he even know I existed? Did he know what he'd taken?"

"It's not something he'd be likely to forget."

"But it could have been. I did not know him then. I knew only what my mother would say, spitting his name, saying terrible things. She told me he was a monster."

"I imagine it was easier, thinking of him like that?"

"Of course," she said. "It was simple. But then, the first time we spoke – I don't know, he was so ... different."

"And that hurt."

"Yes."

"But that changed."

She tensed, and I wondered for a moment if she'd go on. She had every reason not to. I wasn't her counsellor, or even the police. I could have said that she owed me a version of the truth, but what did that mean really? Perhaps all she wanted was someone to listen to her, though, because after a pause she began to speak once again.

"It did not change for a long time," she said, hesitantly. "At first, I almost could not breathe when we talked. But I learned to control myself, to shut part of me off. And then I found that I wanted to hear what he had to say."

"Freud would have loved this."

Kim stomped her feet into the ground and hugged herself more closely. She seemed to be shivering.

"We could go inside," I suggested. "You could tell me the rest in there."

"No. It is good out here."

"You like discomfort?"

She shrugged.

"So when did you decide to take the diamonds? Because that was the plan, right?"

She looked at me, horrified.

"Oh, maybe at first you thought about harming him in some way, perhaps even killing him, but the way I see it that changed when you started to like him. I'm guessing you convinced yourself that the best way to spite him was to take the one thing he'd been waiting twelve years to get his hands on. And, of course, it couldn't hurt that the diamonds were worth a small fortune."

"No," she said, and glanced at her feet.

"Oh, I think so. I think that's exactly how it went. Only you started asking too many questions and Michael got suspicious. And then he got a friend to dig around and that friend happened to find something truly shocking – the girl who'd become so attached to him was the girl whose father he'd murdered."

Kim shook her head slowly, as if trying to deny the logic behind what I was saying.

"The thing I don't get is why he left himself open to it all. Why carry on with the charade?"

"He loved me," she said, in a flat voice.

"Oh, I'm sure that's what he told you. Question is, why did you pretend to believe him?"

She started crying then, though not in a showy way. Tiny convulsions took hold of her and she quivered by my side, face lowered, mucus glistening in her nostrils. She bit down on her lip again, harder this time, but I tried not to let it get to me.

"You didn't kill him," I said, suddenly sure of it now.

"No," she whispered.

"Because you couldn't. Even if part of you welcomed it when you saw him that way. That's why you lost it, I think, seeing that something you'd wanted so badly had come to pass. And it's okay. I really think it is. Although the truth is I don't altogether care. All I want right now are the three monkeys. And I think you have the third one."

She looked at me, bewildered. "No."

"You're telling me it's not in your apartment, that if we went up there right now I wouldn't find it in among your things?"

"I don't have it. And what does it matter anyway? You told me you do not have the others."

She looked at me, her jaw set and her teeth clamped together, and I saw some kind of challenge in her eyes. She suspected me, for sure, and I couldn't really blame her. But then I didn't have time to think anymore, because I heard a screech of brakes and turned just in time to see a familiar white van lurching in my direction.

"You called them?" I shouted. "Before you came out?"

Something in her eyes told me I was right. I glared at her, then grabbed her by the arm and threw her towards the wide man just as he jumped down from the driver's cab with the baseball bat in his hands. He stumbled, but pushed her aside and hurried on, raising the bat over his shoulder and swinging hard as he stepped close to me. This time I knew what was coming and I danced back, sucking my stomach right in to avoid the blow, then rushed forwards and slammed him into the bonnet of the van and bear-gripped him before he could bring the bat back for a second swing. I hoisted my knee into his gut, hoisted it again at his groin. He dropped the bat with a groan and slumped down but still had enough fight to reach up and grab for my neck, squeezing my throat in his gloved hands. I tried to prise his fingers away, meanwhile pushing against his face and poking at his eyes, but he arched his head back so that I couldn't quite reach and before I could get free the thin man had joined in and forced my arm back at a wild angle, threatening to break it near my shoulder. I gargled in pain, flailing uselessly with my legs and stumbling backwards, in danger of toppling over the edge of the bridge. I was just at the point of submission when I heard a loud bang in the night sky and strained my eyes until I could just glimpse Stuart holding the smoking handgun I'd taken from the wide man's apartment above his head.

"Let him go," he yelled, doing a passable impression of a loose cannon. "Let him go right now, God damn it."

The wide man and the thin man froze, still holding me by the neck and the shoulder.

"Let him go," Stuart repeated, this time cocking the gun and levelling it on the thin man.

Slowly, the pressure on my neck and my arm began to ease and before long they'd released me enough so that I was able to step away from them. I swallowed cautiously and gingerly rotated my shoulder in its socket.

"Let's get out of here," I croaked, waving my healthy arm at Stuart.

But Stuart had other ideas. As I watched, he stepped across the bridge and grabbed Kim by the hair, yanking her head back and pressing the gun muzzle against her forehead so that her skin puckered around it. She stared at me, wide-eyed in alarm, and I looked back the same way as Stuart hissed, "Where is it? Where's the third monkey?"

She shook her head, unable to speak.

"She doesn't have it," I told him, as calmly as I could.

"Where is it you bitch? Tell me or so help me I'll pull the fucking trigger."

She whimpered, words failing her. By now, onlookers had spilled out onto the street from the café and it wouldn't be long before one of them called the police or thought about playing the hero. I couldn't imagine trying to explain this one to Burggrave.

"She doesn't have it," I repeated, louder this time. "Let her go. I know where it is. Believe me, there's only one place it can be."

He looked around, beginning to register what I was saying to him, and at last his grip started to loosen on her hair.

"Come with me," I said. "We have to go now."

He lowered the gun from Kim's temple and un-cocked it in an almost trance-like way, as if the mechanics of what he was doing could distract him from the mess he'd just made of the girl slumped on the ground in front of him. He watched over her, unmoving, and I stepped forwards to free the gun from his limp hand. I gave his wrist a squeeze, motioned for him to come with me. When he still didn't budge, I tugged on his arm and dragged him away in the direction of the nearest busy street.

Twenty-Eight

At mid-morning the following day, I followed two teenage girls in through the front security door of a modern apartment building in the south of the city. I paused by the mail boxes just long enough for them to step into the elevator and for the elevator doors to close behind them, and then I climbed a communal staircase up to the second floor of the building where I walked through a fire safety door with a reinforced glass portal in it and passed three identical-looking wooden doors before I found the one I was after.

There was a peep-hole at eye-level in the centre of the door and a brass mortise lock beside my hip. I rapped on the door twice and when nobody came to answer it I checked both ways along the corridor, making sure it was clear, and then I put on a pair of my disposable gloves, removed my picks from my coat pocket and set to work on the lock. It seemed a fair while since I'd tackled a really up-to-date lock but it was no more difficult to coax open than any of the others I'd dealt with recently. And aside from the low-level hum of an air-conditioning unit housed somewhere above my head, the corridor was very quiet, so I didn't even need to lower my head to hear the pins engage. When the final pin clicked into place, I twisted the cam and the bolt snuck back obligingly. Then I eased down on the handle, stepped inside the threshold and locked the door behind me.

The apartment I'd entered was in near-darkness and I could barely see a thing. I fumbled around on the wall for the main light switch and when the overhead light came on I found myself at the beginning of a magnolia painted hallway. There were several pairs of shoes by my feet and a hooded top hanging from one of the wall-mounted coat hooks by my side. Just ahead and on the left was a doorway that led into a compact, windowless kitchen. I turned on the lights inside the kitchen and scanned the fitted ash units and the chrome oven and hob. The kitchen surfaces were covered in dirty plates and coffee mugs and there was a blender that still had the residue from a breakfast smoothie congealed on its insides.

I moved back into the hallway and passed a bathroom, then turned left and entered a relatively large, L-shaped living room with a plush beige carpet, a state of the art flat-screen television, a glass coffee table and a black leather couch. The floor to ceiling curtains were drawn, which explained why it was so dark. I left the curtains like that to avoid attracting any unwanted attention and then I retraced my steps to investigate the final two doors in the apartment. The first door contained a closet that was filled with all manner of household junk: a vacuum cleaner, an ironing board, more shoes, some coats, hats and scarves, and a step ladder. The second door led into a bedroom that was just large enough to contain a double bed and a flat-pack wardrobe and chest of drawers. The bed was unmade and there was a pile of dirty clothes on the floor. By the side of the bed was an alarm clock and a paperback novel.

The bedroom struck me as being as good a place as any other to begin and so it was there that I started my search. Dropping to my knees, I pushed the duvet out of the way and shone my pocket torch beneath the bed. There was a stray white sports sock and a world of dust and carpet fluff but that was all. I felt all along the side of the bed box, checking for storage spaces, but I didn't find any. After that, I felt inside the pillowcases and then inside the duvet, and from the odour of stale sweat that hit me like a blow to the nose, I was glad to be wearing my gloves. When I didn't find anything there either, I turned my attentions to the wardrobe and after that the chest of drawers, removing each drawer and checking behind and underneath them in the usual way. Then I pulled the wardrobe and the drawer unit away from the wall and shone my torch behind and after that I went and fetched the stepladder from the hallway closet and scanned the top of the wardrobe. Finally, I sorted through the dirty laundry on the floor, pockets and all, until I was satisfied that the bedroom was a dead-end, and then I went and put the step ladder back just where I'd found it.

From the bedroom, I moved onto the living room. On the surface, at least, there wasn't so much to search in the living room, and my mind soon began to wander. Not unusually for me, I found myself thinking about my book again. It felt like a long time since I'd thought about it properly and as I went calmly about my business, I began to retread the plot twists that had led to my problems in the first place. Before very long, I found myself wondering if there wasn't a simple way out of it after all. It would take some work, but maybe I could rewrite the beginning of the story to make things easier on myself. The problem with that, though, was that I didn't want to make it all too easy for Faulks or my readers to work out who the killer was. But there had to be a balance to be struck, a way to accommodate logic without killing the book altogether. Perhaps I could dispense with the briefcase, I thought. It could be replaced with a carrier bag from a well-known store and that way Faulks could pick up a duplicate without any trouble. Or maybe the butler's hand was left at the scene in the first place. That wasn't as interesting, I guessed, because part of the mystery was how the murderer had got into a safe guarded by a fingerprint scanner that Faulks himself had been unable to access. Would Victoria go for it? More to the point, would I be satisfied?

The honest answer was no. Really, I should have been looking for ways to push myself and make things more difficult rather than jumping at easy solutions. But I was so fed up with having an almost-finished manuscript on my hands that it was a tempting option. My publishers might not agree, though, and where would that leave me? Back at square one with four months work written off and not a bean to show for it.

A change of scene could help, mind. Italy still appealed to me and if I went there maybe there was a chance I'd find the inspiration I was looking for. And even if I didn't, the weather would be brighter and the winter nights less severe. Plus there were Italian women to think about. Dark-haired, olive-skinned. Wonderful legs, as a general rule. And I'd always wanted to pick up a little of the language, ever since I'd seen Roman Holiday for the first time. I could have my own Roman Holiday. I could maybe do Gregory Peck, give or take a few degrees of smooth. And so far as I was aware, there were no meaty Italians looking to swing a baseball bat in my direction at any time soon.

I wondered how many times Gregory Peck had appeared on the television that dominated the living room. Not enough probably, which was a shame, because it was a fine machine, with something like a 42-inch screen, and I supposed it could give Gregory a pretty fair hearing. As great as it was, though, it didn't help me find what I was looking for and neither did the couch or the glass coffee table or the pile of newspapers and magazines hidden behind the door.

I bypassed the bathroom, figuring a bathroom couldn't come good two times in a row, and I passed over the storage closet too, because tackling all the junk inside of it looked like way too much work and I was content for it to be an absolute last resort. That only left the kitchen, where the smell of dried food on all the dirty crockery was potent enough to make me turn up my nose. There might not have been much evidence of home cooking going on but that didn't mean there weren't plenty of places to search.

The bin was filled to overflow with ready-meal containers, I noticed, and when I checked inside the microwave I saw that it was peppered with fatty residues. The wall-mounted cupboards contained an extensive selection of cereal brands, as well as bread loaves of varying degrees of decay, and several packets of the chocolate sprinkles that Dutch people spread onto slices of bread as a breakfast treat. The base cupboards held a small collection of cleaning products, a few baking trays and saucepans and the odd can of tinned food. I checked inside the oven and behind the housing of the extractor fan and then I gave the lengths of wooden plinth above and below the kitchen units a solid prod to make sure that none of them had been loosened. After that, I opened the fridge door and almost gagged on the eggy smell that wafted out at me. There was a carton of milk and some processed cheese and a half a chocolate bar inside. At the top of the fridge was an ice box. I pulled down the plastic flap on the icebox and pushed a bag of frozen mixed vegetables to one side. Nothing. Then I straightened and happened to look down into one of the slots in the electric toaster and, stone me, there he was, hands covering his eyes as if he was just waiting for me to shout peek-a-boo.

I can't tell you how good it was to see him again. What I can tell you is that I whooped and did a silly little jig and followed that up with a seriously bad moonwalk. Because to hell with my book, there was at least one case I could solve all on my lonesome.

TWENTY-NINE

I had a few more errands to run after leaving the apartment, and one of them involved me teaming up with Stuart for an hour or so. Once we were done, I left him to carry out a job of his own devising, giving me just enough time to return to his building and place a series of phone calls.

The first number I dialled was for the central police station and from there I asked to be transferred to Detective Inspector Riemer's direct line. After a wait of around a minute or so, during which time I was treated to intermittent bursts of recorded Dutch soundbites, I was finally put through.

"Mr. Howard," Detective Inspector Riemer began. "You have some information for us?"

"You remember me then," I said.

"Of course. I was just reviewing the notes on your interview."

"Ah. I should imagine that makes for some fascinating reading."

"The report is quite short, in fact. I see you would not answer many questions."

"Would you believe me if I told you I'm shy?"

Riemer paused long enough to let me know exactly what she thought of my response.

"What if I said I had the impression Inspector Burggrave had already formed a somewhat biased opinion of me?"

She sighed. "I do not have time for games, Mr. Howard. What did you want?"

"Oh, not much. Only to say that I think I know who killed Michael Park."

Riemer hesitated. I could picture her tense and crowd around the telephone receiver. "Will you agree to be interviewed?"

"In a sense," I said. "If you'll meet with me."

"When?"

"Four o'clock this afternoon. And bring your deluded colleague along too, will you?"

After providing her with the necessary details, I rang off and called the next name on my list. The conversations I found myself conducting all followed a similar format and without exception everybody I called seemed reluctant to meet me. If I was a more sensitive type I might have developed a complex about that but the truth is I've never been one to take things to heart and fortunately I can be a stubborn fellow when the situation demands it. In point of fact, every single person I called showed up in the end, which I'm enough of a realist to admit probably had more to do with the lure of the diamonds than any reputation I'd developed for throwing a good party.

The venue was one of Stuart's masterstrokes. We were in the old central warehouse at the disused Van Zandt complex. All about us were broken storage crates, dusty wooden palettes, buckled metal trolleys and empty oil drums. The floor was covered in an ankle-high scree of waste and dust and fallen ceiling plaster and the temperature was no warmer than outside, since there was no heating to speak of and a good deal of the windows were smashed through, allowing the bitter gusts of winter air that scoured the surface water of the Oosterdok to whip around us.

To give the scene some order, I'd gone to the trouble of arranging a number of crates and palettes to form a rough semi-circle in front of me but my efforts didn't appear to have made my guests any more comfortable. Kim, for one, could have done with a hat and scarf, because she was obviously cold. Her chin was tucked right down inside the collar of her puffa jacket, her fine legs were crossed at the thigh and she was blowing warm air onto her cupped hands. I couldn't ask her how she was feeling, though, because she'd evidently decided to have nothing to do with me or anyone else for that matter. Her hundred yard stare was a good one, but that was no surprise given she'd been practising it since her arrival.

The wide man and the thin man were sat opposite her, sharing the same crate, and I noticed the thin man had found the time to replace the leather jacket I'd taken from him. I knew from experience now that the jacket wouldn't provide much warmth but maybe that wasn't the point. Perhaps it was all part of a uniform he and his broad companion had devised for themselves years ago, even if only on a subconscious level. I could imagine them both getting ready to head out for some general villainy and the procedure they might go through. Van keys? *Check*. Bovver boots? *Check*. Baseball bat? *Check*. Shall I wear the leather jacket? Oh go on then.

Talking of clothing, Inspector Burggrave and Detective Inspector Riemer were the most suitably attired, each of them wearing standard-issue police coats with dense fur linings. They also seemed the most inconvenienced by our get-together and gave the impression I was keeping them from far more pressing matters. That was nonsense, of course, but they were police officers after all and it would be bad form to appear pleased about being asked to show up someplace on anybody else's terms. So they kept pacing around in circles and checking their watches and mobile telephones, and just for that I held off on starting for at least two minutes longer than I needed to.

Stuart was sat just to my side and, like me, he was dressed in a thick, roll-neck jumper, though his was several sizes larger and many times more distended around the gut. He'd teemed the jumper with a woollen sports jacket with leather patches at the elbow and he had a very Rutherford-style paisley handkerchief poking out from his breast pocket. His final prop, a leather-bound briefcase, nestled on the floor beside his feet, and if anyone had had cause to look inside, they would have found it was as empty as the wide man's head. Stuart looked entirely at ease, which he was entitled to, since he was the only person beside myself who knew anything of what was about to unfold.

Next to Stuart was my final guest, Niels Van Zandt. To my mind, Mr. Van Zandt looked more fragile than he had done inside his home, his milky eyes watchful and ever ready, but I could also tell that part of him was caught up in the thrill of being back inside his family's old business premises and, so far as I could make out, he seemed no more aware of the cold than he was of his own breathing. He wore only a cashmere sweater and corduroy trousers but from the easy way he was perched on his oil drum, gnarled hands lightly gripping the top of his cane, you would have thought he was comfortably reclined in front of the open fire in his study. Part of me wished I was there myself – I could have done with a mouthful of bourbon to settle my nerves before I began.

"Thank you for coming," I said, looking around the group of people in front of me and showing them my palms in a welcoming gesture. "Some of you are acquainted, I believe, though I hope you won't mind if I hold off on the wider introductions for now. Suffice it to say that this gentleman on my right," I said, motioning towards Stuart, "is Henry Rutherford, my lawyer. Mr Rutherford is here to ensure that everyone understands that I won't be incriminating myself by anything I may say here today."

I looked at Burggrave and Detective Inspector Riemer and waited for both of them to acknowledge what I'd said. They did so, reluctantly.

"For the record," Stuart cut in, warming to his role, "the two police officers present have indicated their willingness to adhere to this understanding."

I thought he might try to get them to confirm it to him verbally but, like all successful confidence men, Stuart knew not to overplay his hand. Burggrave and Riemer contemplated him with evident distaste but he took it in his stride. As Rutherford, he could rise above such things. In truth, he was so comfortable in his performance that Kim must have found it difficult to reconcile the pompous individual before her now with the crazed gunman who had held a pistol to her head.

"As most of you know," I resumed, "the building we are in used to be the main storage and diamond cutting facility for Van Zandt Diamonds. Mr. Niels Van Zandt," I went on, gesturing towards the resilient old gent, "is the nephew of Lars Van Zandt, the founder of the family diamond business. Mr. Van Zandt has agreed to join us today for the sake of clarifying a few points that might otherwise be taken as conjecture. Thank you again for coming, Mr. Van Zandt."

Van Zandt bowed his head and gave me a queer little wave, faintly regal, as if he was granting me permission to continue. If I was a military man I might have given him a quick salute but I've never been able to carry off that sort of thing so I just nodded, as if doffing an imaginary cap in his direction. He seemed to be enjoying my deference, so I went on with the charade.

"Having had the pleasure of being able to talk with Mr Van Zandt, I can tell you that his family established their jewel trading business at the beginning of the nineteenth century. Their core activities involved them in purchasing uncut stones from the former Dutch colonies and refining them here in Amsterdam before selling them onto high-class jewellers and diamond retailers throughout the world. Unlike a number of their competitors, they were hugely successful and rapidly became the most powerful of the Dutch diamond merchants."

"Did you call us all here for a history lesson?" Riemer asked, sharply.

"Not at all," I assured her. "Though I think the background may help a little. And I must confess that I found it all rather fascinating when Mr. Van Zandt spoke to me. I don't think it inaccurate to say," I said, acknowledging Van Zandt again, "that Van Zandt Diamonds were one of the greatest companies this country has ever known."

Van Zandt nodded, a contented look upon his face.

"And, as all of us are aware, Michael Park, the American, was sent to prison for killing a security guard here, most likely while attempting to steal uncut diamonds from the Van Zandt strong room. The unfortunate security guard's name was Robert Wolkers. And this," I said, gesturing to Kim, "is his daughter, Kim Wolkers."

Everyone looked at her in that moment, though Burggrave and Riemer's heads turned fastest. Kim remained cool, neither acknowledging nor denying it. Her eyes moved only from the point of oblivion she'd been focused upon to the ground between her feet.

"This is true?" Van Zandt asked, looking from Kim to me and back again.

Kim didn't react so it was left to me to confirm it.

"Then you have my sympathies," Van Zandt went on, his voice sombre. "My family were very saddened for you. I know that everyone on the board was most sad, though I believe they made a generous payment to your mother."

Kim looked up and glared at him, the severity of it jarring something in his watery, old-man eyes.

"She was using the name Marieke Van Kleef for some time," I said, directing my explanation to Burggrave and Riemer, before they could launch into any disruptive questioning. "I could explain why now, but that would put us ahead of ourselves. And what I'd really like to do, if you'll all indulge me, is to skip to the part where I became involved."

I scanned the faces surrounding me, though I didn't expect any of them to interrupt. They all wanted answers, even if, in Van Zandt's case, it was more out of curiosity than necessity. The wide man and the thin man still hadn't said anything yet, but they hadn't seemed at all surprised when I revealed Kim's real identity. I could see they were uncomfortable, though, because they kept casting looks in the direction of the doors they had come in by, and the thin man was sat with his hands clenched together between his legs, his feet tapping out a nervous quick-time on the concrete floor. Both of them were facing away from Burggrave and Riemer, subconsciously shielding their features as though they were worried they might be recognised from some long-buried mug shots.

"For the purposes of this afternoon, I want you to assume," I said, turning from them to look at Stuart so as to give some emphasis to the assumption part, "that as well as being a writer, I have certain talents of a less than entirely legal nature."

"You are a thief," the wide man announced.

"On a purely theoretical basis," I replied, "I will agree with you."

Burggrave turned and looked pointedly towards Riemer. She ignored him but it didn't prevent her from giving me an ice-like glare. I shrugged, as if my criminality was nothing more than an unfortunate ailment I'd picked up some years before and had never quite been able to shake.

"Working on this assumption," I went on, "let us suppose that Michael Park contacted me, via the website I run, and asked me to meet him at Café de Brug, where, coincidentally, the beautiful, tragically orphaned Ms. Wolkers also happened to work. Let's also say I showed up and over the course of a beer or two Michael asked me to obtain some items for him – the items in question being two monkey figurines located in the homes of these two gentlemen."

I cast my hand in the general direction of the wide man and the thin man. Somewhat ridiculously, I still didn't know their real names, so I couldn't introduce them as I might have hoped.

"I'm afraid I still don't know your names," I said, and received a derisive snort from the thin man.

"But we know them," Riemer interrupted, surprising me as much as them. "I have reviewed a file on them only yesterday."

The two men looked at one another. The wide man shook his head minutely, as if telling his companion it was nothing to worry about. I wasn't so sure about that.

"Would you care to elaborate?" I asked.

"It is police business."

"Tsk," Van Zandt cut in. "Some people say there is too much of this "police business" and not enough police work."

"If you have a complaint, sir," Riemer began, "there are appropriate channels."

"Quite," I said, "and more convenient times, if you'll forgive me for saying so." I smiled meekly at Van Zandt and, in time, he graced me with another of his considered nods. "And, to be honest, the names of these gentlemen really don't concern us a great deal. During the last week or so, I've discovered that names can be untrustworthy things in any case. The only thing that really does matter is that these gentlemen had the monkey figurines Michael wanted."

"Can you describe them?" Riemer asked.

"It's not important."

"We will be the judge of that," Burggrave said.

"With respect," Stuart told him, "I don't think you're here to be the judge of anything. At least not yet, anyway."

"Rutherford's right," I said. "But for the sake of clarity, they were so big." I held my hands a few inches apart. "And they were made of plaster of Paris. The one Michael had was covering his eyes. It was part of a set of what we English call the Three Wise Monkeys."

Burggrave turned to his superior and began talking in Dutch, moving his hands at the same time to first cover his mouth and then his ears.

"Yes, yes," Riemer said, in English again, as if she was talking to a fool. "Everyone has heard of them. They are worth money?"

"I didn't think so," I told her. "But Michael offered me a generous sum to obtain them for him nonetheless. At that point, I should say, I had no idea who he was, least of all that he was a thief himself. But it didn't matter a great deal because I turned him down. He said he needed the job carried out the following night and the time-frame bothered me a great deal. Unfortunately, he gave me the addresses where I might find the monkeys anyway."

"Why did he do this?" Burggrave asked, trying, I thought, to regain some credibility after being slapped down by his superior.

"He said he hoped I would change my mind. Sadly for me, I'm afraid I did just that. The following night, while Michael was dining with these two gentlemen at Café de Brug, I let myself into their homes and relieved them of the two monkey figurines in their possession. Problem was, when I got back, Michael was gone. That was when Kim appeared and told me he'd been frogmarched to his apartment by our friends here."

"It is not true," the wide man said. "We walked to Michael's home with him, but he invited us to do this."

"Yes, I thought that might be the case. I guess maybe it was getting close to the time we were supposed to meet and perhaps your meal hadn't finished as soon as he'd hoped. Tell me, when you reached his apartment, did he make some kind of an excuse, feign an illness perhaps?"

The wide man shrugged, as if I was close enough.

"That wouldn't have been long before Kim and I arrived. She wanted me with her because Michael had deviated from the plan he'd explained to her and she was worried. Partly her concern was for Michael, but in truth it was more for the monkeys." I glanced over to her but still she refused to look at me. "When we arrived, we found him badly beaten in the bathroom."

"So these men killed him," Van Zandt said, as if it were perfectly obvious who had committed the crime.

"I assumed so," I agreed. "In fact, I was sure of it and I thought

I knew why. They didn't know I'd stolen their monkeys, you see, so it seemed to me they were after the monkey Michael had. For some reason, the figurine was important enough for them to kill him and that was why he'd been so concerned to have me steal the monkeys when I did."

Burggrave removed his hands from his coat pockets and reached for the handcuffs suspended from his belt. Riemer stopped him with just a touch on his arm and a shake of her head.

"You no longer think this?" Riemer asked me.

"No. And for several reasons. One is that a few days after I was arrested on suspicion of beating Michael, quite wrongly I might add, these two gentlemen abducted me and held me prisoner in their apartment. When I was there, they told me they hadn't done it."

Burggrave scoffed and threw up his hands. "And this was enough for you?"

"No, of course not. But that changed when I discovered that they thought I had the third monkey, the one that belonged to Michael. That was interesting. I mean, if they thought I had it, then it meant they didn't."

"This does not mean they did not kill him," Riemer said flatly. "They maybe killed him because he would not tell them where this monkey was."

"I thought of that too. But see, if the monkey was important enough for them to kidnap me to find it, I couldn't understand why they would have beaten Michael so badly that he couldn't tell them where it was."

Riemer nodded slowly, as if she was willing to go along with me for the time being.

"And when I told them the truth, about Michael hiring me to steal the figurines from them, they didn't believe me at all. It was as if something like that was unimaginable to them, as if they trusted Michael implicitly."

This time, I caught the wide man and the thin man nodding along with me.

"Why would they feel that way about him, I got to asking myself? And pretty soon the answer was obvious. Actually, I was kind of embarrassed I hadn't thought of it before. These men weren't just friends with Michael, they were colleagues."

For a moment, I thought I might lose them both. They certainly became more agitated, shifting in their seats. Then Riemer said something that caused all of us to stop and turn.

"We know this already," she said. "It was in their files."

"So why didn't you arrest them for Michael's murder?"

"This is also police business."

"You see!" Van Zandt said. "When they do not know the answer to something, this is what they say. When they make mistakes, this is what they say. It is police business. Pah."

"They also say it," I told him, "out of force loyalty. This was Inspector Burggrave's case, wasn't it, Detective Inspector Riemer?"

Riemer didn't answer. She just stared hard at me, as if she could silence me through willpower alone.

"No matter," I told her. "I'm only just getting to the heart of my story anyway. We need to skip back in time again, you see. To the attempted robbery when Robert Wolkers was killed." I turned back to Van Zandt. "I believe the main diamond storage facility was just about where we are now, is that right Sir?"

Van Zandt dithered.

"Should I repeat the question?"

His eyes narrowed and his lips thinned. He seemed to be reassessing me from some new perspective. "It is company policy not to ..."

"Oh crap," I said, interrupting him. "We've been through all that. You told me once before already. So let me ask you again – the main diamond storage area was around about here, correct?"

Van Zandt held off on replying. Even my best no-nonsense stare couldn't persuade him. Riemer's, though, was of a different order.

"Answer the question," she commanded, planting one hand on her hip and sounding as though her patience was running thin.

Van Zandt gaped at her but she wasn't about to relent. He turned back to me with the look of a child who'd been scolded.

"Yes," he managed

"Good. Would you be kind enough to describe it for us?"

Van Zandt sighed, and rolled his eyes, but there was something pantomime about it. Just as in his study, I got the distinct impression he was more than willing to talk once he was the centre of attention.

"As head of security, I designed the system myself," he began, using a churlish voice, as if this was the hundredth time I'd made him run through it all. "There was a large room made of steel, like a giant safe."

"A strong room, I believe we agreed."

"Yes, a strong room, you may call it. The walls were made of steel, many centimetres thick. The floor below was concrete. Around the steel was a cement skin. Beyond that was a steel cage."

"And how was this facility used?"

Van Zandt tutted, as if I should have known he was coming to that part.

"At the end of each day," he went on, "all the diamonds in the factory were locked inside this room and the cage was locked around it. There were always guards on duty."

"Yes. It was a very comprehensive system, though in practice quite simple."

"Simple is good," he told me. "Simple can be strong."

"Quite," I said, casting a knowing gaze towards the wide man. "And presumably the lock on the strong room was a good one."

"As I told you before, there were many locks. They were of the highest quality."

"I'm sure. Could the bars of the cage be cut?"

"We discussed this."

"That's right. I believe we agreed bolt cutters would be no good, that it would take a blow torch to cut through the steel rods."

"Even that may not work."

"And, as you said, there were always guards on duty. Guards like Robert Wolkers."

Van Zandt nodded.

"How many?"

He hesitated, perhaps sensing a change in my tone. "At night, there were two."

"And on the night that Robert Wolkers was killed, how many guards were there then?"

"Two, of course."

"You're sure?"

His cheeks puffed up at that. "There were two guards."

"Well that's interesting. Because I happen to know for a fact there was only one."

Van Zandt stamped his cane into the ground, as if he was hoping to impose a full stop on the end of whatever it was I was planning to say next. "Two guards," he said, simply.

"Oh there were meant to be," I told him. "There's no doubt about that. And I'm sure the records you kept back then showed the same thing. And I know the newspaper reports of Robert Wolker's murder did because Mr Rutherford and I checked them when we went to the city library just the other day. The second guard's name was Louis Rijker. Mr Rijker, I'm afraid, passed away a little over two years ago. Coronary heart failure. Fortunately for us, though, Rutherford was able to make contact with his mother."

I nodded to Rutherford and he stood up from the crate he was sat on and walked away from the group of us towards the oblong of daylight filling the doorway on the eastern side of the building. Outside of that doorway was a yard and in that yard was a taxi cab, engine idling, with an anxious looking widow sat inside of it.

While I waited for Rutherford to return, I scanned each of the faces surrounding me and then I checked my watch and finally contemplated my own feet. There was nothing more to say for a moment or two and the silence felt oddly oppressive. It seemed to fill the warehouse interior almost to choking point, as if a gas main had been left on, and part of me was worried that if Rutherford and Karine Rijker didn't appear in the doorway soon someone might say something incendiary and blow everything apart.

Then I heard a car door shut, the sound like a muffled gunshot in the distance, and shortly afterwards the two of them appeared. Karine Rijker's flat shoes scuffed against the concrete floor like sandpaper and she seemed to take an age to reach us. One hand gripping onto Rutherford's arm for balance, the other holding a bulging leather handbag, she threw her weight between her feet like a chef separating a large egg yolk between two broken shells. Her outfit was almost identical to the one I'd seen her wearing at her apartment. She had on a blue housecoat with a floral design beneath a discoloured, padded overcoat, and her swollen legs and ankles were sheathed in thick stockings that bunched up around her knees. The wig on her head was not a good one, looking matted and threadbare all at the same time, and though she'd gone to the trouble of applying make-up, it looked for all the world as if she'd learned her technique at clown school.

"Mrs. Rijker," I said, holding out my hand to assist the old woman once she'd neared our small circle of friends.

She gripped my wrist tightly, handbag swinging from her forearm, then grasped for my elbow, and as soon as she was steady Stuart and I lowered her down onto a palette we'd positioned on top of two wooden crates for that very purpose. She sat there in quite a civilised manner, with her handbag on her knees. The only sign that she was fretting was the way her fingers gripped her bag, the leather straps wrapped tightly around her hands.

I crouched and looked her right in the eyes, then smiled as reassuringly as I could and patted her knee. The old lady contorted her painted features into a graceless parody of my own expression, the wasted muscles beneath her skin doing their best to hoist her jowls into something other than a hangdog expression. Not wanting to prolong this sudden fit of gurning, I found my feet and turned back to the others once again.

"For the next few minutes," I said, "you'll have to forgive me my awful Dutch and understand that Mrs. Rijker doesn't speak English. We thought it best you heard her story in her own words and in light of that I'll be quiet now and leave her to tell you what it is she came here to say."

And at that point, I nodded to the old dear and, after she'd hesitated for just a moment, Stuart said something to her in a gentle tone that prompted her to clear her phlegmy airways and begin. What she told them didn't take a great deal of time, but cut out as I was from the nuances of what she said and the way in which she said it, her halting speech seemed to take longer than I'd anticipated. She was nervous and uncertain and every once in a while her voice would croak or catch and she'd look down at her fingers kneading away at her handbag. That's when Stuart would place a hand on her shoulder and encourage her to go on, speaking to her as if she was a child in his care and all he wanted was for her to share what was troubling her before any of us could be in a position to help.

What was troubling her was simple enough, though that wouldn't have made it any less traumatic. She was explaining the very things she'd resisted saying for years, after all, facts she'd buried deep in her psyche. Her son, Louis Rijker, she would have told them, had been a security guard at the Van Zandt factory. He wasn't a wildly successful individual but he valued his job and he liked that it enabled him to support his ageing mother as best he could. The two of them relied on his wage to keep a roof over their heads and food in their cupboards and he was willing to do most everything he could to keep things that way. So when someone approached him one day and offered him the chance to make a little extra money on top of his weekly wage, he was tempted. All he had to do, they said, was disappear for an hour during one of the night shifts he'd be working. If he could keep his mouth shut about being absent, whatever the consequences, there was a good deal of money in it for him. If, though, he told anyone about the arrangement, the consequences would be severe. The threat was nothing specific but he got the distinct impression it was genuine.

Faced with that choice, poor Louis agreed that on the night in question he'd make himself scarce. When he returned, of course, he found Robert Wolkers shot dead beside the Van Zandt strong room. In his police interview, he cobbled together a cover story about being off on a routine check of the warehouse when his colleague was shot. The lie was a gut reaction to the situation he'd found himself thrown into but it was a line he soon found himself compelled to stick with. The morning after the night of the killing someone broke into the bungalow he shared with his mother and pulled her from her bed and made it all too clear to the pair of them what kind of repercussions they could expect if he ever told the truth. So he never did. But it was his mother's firm belief that the guilt and the fear he'd endured for the best part of a decade was what led to his increased blood pressure and his insomnia and his stress and, ultimately, to the all-out failure of his heart.

As she concluded her tale, the old lady's words began to fracture and peter out. Sobs took hold of her and she fished a tatty rag from the sleeve of her housecoat and dabbed at her eyes. It was at that point Riemer looked at me and said, "She is finished. You have heard what she has to say?"

"Yes," I said. "And for what it's worth I happen to believe it."

"There is no reason to believe otherwise."

"No," I said, "there's not."

"But what difference does this make?" Kim said, finally looking up at me, her voice hoarse as she spoke for the first time. "What does it change?"

"It's another piece of the puzzle," I told her, as reassuringly as I could. "Another clue to what happened that night."

"But we know what happened," Van Zandt said.

"Do we? I think we know very little. And that includes one very important factor – the nature of what exactly Michael Park got away with on the night Robert Wolkers was killed."

I met Van Zandt's gaze and held it. I thought he might look away but he was a wilful old bastard and arrogant enough to think I might not pursue it. I've been known to be a touch arrogant myself sometimes, though, and I wasn't about to relent.

"The popular rumour was that your family lost a small fortune, Mr. Van Zandt. The theory was Michael got away with a pile of jewels after killing the only guard brave enough to challenge him. And the fact Van Zandt never publicly acknowledged this was as good for many people as a flat-out admission."

Van Zandt bristled. "We did not talk about company security. You know this. It was an important rule to us."

"Important because your security wasn't good enough. The truth is you could have ten strong rooms made of reinforced steel, one inside of the other, but the whole system would still only be as secure as the men who guarded it. And when there was only one man, and that man was corrupt, well, the whole thing was a bit of a joke now, wasn't it?"

"You should not speak like this," Van Zandt said, lowering his voice and casting a sideways glance towards Kim. "Not in front of her."

I made myself look at Kim then and what I saw on her face was enough for me to pause. Her lips had thinned and her eyes were moist and unfocused, as if she was looking beyond the scene in front of her right now, back to the scene that had unfolded twelve years beforehand when her father had been killed. The father she'd told herself she'd avenge. The father who just happened to be a crook.

"Forgive me," I told her, "but it's true. It had to be. Good thieves always look for the simplest solution to steal something. And your father was that solution. He had you to look out for, your mother too. Suppose Michael offered him a share of what he stole? Suppose he told himself it would just be that one time, that once would be enough? Except he didn't realise what that really meant. Because men like your father never do. In schemes like this one the take gets split between as few people as possible. And these two benefited from that."

I pointed to the wide man and the thin man. The thin man wheeled around and checked Riemer's reaction, a hunted look on his face. The wide man just leaned back in his chair, crossed his size-able arms in front of his chest and stretched his booted feet out onto the floor in front of him.

"Some thieves work alone," I went on. "Michael didn't. He liked to have back-up. People to help him carry his score. People to help him store it and move it on. Some muscle if it was necessary. In Amsterdam, that's what these two were."

The wide man gave me a crooked smile, as if I was amusing him greatly.

"See, one thing always bothered me. Michael had been in prison for twelve years and he was only out for a matter of days before he contacted me. But he knew the job he wanted doing inside out. He knew where you lived and he knew what kind of security you had. He knew one of you kept your figurine in a safe on a boat. He knew the other one had been keeping his figurine under his pillow and that there were three good locks on your front door. He knew there was no alarm at either property. But how could he know all that? He was friends with the two of you, he told me as much, but he wouldn't know it even if he'd visited you since his release and there's no way you would have told him."

I ignored the wide man's grin, determined to keep my composure.

Partly it was for Kim and partly it was for Michael himself. None of this was a laughing matter. The man had been killed for Christ's sake.

"There was only one way he could know," I said, "and when I found out he was a thief it made perfect sense to me. The fact is Michael knew because he'd been inside your homes before me. He'd already broken in and found the monkeys. Truth is, he'd done more than simply case the job – he'd carried out a dummy run."

I paused and looked confidently at the wide man. As I studied him, I had the sense that a little of his bravado was beginning to ebb away. I wanted the drip-drip effect to become a flood. I wanted him to see things the way I did. In some ways, Victoria had been right – there was a kind of bond between Michael and me. It wasn't just that we shared the same profession – it was that we were a part of the same world, and it wasn't beyond the realms of possibility that someday somebody might want to beat the life out of me for something I'd taken.

"So then the question became," I went on, the words sounding faintly robotic to me, "why didn't he take the monkeys when he could? They were right there for him. He could have just reached out and grabbed them and been clean away before you knew anything about it. But he didn't." I paused again, staring at the wide man with more determination this time, wanting him to get how important this really was. "Then I remembered something else he told me. He said that you wouldn't suspect him of being involved in stealing the figurines even if you found them missing the moment after I'd taken them. He said the reason was simple: you trusted him. And I asked myself, where does trust like that come from? The answer, of course, is it comes from working together. It comes from being a part of a unit. And as Inspector Riemer has confirmed now, the three of you were a gang. Who knows how much you stole together? My guess is a fair amount. But the real score came here, on the night Robert Wolkers was murdered."

I gestured at our surroundings, turned a complete circle and inhaled deeply, as if something of that time still lingered. I looked once at Karine Rijker and then I glanced up at the steel rafters in the ceiling and went on.

"The truth is I've spent a lot of time thinking about that night. I even came here and walked around and cast my mind back to how I imagined things had gone. And do you know what I decided?"

I met the wide man's eyes again. There was something different in them now. Intrigue perhaps, and maybe a touch of apprehension.

"I decided you'd waited for a night when Robert Wolkers would be here on his own, at least for a little while. Maybe it was a case of waiting for him to tell you when it could happen or maybe you set the date and the time but, however it worked, Robert Wolkers was here by himself when the three of you turned up and he was the one who watched over you while Michael tackled the locks on the strong room. Once you were in, you took as much as you wanted, maybe even all of it. Then you killed him."

Out of the corner of my eye, I could see the thin man shaking his head manically. The wide man just squinted at me and said very calmly, "It is not true."

"No?"

"We did not kill him."

"Hmm. Well," I said, abruptly lightening my tone and shrugging my shoulders, "that was only my first idea. Guess I should have known not to trust it. There's this book, you see, my latest novel, and I've been stuck on it for a while now. I've come up with maybe six possible solutions of whodunnit and how and none of them work. So why should solving all this be any different? I mean, I'm not going to strike lucky first time, am I?" I pointed at the wide man, then wagged my finger as if the two of us should have known better. "As it happens, I didn't really think you did it. Why would you? What possible motive could you have? It's not as if Robert Wolkers was going to give you up – he had as much to lose as anyone else. And let's not forget Michael always denied it was him. And besides, we haven't even factored in the mystery of the missing murder weapon, yet – the smoking gun, as it were.

So I had a second theory. And at first, it seemed pretty outlandish, the kind of thing I might come up with for a book and then discard because it was just too far fetched. But the more I found out, the more it began to make sense to me. And then I worked on it some more, finessed it, removed a bum turn here and there. And guess what? It started to seem like the only way it could possibly have happened."

THIRTY

"The way I see it," I went on, "Robert Wolkers was the one who contacted Michael, not the other way around. He told him who he was and what he did for a living and he told him there might just be a way they could help each other out. Michael, I'm guessing, didn't like it at first. Most professional thieves find their own jobs. That way, they don't have to rely on other people getting things right and they don't have to share their take either. But, we're only human, and no doubt he was tempted by the proposal Robert Wolkers put to him. He had an in to the Van Zandt strong room and Michael was a diamond purist. He probably thought about it for a little while and decided he wanted a piece of it but he didn't want to take the risks all by himself. If what he'd heard was true, there'd be more than enough diamonds to go round and he could do with some back-up. So he found two local rent-a-goons and before very long he'd formed his very own gang."

I paused, and checked on the faces surrounding me, wanting to be certain that I wasn't about to lose any of them. That seemed unlikely. I hadn't held an audience like this since I'd given my first book reading – to two die hard fans and an embarrassed book store owner on the Charing Cross Road. If I wasn't careful, all this attention would go to my head.

"Wolkers," I continued, "would have known some of the systems they had in place at Van Zandt's, and he could easily have found out when shipments were due and what they were likely to contain. My theory is he waited for a large delivery and then he made sure that the guard who was supposed to be on duty with him would conveniently disappear for an hour or so. Then all he had to do was stand guard as Michael and his two Dutch friends tackled the steel cage and the strong room. With enough time on his hands, a skilled thief can get into any safe or strong room in the world. After all, a safe is only as good as the lock that secures it and sadly that lock is always susceptible to being forced or picked open. Once Michael had applied his own particular expertise, the gang emptied the strong room and, since they no longer had any use for Robert Wolkers, they killed him and made their escape with the haul of a lifetime."

I heard a sharp intake of air and turned to see Kim wincing, her eyes screwed tight and her fists balled together, nails pressing into her skin. It was hard not to say something then, to try to appeal directly to her in a way that would make things somehow easier. Instead, I pressed on.

"There were too many jewels to put on the market immediately, though, and now that Robert Wolkers was dead, there was a lot more heat than they would have liked. The police had a hot new officer on the case, a guy called Burggrave, and he seemed to be solving everything he was asked to look into."

Burggrave's ears pricked up. He straightened and his eyes narrowed behind his angular specs, as if someone was scratching his back just right. I tried my best to ignore it, focussing on Detective Inspector Riemer instead.

"So the gang had to go to ground and, in the meantime, they agreed to store the diamonds somewhere safe. There was a place in Chinatown they'd heard of and, although it wasn't ideal (because nothing ever is when one of your gang is a talented thief), they were each as confident in it as they could be. They couldn't use a bank, because a bank would ask too many questions and require ID, but the place they found was just as secure as a bank without any of the hassles."

I turned to the wide man and the thin man and continued my explanation to them, trying to make them see I had it all figured out. They were listening closely now, waiting to hear what I said next and whether they'd need to deny any of it.

"In a neat twist of fate, the strong boxes that were used in this establishment required three keys to open them. It was ideal: each member of the gang could hold a key and be sure that none of them could make off with all of the jewels by themselves. The keys looked like this," I said, pulling two keys from my pocket and placing them in my palm to show to the group. "But, before they were given out, they were encased in quick setting plaster that was poured into moulds in the shape of the three wise monkeys. See no evil, hear no evil, speak no evil. It was the proprietor's way of saying that they didn't care what you kept in their facility – they weren't about to ask any awkward questions. The two keys I'm holding were inside the two figurines that I stole for Michael. That's why the third monkey was so important. Whoever found it could get their hands on a treasure trove of Van Zandt diamonds from the early nineties. And that, it seems, was worth beating Michael to death."

I handed the keys to Riemer and watched her weigh them in her hand. A few flecks of plaster were still attached to the coppery metal, giving my story a ring of authenticity. After a moment, she looked up from the keys and stared hard at me.

"But you said before that they didn't kill the guard," she said, motioning towards the wide man and the thin man.

"Yes," I conceded, turning then to check on Karine Rijker. There was alarm in her eyes, though only because I'd looked directly at her for the first time in quite some while. I certainly didn't get the impression that the English we were speaking meant anything to her, so I returned my attention to Riemer.

"I'm afraid that's where it all gets a little more complicated. To be honest, what I've just told you was like my first rewrite of the ending. But when I thought about it some more, when I really probed into the logic, it just didn't add up. So what I did was I came at it from a different angle. I thought of something I hadn't dealt with and I asked myself the question it posed. Do you know what that question was?"

"Why did they kill my father?" Kim asked, from nowhere.

"No," I said, shaking my head and softening my tone. "That wouldn't have helped. They could have killed him to tie up a loose end or to cut him out of the deal or just because one of them was a hot-head. It left too many possibilities. No, what I asked myself was this: where did the gun come from?"

"They could have been carrying it," Burggrave suggested.

"They could have, yes. And then they could have dumped it afterwards. But why? I've yet to meet a burglar who carries a gun with him on a job. And I know from experience that these two gentlemen favour baseball bats over firearms anyway. So I began to wonder, what if Van Zandt had made their guards carry guns."

"Pah!" Van Zandt said, throwing his hands up in the air and then letting his cane thud down again, as if now I really had lost my mind.

"That would be illegal," Riemer told me, interrupting his performance. "There are strict laws about this in the Netherlands."

"I imagined as much. But let's suppose the head of Van Zandt security was more concerned with protecting his jewels than obeying the strict letter of the law. Let's suppose he offered his guards the means to protect themselves."

"It is not so," Van Zandt said, authoratively.

"Makes sense to me," I told him. "You always liked to keep security matters here confidential. You liked to keep things under your hat. Take the night of Wolkers death – you suffered the biggest robbery the company had ever endured and yet you refused to co-operate openly with the police, or to publicise the crime in anyway."

"That was a decision of the board. Our concern was for the privacy of Mr Wolker's family. It was a difficult time."

"Yes it was. But it also let you bury the news that Van Zandt had armed one of its guards with the gun that killed him."

I looked towards Stuart, then motioned towards the handbag Karine Rijker was clutching so tightly.

"Rutherford, could you oblige?" I asked.

"Of course," he told me, and then he lowered his face and said something in Dutch to the old woman. She listened for a moment, then nodded furtively and popped open the clasps on her handbag, parting the leather with great care and reaching inside very slowly, as if she had something incredibly fragile in there. Her hands emerged from the bag in much the same fashion, cradling a package wrapped in what appeared to be an old tea towel. She handed the package to Rutherford and he passed it onto me. As carefully as I could, I unfolded the material until I was holding the object it contained by a corner of the fabric.

"This is the gun that Louis Rijker was provided with by Van Zandt security. He kept it in his wardrobe after he finished working here, in case the men who'd threatened his mother ever showed up again, and there it stayed until Mrs. Rijker was sorting through his things following his death. I'm as sure as I possibly can be that Robert Wolkers was killed with an identical gun. And it was a weapon his employer provided him with."

"This is just talk," Burggrave said, looking towards Riemer. "The gun that killed him was never found. It is a pointless discussion."

"Well, it would be," I said, meanwhile setting the gun down to one side and slipping on one of my disposable surgical gloves. "If it weren't for this."

The "this" I was referring to was a second handgun and I pulled it from my back pocket and held it in my gloved hand by the trigger guard, so that it was suspended in the air before them all. Every set of eyes seemed to be fixated on it, as if I was a stage magician about to perform a world-renowned act.

"I'd be willing to bet serious money that this is the gun that killed Robert Wolkers," I went on. "And it was the gun that Van Zandt armed him with. As you can see, it's identical to the gun Mrs. Rijker brought with her here today. And do you know where I found it? In your apartment, sir," I said, turning to face the wide man.

The wide man sat upright for the first time. "But it is not mine," he said, sounding genuinely perplexed.

I waited a moment before responding, interested to see if his composure would slip any further.

"I have never seen this gun before," he added.

"Oh but you have," I told him. "Though you seemed equally surprised by it on that occasion too. You see, it was the gun I pointed at you when I made my way out of your apartment, just after you'd kidnapped me. I could see in your eyes that you had no idea how I'd found a gun. After all, there was no gun on me when you searched me before tying me to that chair in your bedroom. The truth is this gun was in the crawlspace in your attic."

I waited again, drawing it out, but he didn't bite. I got the impression it was because he was genuinely puzzled.

"I first came across it when I was searching your room for the figurine on the night I robbed you. It was in your trunk originally, but I hid it in the attic because I happen to have a habit of concealing any weapons I find. Awful things, guns – they can do such terrible damage. But I admit, you seemed very surprised when I came out of your room with it. And I don't mean surprised because you'd gone looking for that gun in your trunk and couldn't understand where it had got to. I mean surprised because you had no idea there was a gun in your apartment in the first place. And I think the reason you had no idea was because Michael put it there."

The wide man's brow furrowed and he squinted at me.

"You don't get it, do you? Michael wasn't just casing the job for me when he broke into your apartment. He was also planting the gun."

There was a moment of silence. His brow became more tangled.

"So he was framing him," Stuart said, in a wistful tone.

"No," I said, turning to him. "Why would he do that? Why spend twelve years in prison without giving up the other members of your gang and then try and set them up once you get out? It doesn't make any sense."

"So what then?" Stuart asked.

"Ah," I said, "well that's the tricky bit. Go back a step. Michael hired me to steal the two monkey figurines, correct?"

Stuart nodded. I looked around again and found the wide man and the thin man nodding too.

"The question is, why did he do that? Yes, it would give him an alibi of sorts with his friends, but why else? Well, at the most basic level, it meant he wouldn't be the one to take them, at least not directly. And I think that was very important to him. I mean, he spent twelve years inside and in all that time you two were patient. You didn't try and get at the jewels. No, you agreed to wait until he was out and then share the take."

I circled my spare hand in a casual, thinking gesture, like a lecturer about to depart from his script.

"Of course, there's a good chance that had something to do with you being unable to move the stones, but it was also something else. You were a gang and you'd developed some degree of group loyalty. Michael wanted to steal the jewels from you but he didn't want to be the one to do it. And meanwhile, he also wanted to leave you the gun, by way of compensation, if you like."

"How was it compensation?" Kim asked, her eyes beginning to glimmer.

"Because it was the murder weapon. It would allow them to put your father's real killer behind bars if he gave them any trouble."

"But I don't understand," she said. "How?"

"Fingerprints," I told her. "The killer's prints would still be on the gun, even twelve years after the crime. Correct Inspector?"

"It's possible," Burggrave conceded.

"Just possible?"

He shrugged. "The killer may have used gloves."

"Of course," I said, striking my forehead with the heel of my palm. "I hadn't thought of that. And did you?"

"What?"

"Use gloves? When you killed Robert Wolkers."

THIRTY-ONE

Burggrave was stunned for a moment, as if he couldn't quite believe what I'd just said. He stood there, eyes wide, head loose on his shoulders. Then, all of a sudden, he pulled himself together and surged forwards as if to hit me square in the face. Before he could, though, the wide man and the thin man stood in unison and blocked his path. Burggrave wheeled around to look at Riemer, who was appraising him coolly, though not, I thought, from an altogether new perspective. He turned from her gaze and glared at me, face reddening.

"This is a lie," he said. "You are a fool for thinking you can say these things."

"Inspector Burggrave was very thorough in his investigation of the killing," Van Zandt added.

"You mean he was very amenable to the way you wanted it conducted," I told him, from over the top of the wall of thugs I was stood behind. "You expect me to believe that an investigator as skilled and decorated as Burggrave wouldn't have found out within two minutes that Robert Wolkers was on the take, that Louis Rijker had been bribed, that, in short, you had a fundamental failure in your security system? Please. He would have known immediately. But he knew that anyway. Because he was in on it too. You both were."

"Nonsense," Van Zandt spluttered, then turned to Riemer. "Detective Inspector, I think you had better put an end to this performance before I instruct my lawyer to sue the department."

"Be quiet," she said. "Let us hear what he has to say."

"But it is slander."

"Enough," she barked. Then to me, she said, "Go on."

"Diamonds are worth a lot of money," I told her. "Everyone knows that. And even the best security system in the world is fallible. So what does a company like Van Zandt do to protect itself?"

"It takes out insurance," Stuart said, the answer suddenly occurring to him.

"That's right," I said. "In fact, it obtains a comprehensive anti-theft policy."

Just then, I realised how tired I was becoming of peering over the shoulders of my two minders and so I patted the wide man and the thin man on their arms, inviting them to retake their seats. Burggrave was still sizing me up, fingers clenching and relaxing, feet set shoulder-width apart, but he couldn't do much with his boss stood beside him and if it came to it, I still had the threat of the gun in my hand anyway. I waited until the wide man and the thin man were seated and made sure that Van Zandt squirmed under my gaze before I resumed.

"Where was I? I asked.

"Insurance," Stuart repeated.

"Oh yes. Insurance. Well, as you can imagine, the premiums on an anti-theft policy for a diamond business are huge. And as the head of security, Mr. Van Zandt had to justify the expense. Well, what better way to explain the cost away than by arranging for a theft? And with a little careful paper management, he could claim for one amount from the insurer and notify the board that a lower amount had been recovered."

"This is enough," Van Zandt said, and forcefully pushed himself up onto his feet. For a moment, he locked onto Burggrave's eyes, the two of them sharing some wordless communion. Then he turned and began to hobble away.

"The difference would be used to line his own pocket," I went on, raising my voice so Van Zandt could still hear. "So you found a likely guard, Mr. Van Zandt, and you offered him a bonus if he contacted a local thief and arranged for a convenient burglary to occur, didn't you?"

Van Zandt ignored me and kept moving in the direction of the exit.

"Isn't that so, Mr. Van Zandt?"

He waved me away with his hand, head shaking, but he didn't pause. As it happened, that didn't matter a great deal because with a wordless jab of his thumb, the wide man signalled to his partner and the two of them were off after the old man, covering the distance to him in a matter of seconds and lifting him clean off the floor by the elbows. Van Zandt struggled and kicked and wheezed, his feet wind-milling in the air, but he didn't have the slightest chance of freeing himself. Within a matter of moments he was pressed back into his seat and this time he was flanked by two gentlemen who weren't inclined to allow him to leave. Thankfully, Detective Inspector Riemer didn't see any reason to intervene. In fact, she was the one who motioned for me to continue.

"But I had to wonder, how did you know which thief to approach? And then I realised, that's where Inspector Burggrave came in. He was a thrusting young officer back then but all those crimes he was solving had started people talking. Was he on the take? You certainly thought so. My guess is you contacted Burggrave and the two of you came to an arrangement and after that all the pieces fell into their neat little places. The scam was set. Arrangements were made for Louis Rijker to go missing for an hour or so. Perhaps that was something the Inspector handled himself or perhaps he knew a local thug who could apply the necessary pressure. However it worked, though, on the given night Louis Rijker followed orders and Robert Wolkers let our unsuspecting thieves into the warehouse and watched over them while they set about their work. From there, things panned out much as I've previously described except, of course, for the aftermath."

I paused, and paced from one side of the small semi-circle of spectators I was stood inside to the other, my rubber soles tapping softly against the concrete floor. I lifted the gun above my head and waved it about, as if it were just an everyday prop that I was using to trigger my mind. I didn't, though, stand too close to Burggrave because I still wasn't sure what his reaction would be. For the moment, he seemed to be waiting to hear more of what I had to say, perhaps believing he could poke enough holes in my theory to end the matter there and then.

"With the strong room empty and the gang long gone," I carried on, "Wolkers still had enough time before Rijker returned to report the theft. First, he called his head of security and after that a call went out to the local police force. Burggrave was the first to respond, naturally. In fact, it wouldn't surprise me if he'd been waiting with Mr. Van Zandt just a short distance away. The two of them would have met Wolkers, as pre-arranged, but unbeknown to the guard, he'd become a major loose end by then. Perhaps Burggrave told him he'd need to be tied up or knocked on the head to make things look more plausible. Before all that though, he'd have to remove his gun and hand it over. It wouldn't do for Van Zandt to be found arming its guards – it would almost certainly invalidate their insurance."

I cut away from the picture I'd been painting and looked from Van Zandt to Burggrave. I tried to close out the image I'd glimpsed of Kim sat between them, her face ghostly white, eyes shut tight and teeth clamped together.

"I'm not certain which of you shot him," I said, "but my guess would be you Inspector Burggrave. Mr. Van Zandt saw himself as a businessman so it's possible he believed the pay off was enough to keep Robert Wolkers mouth shut. Maybe he even had ideas of carrying out the same scam again at some point further down the line. But it was all too risky for you, Inspector – there was no way you could bungle the investigation of such a daring robbery. So you killed Robert Wolkers and after that you made your first serious error."

"Killing my father wasn't enough?" Kim said, in a hollow voice.

"Excuse me," I told her, "you're right. My phrasing was clumsy. I should have said he made his first tactical mistake. You see, he agreed to cover up the use of the gun altogether."

I met Burggrave's gaze and held it. I was right – I knew it – but he still wasn't giving anything away. Van Zandt could be broken by a skilled investigator, I hadn't the slightest doubt about that, but Burggrave would present a real challenge. In this particular arena I'd devised, he was like a prize fighter, a real old bruiser, and it was beginning to feel like I could give him as many jabs as I cared and he still might never go down.

"I'm sure that originally the Inspector would have planned to ditch the gun, perhaps in one of your many canals, but for some reason, most likely more money, he agreed to entrust its destruction to Mr. Van Zandt. Once he'd handed over the gun, he would have had just enough time left to put some finishing touches to the scene before more officers arrived. Then, over the course of the next twenty-four hours, he set about framing Michael for the crime, even sprinkling a few diamonds that Mr. Van Zandt had held back from the latest delivery around his apartment. It was amazing how quickly he was onto the thief's trail – made all the papers. Only, it was less amazing when you knew how he'd got onto Michael in the first place."

Finally, Burggrave spoke. "I hope your books are many times better than this," he told me. Then he turned to Riemer and waved his hand in the air. "It is an illusion. A fantasy."

"I don't think so. Although no doubt this gun can be the judge of that," I said, drawing everyone's attention to the pistol in my gloved hand once more.

"You could buy this gun anywhere," Burggrave said.

"We'll see," I told him, and allowed myself a smile. I was still enjoying how much it was irritating him when Kim interrupted us.

"Tell me the rest," she said, in a pleading voice. "I want to hear it. There is more, yes?"

"A little," I admitted. "Take Michael, for instance. He knew he hadn't killed anyone – in fact, he knew your father was still alive when he left here. So he had to figure something was up, especially when Burggrave found those cheap jewels in his home. But what could he do? And besides, I happen to believe that somewhere in his head he felt culpable for the murder in the way a less moral man might not."

Van Zandt made a snorting noise, as though the credibility of what I was saying was being stretched ever thinner.

"You scoff," I told him, "but I think it's true. He might not have pulled the trigger and he might always have denied being guilty, but part of him still felt a sense of responsibility for what happened here. I guess that's because the job had smelt a little off to him from the start. Maybe that had something to do with why he did his time, but don't be fooled into thinking he went in blind. Michael was an intelligent man, Mr. Van Zandt. The top thieves usually are. And all through that time he spent in prison he was thinking about what had happened, putting the fragments of what he knew together, weaving them into a greater overall understanding. And when he got out, I think one of the first things he did was he broke into your rather impressive home near the Museum Plein. And do you know what I think he found? I think he found that you hadn't destroyed the gun at all – I think he found that you'd simply hidden it in your house, though not particularly well. Who knows why you held onto it? Perhaps you thought it might give you something over the Inspector here. But keeping it turned you into the foolish one. And as soon as Michael found it he must have had an inkling that it could frame you or Burggrave for the murder he'd gone down for. So he took it and a few days later he left it in an apartment belonging to one of his former gang members."

"It makes no sense to me," Riemer cut in. "Why would he not bring the gun to the police?"

"The same police who'd framed him?"

"If that is what he believed, he could have found a different officer, someone he felt he could trust."

"Well now," I told her, "I'm not sure that all of your colleagues are as decent and noble as you Detective Inspector."

She stared at me flatly.

"Will you give me the gun?" she asked.

I chewed on my lips and studied the piece of hardware at the end of my arm. I was growing used to it; the stock was well crafted and it felt snug in my hand. But I could see why Riemer might object to me waving a gun about willy-nilly, especially if it had the capacity to prove the things I said it could. I turned to Burggrave and gestured at him with it.

"You won't mind, I assume," I told him.

"Of course not," he said, rather stiffly.

"Well then I don't see why I shouldn't hand it over to you Detective Inspector Riemer. You are wearing gloves, I see."

I offered the gun to her and she snatched it from my outstretched hand, releasing the cylinder and emptying it of bullets. Then she returned the cylinder to its housing with a flick of her wrist and slipped the gun into one of her coat pockets.

"And the other one," she said.

"I don't see why not," I told her, and motioned for her to go ahead and pick up the gun Karine Rijker had removed from her handbag.

Riemer stepped forwards and gathered the pistol, going through the same process to check it was empty, then slipping it into another of her coat pockets.

"You will remember which is which, I take it."

"You have finished your story?" she asked.

"Calling it a story's a little pejorative in the circumstances, don't you think? And I'm afraid there's just the small matter of more recent events to clear up, if you can bear with me."

"I'm listening."

"Good. Well, your colleague here, Inspector Burggrave," I said, acknowledging the tensed figure to my right, "would have spent a lot of time over the twelve years Michael was in prison thinking about all those diamonds Michael got away with. They had to be hidden somewhere and if he could just get his hands on them their value would dwarf whatever money he'd been paid by Van Zandt. Of course," I said, gesturing to my newest guardian angels, who were still flanking the old man, "he couldn't exactly go investigating these two gentlemen in case things didn't tie up as neatly as they had done before. But perhaps he could still work some avenues, ask a few contacts in the prison system to see if Michael ever let anything slip. Michael never did, he was careful, but talk got around about a small monkey figurine he kept in his cell. Maybe Burggrave knew what that meant right away – after all, I get the impression he'd made plenty of money over the years that he couldn't exactly pay into his current account – but even if he did, he couldn't do anything without all three keys. The Chinatown facility doesn't exactly yield to police jurisdiction, especially not when the officer who wants to look inside their strong boxes doesn't want anyone on the force to know about it. And Burggrave couldn't get access to Michael's figurine inside the prison system. It was ironic really – Michael found the most secure place in the world to keep his key."

I smirked at Burggrave and shrugged my shoulders in a showy way, wanting to rile him that bit more. I could tell from his expression and the way he was trembling very slightly that if we were on our own right now, I would be in trouble.

"So what were you left with? Well, you had twelve years of corrupt policing business to take care of and, at the end of that time, Michael was released. From that point on, I imagine you kept him under watch, following him around the city, finding the bed-sit he was holed up in, noting the details of the young girl he seemed to be seeing. You would have gone on like that, watching him endlessly, obsessively even, until one night, you would have seen Michael having dinner at Café de Burg with the exact same men he'd stolen those diamonds with in the first place. I can't know exactly what happened, I admit, but it doesn't seem beyond the realms of possibility that you would have seen the group of them leave and followed them back to Michael's apartment. You would have seen them go into Michael's building and you would have seen these two gentlemen come out shortly afterwards and I guess you might well have decided that this was it, that if you didn't act now you'd miss your chance forever."

I stopped, hoping he might interrupt in some way, but he said nothing. Maybe that had to do with how angry he'd become. Seething is the only word to describe it. His face had turned puce and spittle clung to his lips. He kept rising up on his toes, as if ready to lunge at me, and I could tell it was an effort for him to keep his arms down by his sides because they kept shaking and all the tendons and arteries were bulging in his neck.

"So you made your way inside the building and you confronted Michael. Perhaps you caught him unawares. In any event, the conversation can't have gone as you'd hoped. There's no way Michael would tell you where the jewels were and I suspect there's a good chance he goaded you about some kind of evidence he had tying you to the murder of Robert Wolkers. You'd have lost it, of course. You wanted to know where the jewels were, where the monkey figurines had got to, at all costs. And at some point I guess you began using force, but still Michael wouldn't tell you what you needed to know. He must have put most of it together by then and the way you were acting wasn't exactly the behaviour of a decorated officer of the Amsterdam-Amstelland police force."

"You will regret this," he cut in, voice quivering. "You cannot say such things without consequences."

"Eventually," I went on, speaking over him, "you took things up a level, even broke some of Michael's fingers like a crude torturer, but it didn't get you anywhere. Michael had spent twelve long years behind bars waiting to get his hands on his jewels and he wasn't about to give up their whereabouts to the man who'd set him up in the first place. Maybe he said as much; it wouldn't surprise me. And you must have known then that it was true. And what else could you do? You couldn't drag him down the station on false pretences in that state and you couldn't let him get away with the diamonds. So," I said, shrugging, "you killed him."

Burggrave shook his head at me, his eyes like blades behind his glasses, perspiration breaking out across his forehead.

"Or perhaps I should say you thought you'd killed him," I went on. "You beat his head against the back of the bath tub until he was unconscious and then you made a quick search of the apartment. Luckily for you, you found Michael's monkey figurine, the one covering his eyes, and I'm guessing you also saw the photocopied passport page that I found moments later when I entered the apartment," I said, giving Kim a warning look so that she wouldn't contradict this version of events, "a page that showed Marieke Van Kleef's real name was Kim Wolkers."

Burggrave screwed his face up in disdain but I was on a roll now.

"I'm not altogether sure what happened next. Either you had just enough time when you heard Kim and me enter the front of the building to climb another flight of stairs or you were already outside the building working out what to do when you happened to see us arrive. Either way, you would have known by then that Kim was the daughter of the guard you'd killed and I suppose you might also have known who I was, since you could have seen me meeting Michael the night before and perhaps even followed me home. Something else you would have known is that we were about to find Michael's body. So you waited until we were inside the apartment and then you made an anonymous call to the police, most likely from a payphone – there's one just along the street from Michael's building. Then, just as you'd done all those years before, you made sure you were the first officer to respond when the call went out."

He inhaled deeply, as though readying himself to pour scorn on what I'd just said. I didn't give him the opportunity.

"Of course, you knew something was up when Kim was the only person you found inside that apartment. To my shame," I said, looking towards Mrs. Rijker as the only non-English speaker, "I'd jumped out the back window on hearing the sirens."

Mrs. Rijker smiled at me brightly, as if I'd just recounted her favourite anecdote. I nodded back, as though acknowledging some form of wordless absolution, then returned my attention to Burggrave.

"Because of my reaction, you made it your business to find me and once you heard from the British Embassy that I had a conviction for theft you began to put two and two together in the way that good police minds are want to do, and you began to wonder if maybe Michael had set these two gentlemen up. And now that he was dead, it occurred to you there was a fair chance I was the one with the two remaining figurines you needed. So you arrested me on suspicion of being involved in Michael's death and you kept me in custody overnight, ignoring Kim's testimony," I said, looking pointedly at Riemer, "that I'd been with her at the time of the killing because, for one thing, you knew she'd made a statement under a false name and for another thing, you knew she was lying. Sadly for you, when the questioning went nowhere you couldn't bend my fingers back to the vertical or beat my head against the wall. But conveniently, you could detain me overnight and it was during that time you broke into my apartment, literally removing the door from its hinges to get inside."

"So now I am a burglar too."

"Don't sound so appalled," I told him. "In my book it's a good deal more civilised than murder. Of course, you'd already been in my apartment once before when you came to question me about Michael's attack but you didn't have time to find what you were looking for then. Now you had the opportunity to search at your leisure, although I'm glad to say you didn't find the two figurines I'd squirreled away."

I looked back at Kim and this time I gave her an apologetic look.

"That temper of yours got the better of you again, though," I resumed, "and you made a real mess of my apartment. There's always a chance you left some fingerprints there while you were doing it, of course, and I was careful to wear gloves when I cleared up."

"If any prints are found," Burggrave said, "they will be from when I first visited your apartment. From the things that I touched."

"Oh, you could argue that," I said. "But then how are you going to explain it if the third monkey happens to be found in your apartment? Your colleagues are there now, I believe, Detective Inspector Riemer?"

Riemer held my eyes, ignoring Burggrave's bewildered look. She nodded slowly.

"What is this?" Burggrave demanded, turning to Riemer and leaning into her face. "You are searching my home! This is all lies. You cannot do this. On whose authority?"

"The Superintendent's authority," Riemer told him, blankly.

They stared at one another for a moment, neither of them conceding anything in the slightest. Their mutual loathing would have been apparent to a blind man, though Burggrave's self-confidence was really quite something to behold. If I hadn't been so sure of myself, even I might have been persuaded that I'd got it all wrong.

"We will see about this," he said, and began to walk away from the group of us towards the double doors on the far side of the building, the tails of his police coat swinging from the back of his legs.

I looked at Riemer searchingly, waiting for her to do something. She held my gaze for some time, giving nothing away. Then, just as I threw up my hands in disbelief and tossed my head back on my shoulders, she reached into her inside pocket and removed a small two-way radio.

THIRTY-TWO

"So," I said, once Victoria had picked up the phone, "I have a view of the Eiffel Tower from my balcony."

"You're kidding."

"Well, you have to lean out and crane your neck, then look through the sitting room of the flat across the way, but it's all there, as clear as day. So long as you use a telescope."

"Oh Charlie."

"But I can smell croissants from the patisserie at the bottom of my building. And I have a wonderful traffic scene from my bedroom."

"Will you be able to write?"

"Of course I will. Once I'm used to it, I won't even notice the noise."

"And you don't regret not going to Italy?"

"Not at all. I ignored Paris for a while, you know. I mean, it just seems so obvious, doesn't it? But it's beautiful here."

"And the women?"

"I hear there are some. They get everywhere these days. Some brave soul should really go in search of their nest."

"The blonde got to you, huh?"

"It's not so bad," I told her. "Just a sucking chest-wound kind of pain."

"Always so dramatic."

"Occupational hazard."

"Charlie," Victoria said, "I still have some questions about what happened."

"More?"

"Just a few. You know how I am with plot holes. Can't rest if something doesn't add up all the way around."

"But the last time we spoke you said you were happy."

"And I was. But then I went home and I finished off a manuscript I'd been reading and climbed into bed and it hit me. Wham! Why did the American do it? Why did he turn on the wide man and the thin man and try to take the diamonds all by himself? It just didn't make sense to me. It didn't sound like something he'd do."

"He was a thief, Vicky."

"I know."

"Taking things was what he did."

"Granted. But he'd mellowed, hadn't he? And if the reason he hired you was because he couldn't stomach taking the monkey figurines himself, how is it he felt just dandy about taking the diamonds?"

"Trust you," I said. "You're too good."

"I am?"

"Yes. Vic, I had eight people in that warehouse with me, two of them trained investigators, and none of them asked me a question like that."

"Does it hurt your theory?"

"Not really. Oh, it hurts the theory I set out for everyone else's benefit. But that's a different matter altogether. The thing is, I'd asked myself that exact same question when I was working things through. And it took me quite a while before I came up with something that I think makes sense."

"And what's that?"

"I think Michael planned to give the diamonds away."

"Sorry?"

"To Kim."

"Oh Charlie. You can't be serious. Why would he do a thing like that?"

"For starters, I think he felt guilty about the way things turned out for her father. More to the point, though, a young girl lost her dad because of a scam he got involved in and that girl was messed up enough to go and work in the prison where his killer was supposedly locked up. When he found out who she really was, I imagine that would have got to him. And then, of course, there's the possibility he really had fallen for her."

"Oh come on."

"You didn't see her, Vic. Sure, she was attractive. But there was something about her, some quality that set her apart in some way. I imagine that after twelve years in prison any man would find her pretty alluring."

"Alluring enough to give her a fortune in diamonds?"

"For him, anyway. My thinking is he wanted to compensate her for what she'd lost. And it wasn't as if the wide man and the thin man would understand that. I think I said before that there was something very appealing about Michael."

"I'm not sure I buy it."

"I suppose it is a little out there. But you know yourself how it is when you fall for somebody. You can throw logic out the window, really."

"Hmm. Well I might be prepared to go along with you half way. Let's say he planned to take all the jewels and run off with her."

"It's possible. Or maybe it was as straightforward as I made it seem in the first place. Maybe, after spending twelve years inside, he felt he deserved all the loot for himself."

"I think I like that explanation most of all."

"Well, that's the difference between us," I said. "The romantic and the mercenary."

"Either way, I don't suppose it matters much now. What with him being dead and the police having all the jewels."

"Mmm."

""Mmm," Charlie?"

"Well, one might say they don't exactly have all of the diamonds."

"But how can that be? You said you let them have the two keys you'd stolen and you told them where they could find the third monkey. Were some of the diamonds hidden somewhere else?"

"Not to begin with."

"Not to ... Oh Charlie, what have you done?"

"Nothing that should surprise you."

"You took some?"

"More than some, as it happens."

"But how?"

"It was easy, really. Once I was sure the wide man and the thin man and Kim didn't have the final monkey, I was pretty confident Burggrave had it hidden somewhere. But before I went to his apartment, I went back to the place in Chinatown and paid for my own storage deposit box up front. It wasn't cheap, I'm afraid, but I had a feeling it would be worth it. Of course, I was given three new figurines to go with my new keys and my new storage box. So then all I had to do was smash open the figurine that was covering his ears and the one covering his mouth and keep those keys to one side. When I found the third monkey in Burggrave's apartment, I switched it for the monkey covering his eyes that I'd been given that morning."

"So the box the police had keys to was empty?"

"Well, no. I had to put some of the diamonds in it. Quite a lot of them, actually. Otherwise my story wouldn't have added up."

"But you took the rest?"

"Guilty."

"Charlie, you're crazy. They'll come looking for you."

"I doubt it. I handed them a murderer and a fair amount of the loot. And I can't see the Van Zandts wanting to publicise any of this. They've been denying the theft out of hand for years, remember."

"Well, I hope you're right, for your sake. Are the diamonds worth a lot of money?"

"They should cover me for a few years, at least."

"I've been slow, haven't I? I mean, that's why you went to Paris, right? To see that man – that fence of yours who got you into all this in the first place."

"Pierre. I'm meeting him this afternoon as it happens. Putting a face to his probably-made-up-name for the first time."

"I could kick myself. Why didn't I think of that connection before?"

"You didn't know I had the diamonds."

"Oh yes."

"And you forgot what I'm really like. You thought I'd solved the crime for free and walked away with a warm, all over glow for my troubles."

"Why not?"

"Because that's not me, Victoria."

"Really? So okay then tough guy, tell me you didn't give any of the diamonds to the blonde."

"I could tell you that."

"But it wouldn't be true, would it? And let me guess: she thanked you in the way that comes most naturally to her and then she ran off and broke your heart."

"Hardly. I told her to go. And if she had any sense she listened to me and got a new fake passport to go with a new fake identity while she was about it. There's no guarantee the Dutch police won't decide to charge her with something, I suppose, but more importantly the thin man and the wide man aren't the type of people you want on your tail."

"Oh yes. What happened to them?"

"No idea, though I'm sure it'll be in the papers if they're ever charged. They may not be, though. At the end of the day, Vic, all I had was a story. It might have been tied together pretty nicely, but it's not the kind of hard evidence Riemer's going to need if she's ever going to bring charges."

"It was a bit more than a story, Charlie. You gave them fingerprints."

"You think? I don't know – twelve years went by. And I handled that gun without my gloves on a few times. Stuart even fired the damn thing."

"Witnesses then. Louis Rijker's mother, for one. It was marvellous how she came through for you like that."

I sucked air through my teeth, as if I'd just been cut.

"What?"

"Honestly? I assumed you'd seen clean through that one."

"Seen through what? I don't get it."

"Well, let me put it this way – you remember my cat allergy?"

"Of course."

"And you remember how I told you I reacted when I went to Karine Rijker's house?"

"Yes, you sneezed."

"Now think back to what I told you about the warehouse."

"Okay, so now you mention it I can see that you didn't sneeze in the warehouse. So big deal. It's hardly surprising the allergy was less severe outside of her home."

"But my allergy's very acute, Vic."

"And?"

"And I can see I'm going to have to spell it out for you. The Karine Rijker who came to the warehouse wasn't the same Karine Rijker I met in the bungalow."

"There are two of them?"

"Just one."

"Then ..."

"She was a set up. A contact of Stuart's."

"But ... but she had that gun – the one Van Zandt had given to poor Louis."

"Because I gave it to her myself."

"But now I'm lost again. Charlie, you're being deliberately obtuse. How did you get the gun?"

"You really want me to go over what I do when I'm not writing again?"

"Oh."

"But if it makes you feel any better I did find the gun in the real Karine Rijker's home. That morning before we met everyone at the warehouse, you remember I said Stuart and I ran some errands? Well, the first was we went back to Karine Rijker's bungalow and Stuart kept her company while I had a quick look around her bed-room. The gun was at the bottom of a wardrobe, just like I said."

"So it was a trick?"

"Half of it was a trick. But the gun was real. And it did match the gun I already had exactly. And I'd be willing to bet a lot of money that I was right about Van Zandt arming his guards."

"Even so."

"Even so, you're disappointed."

"A little. It seems kind of – "

"Sordid."

"I was going to say underhand."

"Well you're right. It was underhand. But I'm a firm believer that sometimes the ends justify the means."

"And Rutherford was happy with all this I take it?"

"Stuart, you mean. I don't think he lost much sleep over it."

"Did he ask for some of the diamonds?"

"He didn't ask and I didn't offer. He made six grand out of me if you remember and I guess he'll use that to fund his next scam."

"Yes, I guess so too."

"So listen, you might not be comfortable with it, but the reality is most of the diamonds are with me now."

"Right. Well, I wouldn't say I was completely uncomfortable with it Charlie because the truth is unless you've found some time amid all this madness to solve your briefcase problem, I'm not going to be selling your book in the near future."

"Oh yes – my book. I'm glad you mentioned that. Thing is Vic, I've decided to scrap it."

"But you can't! I wasn't serious, Charlie. You just put my nose out a little – keeping me in the dark like that. You'll figure the book out soon enough – you know you will. We can even work on it together now you've got a little more time on your hands."

"But my heart's not in it. The truth is I have another story I want to tell. I all but nailed the plot back in that warehouse in Amsterdam, you see. And with a few name changes here and there, and maybe the odd choice scene to spice it up a bit, well, what do you think?"

"A fictional memoir? I don't know Charlie. It could work, I guess. But you'll need a good title."

"Funny," I said. "I've been thinking about that too."

ACKNOWLEDGEMENTS

Thanks to Mum, Dad, Allie, my family and friends. Thanks in particular to everyone who read the manuscript, to Andrew, April, Ben, Kaushik, Paul, Simon and Will, and especially to Debs and to Jo.

Special thanks to Susan Hill, Jessica Ruston, Lynne Hatwell, Scott Pack and all at Long Barn Books and Sheil Land Associates.